Everything That Glitters Ain't Gold

Everything That Glitters Ain't Gold

by Shara Lamar

Proofreader

Cassandra D. Finley

Senior Publisher

Steven Lawrence Hill Sr.

Awarded Publishing House

ASA Publishing Company

A Publisher Trademark Title page

ASA Publishing Company
Awarded Best Publisher for Quality Books
105 E. Front St., Suite. 203, Monroe, Michigan 48161
www.asapublishingcompany.com

Copyrights©2011 Shara Lamar, All Rights Reserved
Book: Everything That Glitters Ain't Gold
Date Published: 07.10 / 03.11
Edition: 1 *Trade Paperback, Revision 1*
Book ASAPCID: 2380545
ISBN: 978-0-9828135-7-7
Library of Congress Cataloging-in-Publication Data

This book was published in the United States of America.
State of Michigan

A Publisher Trademark Title page

Dedication

This book is dedicated to my mother, *Maggie May Lamar*.

Thanks for being there for me throughout this whole process. You're not only my mother, but you are my best friend as well. Words cannot describe the love and respect that I have for you, you are my hero. Without you, I would not have accomplished any of my dreams; thanks for being my number one fan.

I love you mommy.

This book is also dedicated to my beautiful sister *Lakeysha Lamar*.
Thanks for all your love, encouragement, and financial support. You are a wonderful sister.

I thank God everyday that you are in my life.

To my brother *Douglas Lamar*.

Thanks for your support and encouragement.

Special thanks goes out to Big Merch, Plezure God Hair Salon, and all of the people who purchased the first copy of the book.

Thanks for your support!

Everything that glitters ain't gold!

Everything That Glitters Ain't Gold

by Shara Lamar

Chapter One

No More Drama (Present Day)

My phone began to ring at five o'clock in the morning, I thought who could this be, with much hesitation I answer the phone.

"Hello," I said.

The operator on the receiver stated. "You have a collect call from Keith Jackson will you accept the charges?"

I said, "NO!" Then I hung up the phone feeling like I had just defeated Floyd May Weather, Jr.

Five minutes later my phone rang again and proceeded to ring every ten minutes for the next hour. I was unable to get any sleep and I had a final exam scheduled for 9:00am. So at 6:30am, I finally accepted the call.

"Bitch, what's wrong with your dumb ass? Why you didn't answer the phone when I first called? Yeah you tough now that a nigga is locked up for a minute huh?"

"Whatever," I said. "What do you want? I have to go to school in an hour." *I lied to get him off the phone.*

"Bitch, I want to know why you haven't been calling my people to see what's been up with me? I've only been locked up for a month and you trying to jump ship. I'm telling you now, play with me if you want and your ass gonna end up fucked up somewhere," Keith said.

"I told you, I ain't fucking with you like that anymore." I whispered into the receiver of my cordless phone.

"What you say, bitch?"

ASA Publishing Company

"I said, I'm straight on you, please leave me alone" was my finally plea for Keith to exit my life forever.

"Yeah alright bitch, I'm not gonna be in this jail forever and when I see you I'm going to kill your stupid stuck up ass." *Click!* That was the end of Keith and me or at least that's what I thought.

8:00am came too quick for me. I could have sworn I had just gone to bed. As I got up, I wondered how in the world did Keith get access to call me that early in the morning. That question had me really scared. I made a mental note to make sure I had my little pink nickel plated .25 that Keith gave me for protection when I wasn't with him.

As I got up to wash my face and brush my teeth, I notice that I didn't put the phone back on the base properly. So as I put the phone back on the charger mount I check the receiver and notice I had some messages waiting. I ignored them and went on with my day. I wanted to believe that I had aced the final exam that I took in Finance class but in my heart I knew, I didn't. All I had on my mind was Keith and his threatening phone call. I knew he couldn't hurt me anymore. He had just gone to jail a month ago for two counts of first degree murder and possession of an unregistered firearm. The police and FED's have been watching him for the past two years. They believe that he has been involved in several murders in the Detroit area and a couple in Youngstown, Ohio. The FED's believe that Keith is the number one cocaine supplier in Detroit. Due to their suspicions, evidences, and a witness; his bond was set at one million dollars cash, no exceptions. As I headed home from school, I decided to stop at the liquor store to get me a pint of Remy Martin VSOP to ease my mind. I pulled my car into the driveway, got out of the car and checked to make sure my gun was securely placed in my purse just in case I had a surprise waiting for me in the house. I've been so paranoid since Keith got arrested. I didn't want to relive the horror that I've gone through again.

As I stepped in the house, I felt a sense of calmness in the air ever since my conversation with Keith this morning. I felt for the first time in a while that I had my life back. I kicked my shoes off, went to the kitchen and grabbed me a glass, a couple of ice cubes, and poured myself a double shot of Remy and headed to the living room. I sat back in my leather recliner and propped my feet up on the ottoman. I turned the stereo on with the remote and turned the volume up so that I could feel the smooth sound of Kem. I sat back and enjoyed my drink. I looked over at the phone and notice my cordless phone message notification blinking. I picked up my phone to check my messages. One was from my mother and the other message was from two familiar voices talking to one another. I couldn't believe what I was hearing. It was Keith and a familiar female's voice that I couldn't identify off hand. I could not believe that he would have a female call me on three-way, but what was more shocking was what they were saying.

"Why are you stressing about her dike ass? She don't want you anymore. She wants a bitch now." The female said to Keith.

"I don't care what she wants. That's my bitch, and she will always be mine till the day she dies," Keith stated.

"But why do you care what she's doing or who she's with? I thought you said I give you the best head you ever had and that when you get out, it will be all about us. Nigga, I've been the one risking my freedom to bring weed and crack up in the county for you to sell, not her."

"Don't be saying that hot shit over the phone. Besides you're not her. She's wifey. You either get with it or get lost. Besides I'm gonna get that bitch when I get out." Keith said.

So, this bitch has been fucking Keith. I wonder how long have they been fucking behind my back. It didn't matter much now. He was facing some long hard time and I would be long gone before he got out. But that scandalous ass hoe, oh I had something for her. I just don't understand how my life has transformed in the last two years. It seems like just yesterday, I was happy and in love with Keith and wanted to have his last name as well as his kids. As I took two Tylenols and sipped on my drink, I thought back to how Keith and I first met.

The year was 2006; I had just come back to Detroit after being away in college for the last four years. I was feeling kind of depressed because I had just graduated from college and had not found a job yet and it had already been five months. So one Sunday morning my mother said, "Tomika, you need to stop laying around the house feeling sorry for yourself." So I decided to get up, get dress and attend church with my mother.

It was a beautiful summer Sunday morning the weather was just right. I can remember it like it was yesterday; it was June 4, 2006, and it was 83° degrees. I had on a cute Donna Karan Capri outfit on, appropriate for church. My mother had on an old lady church suit that I can't believe she wore on a beautiful day. We arrived at church ten minutes late. So you know what that meant, either go up stairs and sit in the balcony, or find a seat in the back of the pew where everyone can see that you're late.

I decided to sit in the back of the church. I didn't care if people knew that I was late, we were in God's house. On my way to my seat, I notice the finest man I've ever seen in my life. He was standing up to let my mother and me pass. He stood 6'2" and he was chocolate. I mean dark chocolate about two hundred pounds *all in the right places* and he was muscular. I nearly passed out!!!! I played it cool and walked past him and I sat down and prayed that he didn't notice me staring at him throughout the service.

After two more services of me waking up early on Sunday to receive the Word of God, not to mention to get a glimpse of that fine man. I've been seeing him there faithfully every Sunday morning; I decided to say something to him. This particular

Sunday, I was in no mood to play games with the unknown man. I decided to approach him after service and introduce myself to him. I figured what's the worst that could happen, he could just brush me off or just ignore me. We were in church so he couldn't be flat out rude to me or could he? All through the service I notice him looking at me. I was so nervous that I wanted the service to go on forever. While the pastor was saying his closing remarks I notice Mr. Big, *that was the nickname I had given him,* walking up to me. I was sweating so bad that you could see sweat under my arms. Anxious to leave, I walked past my mother and told her that I would wait for her in the car.

As I proceeded down the steps outside, Mr. Big tapped me on my shoulder. I turn around to see him smiling like a kid in a candy store. He said, "Excuse me Miss, what's your name?" We both laugh knowing that he was trying to be slick reciting a chorus from Jay-Z's rap song.

After we stared at each other for a moment or two, I told him my name. He then told me his name and proceeded to ask for my phone number. I told him that I didn't give my number out to strangers. He said, "I'm not a stranger you've been seeing me here at church for a month now and I know you want my number as well."

He had just pulled my hoe card.

So without much fuss, I gave him my cell phone number and hoped that he would call me that night. After getting my number, he was a gentleman and walked me to my mother's truck.

I couldn't help but wonder what type of car he was driving. So while my mother was standing in front of the church gossiping, I pull out of the parking lot to see what type of car he got into, and just as I predicted it was a luxury car. He got in the driver side of a dark green Audi A8, my mouth dropped when I saw him drive off. I hate to say it, but in my mind I was thinking about money. I knew he had to have money. How he gets his money, I didn't know. I just assumed that by him being a church going man, he must have a good job in the corporate world. When my mother got in the car, I told her all the details of me and Mr. Big's conversation.

"Well now I know his name. I can stop referring to him as Mr. Big. I guess, I watch too much Sex and the City." My mother told me to be careful of Keith. She said, "It's something about that man, I just don't like. You know the devil comes to church too."

With that said, I went on talking about Keith and his car. Later on that night, I laid in my bed waiting for his phone call. He never called! Six days went by and no word from Keith. I figured I would see him at church tomorrow and he would give me some lame excuse of why he hadn't called me yet.

Sunday morning came and I was dressed to impress, my mother wasn't feeling good so I went to church alone. As I walked into the house of God, I felt uneasy. I thought to myself, *"Am I coming to church to see a man?"* Right then and there I decided that I would start coming to a different service, just so I wouldn't be enticed by Keith and I could fully receive the Word of God. Since I've been coming to church, I really enjoyed the services and how I felt afterwards. I didn't want Keith to put a sour taste in my mouth about church.

I took my seat and began to join in, in the praising of the Lord. When the service was over I turned around to see Keith standing right behind me. I smiled and said, "Hi" to him, he waved and continued to walk out of the church. I felt just like a fool. This really made me want to change what time I would attend church from now on. Sunday came and left, now it was Monday morning and I receive a phone call around 9:00am, it was from one of the well-known news station in Michigan. The young lady on the phone stated that she would like to set up an interview with me and one of the producers at the news station.

Immediately I agreed and I had a job interview set up for that following Thursday morning at 10:00am.

I was so excited that I wanted to celebrate. So I called my girl Simone to see what was up for the night. Simone and I have been friends for at least eight years. I first met Simone in Junior High. We were both beginning the last year in there. Simone and I are totally opposite from one another. From the way we dress to the way we look.

Simone is high yellow with long black hair and grey eyes. She wears a size double-D bra and has a petite shape. There's just one problem with her body, she doesn't have a butt. She is as flat as a pancake in the back. To all the guys in the D, she's a dime piece, but her attitude makes her a six or a seven piece. I, on the other hand am brown complexioned. I have long brown hair with blond highlights and I wear a size 36C bra. I have a nice shape and a cute little butt, my weight fluctuates a lot. So at that time, I weighed about 150' to 160' pounds, I would be consider thick. I liked to wear blue jeans and a nice pair of boots. I like for my outfits to be brand named, but like most college graduates who don't have a job, anything that looks cute and is cheap, I like it. Simone likes to wear tight fitting dresses and cat suits all the time. All her clothes have to be brand named. If it didn't have an expensive label attached to it, she would not wear it. Simone and I haven't hung out in a while since I've been back home. Because I've been depressed about not having a job, I just didn't feel like hearing about all the ballers that she's been dating and all the money she gets from them. I guess I had a little jealousy in my heart.

Simone works part-time as an administrative assistant at a Law Firm downtown, but her real income comes from tricking. She has tricked with some of the biggest basketball and football players in Detroit. It goes without saying that Simone is about her money. After telling Simone the good news about my job interview, we made plans to go to this new bar downtown called

The Spot. It was Simone's idea to go there. She said it was a nice restaurant bar that served good food and has live entertainment and of course niggas with money was going to be there. So I told Simone that I would meet her at her house around 8:00pm and we would ride in her car. I wanted to ride in Simone's car because I had an old ass 1993 Grand Am and Simone had a 2005 328i Sedan BMW. Simone kept a nice ride ever since she turned sixteen and received her driver's license. I was happy for Simone's success, but I knew the way that she made her money would cause serious harm to her in the future.

Chapter Two

The Spot

I arrived at Simone's house a little after 8pm. I pulled in the garage and gave the security guard Simone's apartment number and my license's plate number, paid five dollars to park and drove in. The first two levels of the garage were so full that I had to park my car on the third level and take the elevator down to the lobby.

When I got to Simone's door, I rang the doorbell several times before Simone came to the door. When I walked in her house, it smelled like marijuana, liquor, and sex. I took a seat on her sofa while she finished getting ready. Simone had a beautiful apartment it was about 1015 square feet with cathedral ceilings. She had a stylish contemporary apartment.

While I was waiting for Simone to get ready, I heard a man laughing in her bedroom. I could not believe this, she knew I was coming over around 8 o'clock and she's back there fucking some nigga. Thirty minutes went by and Simone entered the living room with some thug ass nigga following right behind her. The man spoke, "What's up Shorty?" I politely said "Hi" and proceeded to give Simone the evil eye for having me wait out here in the living room while she's sucking and fucking, and who knows what else in her bedroom. He then started to ask me 21 questions.

"What's your name Ma?"

"My name is Tomika, why you ask?"

"I just wanted to know who my girl, Simone is rolling with."

"I hear that," I said sounding very sarcastic. Then I asked him what his name was.

"My name is John, but everyone calls me Blunt."

"Why do people call you Blunt?" I asked.

"Because that's all I do is smoke blunts." And then he started to laugh. I felt stupid for asking him that, *but if you don't ask you don't know*. Blunt sat down next to me and started to roll up a blunt. He was an alright looking guy. He stood about 6 feet tall. He was light complexioned with hazel eyes *which probably help him get females*. He had a nice build but I guess what would make him stand out from being average was his attire.

Blunt had on some Red Monkey jeans, a red and black Red Monkey T-shirt, and some black Prada boots on. He didn't have on any earrings which is a plus for me. Blunt had an iced out Versace watch on, a white gold chain on- that hung to his belly button with a big charm that was the shape of Michigan, the mitten, and that too was iced out with yellow diamonds. He had a pinky ring to match with yellow diamonds. You could tell he was getting money.

Blunt asked Simone did she want to hit the blunt before she left. She said, "I'm good, me and my girl Tomika about to go to the bar and get fucked up."

"What bar y'all going to? Maybe, I'll stop by and kick it with y'all for a minute."

"We're going to **The Spot**. You know the new bar about three blocks away." Simone said. Blunt finished rolling his blunt while Simone put her high heels on and checked her make-up in the hall mirror.

Simone was dressed to impress. She had on a red mini skirt with a red and white blouse that hung off her shoulder, and of course it was brand named. It was a Christian Dior outfit and she had the matching handbag and heels to accessorize her look. I felt as though I was under dressed. She told me that the dress code was casual and comfortable. I had on some cute snug fitting Evisu pants and a tight fitting white blouse that was low cut so that my cleavage would show a little, and to set the outfit off, I had a pair of white Kenneth Cole heels on with a white Kenneth Cole purse to match. I thought that I was looking sexy until I saw Simone. I wanted to go home and change, but I figure it would be a waste of time because I would never have anything to put on that would look as good as Simone's outfit. I said to myself, "Once I get my hands on some money I would buy me a ton of clothes." But one thing that I had that Simone didn't was an ass and my ass looked good in the jeans I had on. I could tell Blunt was thinking the same thing. After Blunt finished rolling up the weed, Simone cut the lights off and we all headed out the front door.

When we got in the car the first thing Simone did was ask me what I thought about Blunt.

"Girl, don't you think Blunt is fine as hell?"

"He's straight," I said.

"He got that doe. I might make him my man. Plus he can lay down the dick like a champ." Simone said. I just laughed at her, than I asked her could Blunt eat pussy. She looked at me like I was crazy then she said, "I don't know. He never ate my pussy." *I couldn't believe this. Simone, the one with all this game can't get this sucka ass nigga to eat her pussy, ain't this some shit.*

When we pulled up to **The Spot** it was off the hook. The line to get in was almost around the corner. I did not want to wait in that line especially with the heels that I had on. Simone paid ten dollars to valet park her car right across the street from the bar. I could tell a lot of ballers were in the bar because of the cars and trucks that were parked in the valet section. There were Range Rovers, Land Rovers, Cadillac Escalades, 760li BMW's, and G, E, and S class Mercedes Benzes all outside. Simone was just smiling when she got out of the car.

As we were approaching the bar, Simone made a phone call and before we got to the door, a man came out and signaled Simone and I to follow him in. All the females in line looked at Simone and I with disgust in their eyes. We had to pay ten dollars each to get in the bar but it was worth it.

The bar had a nice atmosphere it was decked out with modern artwork and contemporary barstools. The only problem I had with it was that it was too packed. It seemed like everybody and their mother who lived in Detroit was in the bar. Everyone was dressed to impress. Simone and I got a table in the dining area because the bar area was just too crowded. The guy who came outside to get us bought both of us an Apple Martini and we kicked it with him while the entertainer of the night, Ms. Jackie Brown, got ready to perform. Simone ordered us two more Apple Martini's from the waitress and an order of Bar-B-Que wings. The waitress returned quickly with a bottle of Moet Rose Champagne and two glasses. Simone and I both looked at the bottle in shock. We wanted to know who the person was that sent the bottle over. Simone said that she knew it wasn't Greg, which was the guy that came out and got us. She said that he was too cheap and his money wasn't long like that. So Simone asked the waitress, "Who order the bottle of champagne for us?" We both looked over to the bar as the waitress pointed to Keith.

I could not believe it, here Keith was at *The Spot* sending over a hundred and fifty dollar bottle of champagne, but he can't pick up the phone to call me. The waitress asked us, did we still want the Apple Martini's. Simone quickly said, "No."

We both wave to him and told the waitress to tell him thanks. After the waitress left Simone said, "I knew he wanted me, he was just playing hard to get."

"You know him?" I asked her.

"Not really, I see him around from time to time at different clubs."

"Oh, so why do you think he wants you?" I said with disgust in my voice.

"Because everytime I see him out, he's always staring me down."

"So why haven't you and ole boy hooked up yet?" I asked.

"I think he has a girl or something like that or maybe he's scared of me," she said. I just laughed.

I didn't tell Simone that I knew Keith. I wanted to find out what all she knew about him. As the entertainer for the night Jackie B started to sing one of Fantasia hits *Free Yourself*, I started in on Simone some more. "Have you and ole boy exchanged phone numbers?" I asked.

"No, we just say hi and bye to each other."

"So why won't you go up to him and spit your game?"

"Girl, he's got too much money for me to play myself and go up to him. A guy like that you have to let come to you."

"How do you know that he has money?" I asked.

"Because he drives around in all the new cars. He's always with the big ballers around the city, and his gear and jewelry be off the hook."

"What does he do for a living?" I asked her.

"I guess he's in the drug game like everyone else that he's around."

"Why are you asking so many questions about him?"

"I'm just being nosy. I've seen him around myself a couple of times. Do you know his name?" I asked.

"No, but I think everyone calls him Monster."

"Monster," I said. "Why do they call him Monster?"

"I don't know," Simone said. I quickly change the subject and started asking questions about other people who were in the club. I could tell that I was starting to irritate Simone.

While we were having idle chitchat Keith walked up and tapped me on my shoulder and said, "Hello."

"Hi yourself, stranger. Thanks for the champagne." I said.

"No problem. Do you come here often?"

"No this is my first time here."

"So what brought you here tonight?" He asked.

"My girl, Simone." *I turned and pointed to Simone,* "She said that it was a nice place and the food was on point, so I decided to hang out tonight," I said.

"That's cool," He said while looking at Simone strangely, he didn't even bother to acknowledge her at the table.

"You're looking good tonight. I just wanted to come over and tell you that before I left."

"Thank you, you're not looking so bad yourself." I said to him. In all actuality Keith looked real good. He had on some brown Gucci loafers, brown slacks, and a tan and brown polo style shirt. On his wrist was an iced out Presidential Rolex watch. I thought to myself *this man should me mine.*

"Well I'll let you two ladies get back to your conversation, enjoy the rest of your night."

"I will, thank you."

As soon as Keith got about a foot away from the table Simone said, "I was wrong girl, he doesn't want me. He wants you."

"What's up with you and ole boy?"

"Nothing, I just met him one time when I was leaving church." I told her.

"I have never seen him talk to a female for that long of a time in a bar or club before, he must like you or something."

"Whatever," I said.

"I'm for real. You need to get on that one."

Simone and I talked some more about Keith and the many men that were in her life for another hour or so, then she signaled for the waitress to come over. When the waitress got to the table Simone asked for the check, the waitress said, "Not to worry about it, ole boy who bought the bottle of champagne paid for the food and other drinks as well." Simone and I looked at each other and smiled. Simone left a ten-dollar tip on the table then we got up and walked out.

While heading to the parking lot, I could feel someone watching me as I approached the passenger side of the car. Before I could get in Keith said, "Do you need a ride home?" I turn around to see him on the driver's side of the midnight blue 760Li BMW that we were parked next to.

"I thought you left already." I said to him with a smile on my face.

"I wanted to make sure that you left the bar safely, just kidding. I had some business to discuss outside with one of my partners and it ran long."

"You're so funny," I said to him.

"Are you going to let me give you a ride home or what?" He said.

"I'm good. I parked my car in my girl's apartment garage, thanks anyway," I said.

"Well at least let me drive you to your car." I turn around to see what expression Simone had on her face and it was the one I expected. She gave me that girl if you don't get in the car with him, I will, look.

"O.k." I said, and then I told Simone to take down his license's plate number just in case she doesn't hear from me tonight.

"You don't have to worry about me doing anything to you, I'm trying to get to know you." He said.

Simone told me to call her as soon as I got in my car, because she was going over a friend's house. *That meant she was going to make some money tonight.* I got in the car with Keith. The interior looked almost as good as the exterior. The car had wood grain all around and it had peanut butter leather seats that felt so good. I thought to myself, I can get use to riding in style. He asked me how far away from the bar was my car. I told him about two blocks away, and then he asked me if I wanted to ride around, so we could get to know each other better. Now by this time it was about 1:00am in the morning, and I didn't want him to think that he was getting some ass. So I played it cool and said, "Yeah that's fine, just don't try to be slick and pull into a hotel."

He just laughed and said, "Girl you are crazy, you don't care what comes out of your month."

We stayed in the downtown area and rode around the river and parked on the island and talked about everything; from what side of town we were from to our families.

He was impressed that I had gone out of state to go to college. I told him how it has been hard for me to find a job in my field, and that I have an interview on Thursday and how excited I was about it. When we finished talking it was around 3 o'clock in the morning. I thought by now Simone would have called to see what I was doing or where I was at. I guess she was taking care of business. Keith drove me to my car and waited for me to pull out of the parking garage before he left. I was so embarrassed to get in my car after riding around in his. He was such a gentleman that it kind of took me by surprise.

As I was driving home, I could have sworn that Keith was following me. I couldn't see his car but I could feel a presence. When I got home that morning, I felt that I knew all I needed to know about Keith.

I told him that I was the youngest of two girls, and how I've moved back here from Florida to live with my mother. He told me that he was twenty-eight years old. His last name was Jackson. He had two brothers, one older and the other younger than him. He grew up on the eastside of Detroit, off of John R and Nine Mile.

He also told me that he was into real estate. He said that he buy and sell houses for a living. He and a childhood friend restore abandoned houses around and in the city of Detroit, and sell them for a nice profit. I really didn't believe him after what Simone had told me about him, but I figure why would he have any reason to lie to me, his story sounded legit.

Simone finally called me around 10am, talking about she hooked up with this football player she's been seeing, and he kept her up all morning eating her pussy. I laughed and told her about Keith and my conversation. She asked me was I going to go out with him again. I told her I didn't know because we didn't go out on a date. We just rode around and got to know each other better. I couldn't wait to see him again. I just hope that he calls me because I didn't have his number and he didn't say anything about calling me. I didn't tell Simone that I didn't have his number. I would have looked like a fool to her. Since she's use to dealing with niggas with that bread and was use to niggas being on her head.

This was new to me, dealing with someone who was on Keith's level and who seems to have a lot going for himself. I'm use to dealing with nickel and dime ass niggas. You know the type, the niggas that got legit jobs, but want to slang weed or a couple of eight balls on the side. Or the corner niggas that's in their late twenties, early thirties, and all they know is the block and haven't upgraded from weed to crack, still stay at home with their mother but drive fifty and sixty thousand dollar cars.

I knew that Keith would be different than the guys that I dealt with in the past. He would be my man, the one I could depend on, my rock. When I got in the house, my mother was tripping on me talking about, she wasn't gonna have a daughter coming in her house all times of the night especially, not coming in when she was about to go to work. I just said ok, went straight to my bedroom, and went to sleep.

Chapter Three

A Career and a Man

Thursday took forever to get here, still no word from Keith. I was getting ready for my job interview when the phone rang. I answered the phone, "Hello, can I speak to Tomika?"

"This is she," I said.

"Hey baby, how have you been doing?" The voice kind of caught me off guard at first, and then I realized that it was my ex-boyfriend from college, Jamal. Jamal and I were together for two years. He had graduated a year before me and moved back to Atlanta where he's from and started teaching.

"I'll be in Detroit this weekend to visit a couple of my partners and I wanted to stop by and see you," he said.

"That sounds good. What about Saturday night?" I replied.

"That should be good. I'll call you when I get there, and we will take it from there."

"Sounds like a plan, have a safe trip," I said, then I hung up the phone. It would be good to see Jamal I thought to myself, and maybe I will get some dick! It's been about eight months now and a girl has needs.

Jamal was a good boyfriend as far as looking out for me and making sure I had everything I needed and wanted while I was in school. There was just one dilemma with Jamal, he's a hoe. I can't count how many times different females would call me at all times of the night and tell me how he was at their house or he had just fucked them or something to that degree. He even had the nerve to get a girl pregnant while he was with me. Jamal made the girl have an abortion, but it still hurt me to know that he was putting my life at risk by having unprotected sex with someone else. That was the straw that broke the camel's back. After that, I went and got tested for all the STD's you could think of, and I made him wear a condom every time we had sex from then on. He still took care of me and made sure that I had everything that I needed until I graduated from college. I was caught in a daze for a minute, thinking about how good the sex was with me and Jamal. Jamal made me cum every time we had sex, if it wasn't from his dick it sure as hell was from his tongue. Jamal had an average build. He stood 5'9" and weighted about 185 to 195 pounds. He dressed like Kanya West. He always had a César fade and kept 360° waves. Jamal wasn't from the streets, but he had a little thug in him. He was from a middle class area in Atlanta, Georgia. He never had to want for anything. Just thinking about him made me hot. I had to shake the thought of having sex off of my mind because I was on the verge of pulling my Perfect Ten vibrator out and getting me a quickie before I went to the job interview.

I arrived at the local news station at 9:45am and was dress for success. I had on a black pants suit from Express, and some black four inch Nine West heels on. I had my hair pulled back in a bun with my one carat diamond studded earrings on that Jamal bought me for an anniversary gift last year. I don't wear make-up. So I just had on some Mac lip gloss. I walked up to the receptionist desk and informed her that I had a 10 o'clock appointment with Mrs. Jennifer Moore. The receptionist told me that it would be a couple more minutes because she was still in her office with her 9:30am appointment. I politely took a seat and picked up an Elle magazine to read. The young lady called my name about ten minutes later to meet with Mrs. Moore.

Mrs. Moore was a very attractive medium height, white woman. She had long strawberry blonde hair that was cut and layered. She would put you in the mind of Courtney Cox from the T.V. show **Friends.** She stood about 5'8" in heels, and she weighed about 150 pounds. She had on a tight fitted blue business suit that complemented her shape.

"How are you doing today, Miss. Smith?"

"I'm fine, thank you."

"Good, well let's get down to business," she said.

"It said on your resume that you have a Bachelor's of Science Degree in Communications and that you have four months of experience from your internship at a local news station in Tallahassee, Florida."

"Yes, that's correct," I said. "I got a lot of hands-on experience behind the scene with an assistant producer, some light PR work, and I provided assistance to the Production Manager."

"That's very impressive."

"Thank you."

"Unfortunately the position that we have available is an entry level position, you would be an Assistant Associate Producer /Receptionist for the Producer. With that said, are you still interested in the position?"

"Yes," I said.

"The position pays $25,000.00-$30,000.00 annually, but it's a great opportunity for growth within this organization, and with your experience I know you will be successful here. With that said, I'm offering you the position. Do you have any questions?"

"Yes, does the company have a 401K Plan?" I asked.

"Yes, for every dollar you invest, we will match it."

"Another question I have is what type of medical benefits do you offer?"

"We offer full health care coverage which includes dental, vision, and health, and our medical provider is HAP. You would start this following Monday thru Friday for training from 8:00am-

5:00pm, then the following week you would start your regular schedule which is 7:00am-4:00pm or longer; depending on what project you're working on. One last thing, this in a non-exempt position, so will I be seeing you first thing Monday morning?" she said.

"Yes you will, I look forward to working here and starting a career with WKPT News."

On my way home, I decided to stop at the mall to buy me something nice for when Jamal comes to visit. As I was turning into the mall entrance, I felt my phone vibrating. I looked down and notice that the caller ID said private. I didn't know who would call my phone private, so I answered with an attitude.

"Hello."

"Hey, how did your interview go?"

"Is this Keith?" I said sounding sarcastic.

"Yes."

"So how did the interview go?"

"Oh, it went good. I got the job. It's an entry level position."

"But it's something you know."

"I can't believe you remembered."

"That's good to hear." He just blew off my comment that I made about him remembering.

"I thought you forgot about me, I haven't talked to you since that night at the bar." I said with much attitude.

"It's not like that. I just had a lot on my mind this past week, but I do want to see you and make it up to you. So what's up for this weekend?"

I said to myself, *nigga I will be getting my freak on this weekend. Getting my ass ate out and everything. I can't believe he wants to do something the same weekend Jamal is coming to town, hell to the nawl!*

"I can't hang out this weekend, I have plans already. What about sometime in the middle of the week?" I asked.

"That's cool, I just wanted to holla at you for a minute. What you doing now?"

"I'm pulling up at the mall."

"What are you about to get from the mall?"

"Nothing just window shopping, I might pick up a few things," I said.

"What mall are you at?"

"Fairlane."

"Oh, o.k. well I'll let you get back to what you were doing. I'll talk to you later."

"Alright, be safe out there," I said.

A couple minutes later I was in the mall looking around when I decided to go to Victoria Secret and find something sexy to wear for Jamal. I picked out a couple of bra and panty sets, and a few thongs that were on clearance.

When I was approaching the line to pay for my items my phone began to ring, again it showed up private. When I answered it, it was Keith asking me where I was at in the mall. I told him Victoria Secret. Five minutes later, I got a tap on my shoulders. I turn around and it was Keith, looking good as usual. He had on a sky blue Lacoste shirt with dark blue jean Lacoste shorts and some white, sky blue, and dark blue Lacoste shoes. It looked like he had a fresh hair cut with the razor line up. He had on a Presidential Rolex on his wrist.

"What are you doing here?" I asked.

"I wanted to see you and I didn't want to wait until next week. I was in the area so here I am."

We had small talk until I got up to the register. When the cashier laid all my items on the counter, Keith couldn't help but look through them. Then he asked, "Who are you wearing this for?" And he held up one of the bra and panty sets.

"You, if you play your cards right." He most likely thinks I'm a hood rat or something for saying that, but he responded by saying "Oh, yeah."

The cashier rung all my things up and said, "Your total is $196.35." I'm thinking in my head *what the fuck,* if Keith wasn't there, I would have quickly put some shit back. But instead, I smiled and thought to myself, "How am I going to pay for this shit?"

All I had in my checking account was $235.00 and I had about five hundred in my savings. I needed to start working quick, my money was running out and my mother was on some bullshit about helping me out. She believed in the ole saying, God bless the child that got its own.

As I was going into my purse to pull out my debit card, Keith had already had two crisp hundred-dollar bills in his hand, giving it to the cashier. While we were waiting for his change I thanked him and he reply by saying, "I'm trying to play my cards right." I laughed, he handed me the bag and asked what did I have plan next.

"Nothing much," I said.

"Well, would you like to have lunch with me?"

I was so happy I didn't know what to do, but I didn't want to show it so I took my time and said, "Yeah, that would be nice."

"Where do you want to go and eat at?"

"It doesn't matter, somewhere close. I'm not in the mood for a long drive."

"Cool, we'll go to Benihana, its right across the street."

"O.K, I'll meet you over there," I said.

When I pulled up to the restaurant, I called Keith to see if he had made it there yet. He said, "No." So I sat in my car and waited for him to pull up. While I was waiting, I called Simone and told her that Keith bought my underwear at Victoria Secret and that I'm about to meet him for lunch.

"Girl I told you that nigga likes you."

"Whatever, he probably just wants to fuck me."

"So what, just make sure you get some money out of him," Simone said.

"Girl you are a trip, I'll talk to you later."

A couple of minutes went by, then a gold Range Rover pull up on the side of me. I didn't pay it any mind, until I notice it was Keith getting out of it. I started to think maybe Simone was right. He must be a street nigga and I don't need that in my life right now, but he just looks so good.

It was around 2pm when we sat down in the restaurant. I wasn't in the mood to eat due to the fact that I was nervous being with Keith, so I just ordered some shrimp fried rice with extra garlic butter. Keith had Yakisoba. He order a double shot of Remy VSOP. I didn't want him to drink alone so I ordered an Apple Martini with Ciroc Vodka.

The time just flew by as we ate and ordered two more drinks each. We talked about everything from cars to fashion. I asked him did he go to church every Sunday. He responded by saying, "Yes, I try to attend church every Sunday, unless important business arise or the weather is bad, but for the most part I attend church regularly. I see you don't."

I was somewhat offended by his comment. "I did go to church on a regular basis too. It's just that I haven't been in a church going mood lately but I've got myself together now, so I will be attending more often than I have in the past," I said.

"I hope so. I enjoy seeing you there," Keith said.

"And I as well," I said.

We then proceeded to talk some more about general issues. I was a little tipsy, and I kept referring to him as nigga and using a lot of profanity. I could tell that he was getting a little irritated by it. He looked me dead in my eyes and said, "You're too beautiful to be using that kind of language. People used profanity when they don't know how to express themselves." After he said that, I apologized.

It was about 5:30pm and we were buzzing from the drinks we had. Keith's cell phone began to ring, he excused himself and answered the call. When he hung up, he had an evil expression on his face. He signaled for the waitress to bring the check. He told me that he had some important business to take care of and he would call me later on that night.

I got home about 6:30pm. The first thing that I did when I stepped in the house was wash my sexy panties and bras that I just got and I hung them up and went upstairs to my room.

I took my clothes off and jumped in the shower. I was so wrapped up in Keith, I forgot all about Jamal until my phone rang and it was Jamal confirming that he would be here on Saturday, and he wanted me to spend the night with him. I told him, I would. We talked for a couple minutes about what we were going to do for the weekend. We decided to get something to eat, catch a movie and head to a hotel.

After getting off the phone with Jamal, I looked down at my nails and notice that I needed a nail and hair appointment ASAP. I called my girl Joy to see if she could fit me in tomorrow. She said no, but she could get me in first thing Saturday morning. I thanked her and hung up the phone. I just couldn't get Keith off my mind. I kept thinking about what he said about me using profanity. I thought to myself, I must have looked stupid and ignorant in his eyes. Hopefully I can make a better impression next time we meet.

Chapter Four

The Jump Off

Friday was my chill day. I caught up on my laundry and cleaned up my bedroom. I knew that I would have a long weekend, and I wanted to be prepared for my workweek on Monday. My room was a mess. I had clothes all over the place. I decided to change my bedspread as well. While I was cleaning up my room and washing clothes, my cell phone started to ring. I looked up at the caller ID and notice it was a 248 number. I answered.

"Hello, can I speak to Tomika?"

"This is she."

"How you doing today?"

"I'm fine, may I ask whose calling?"

"This is Keith."

"Hey, I didn't know it was you, since you always call from a blocked number."

"Well it's me; I figured that I could trust you with my cell number."

"Ha-ha!" I said.

"So what's going on with you today?"

"I'm chilling, just cleaning up my room. Doing a little laundry."

"I was calling to see if you wanted to get some breakfast."

"I have a better ideal, how about you come over and I'll make you breakfast."

"That sounds good. But just so you know, I don't eat pork at all."

I thought to myself, "Ain't this some shit, all I had in the refrigerator was pork sausages and pork bacon." "O.k. that's cool. What else don't you eat?"

"I don't eat beef either, just chicken, turkey, and fish."

"Well give me about an hour and I will have breakfast ready."

"That sounds like a plan. Where do you live?"

"I live on Marlow between Joy Road and Tireman, the address is 5678 Marlow."

"You live in the hood."

"If you say so, I'll see you in an hour."

"Bet."

I didn't have much time so I jumped up and threw on some sweat pants and t-shirt, grabbed my car keys and headed to Farmer Jacks. There I got turkey sausages, turkey bacon, some potatoes, and onions. I paid for the food with my debit card. I made a mental note that my money was getting shorter and shorter. I got back home in about twenty minutes. I cut up the potatoes and onions put them in the skillet, put six pieces of turkey bacon on a bake tray with six turkey patties, turned the oven on 400° degrees, and put the tray in the oven. I then boiled some water for the grits; crack my eggs open, added cheese, salt, pepper, and a hint of milk with the eggs.

Keith got to my house at 10:45am. The food was ready, but I needed to take a shower. I opened the door and lead him in the house.

"You have a nice house."

"Thank you, but my mother has a nice house."

"You know what I mean."

"Yeah, I'm just messing with you, but I have to jump in the shower real quick, if you want to eat now you can. Everything is ready and in the kitchen."

"Naw, I'm cool. I'll wait for you."

"Alright I'll be back in a minute." As I went upstairs to take a shower, I was hoping that Keith would follow me upstairs but he didn't. I got in the shower, washed the necessary areas then I got out. I put on a wife beater and some sweat pants and I pulled my hair back in a ponytail. Sprayed some Victoria Secret body spray on and went down to the kitchen. When I walked in the kitchen, Keith had my food on a plate and a glass of orange juice. I smiled at him and said, "Thank you.

He said, "No problem. It's the least I could do. Now let's bless our food, I'm starving." We ate our food in silence. After we were finished, I washed the dishes and he chilled in the living room watching T.V.

"You really have a nice house," he said.

"Just cause I live in the hood; let you tell it, doesn't mean I can't have a nice home. I lived in a three-bedroom colonial style house with one and a half bathroom with a finished basement with a picture window in the living room, two bedrooms were downstairs, and one bedroom/den was upstairs. Since I came home from college, and my sister moved out, my mother turned one of the bedrooms downstairs into a computer room and let me have the upstairs room all to myself."

Keith admired all the African paintings and sculptures that were all over the house. After I finished washing dishes, I joined Keith in the living room and sat on the love seat right across from him. "What's wrong? I don't bite. You could have sat next to me."

I smiled shyly, got up and moved to the couch with him, videos played in the background as he asked me a series of questions. "I'm not in the habit of playing games or wasting time, so do you have a man or anyone you're dedicated to?"

"No, why would you ask me that? If I had a man, I wouldn't have invited you over for breakfast, and I sure as hell wouldn't have gone out with you yesterday."

"True that."

"So, what about you? Do have you a woman or should I say, do you have any women?" I asked.

"No I don't have a woman. I have many female friends that I deal with for numerous reasons, but no one I can call my woman." That right there let me know that he has a lot of women on his team.

"Well that's interesting to know, I don't want to have any encounters with your women friends. So, I hope you have them in check and they know how to play their position," I said. Keith just laughed.

"What do you know about someone playing their position?"

"I know a lot, I've dealt with guys who kept a lot of women around, as so called friends. I know how the game goes."

While I was talking, Keith's cell phone was vibrating off the hook, he finally looked at it then said, "Ok, Miss Lady, I gotta go. So I'll holla at you later on."

"That's what up," I said.

Saturday came just as fast, I got up threw on an Apple Bottom jogging suit, and some Apple Bottom flip-flops and grabbed my red Coach purse and headed to my hair appointment. I arrived at the hair salon, which is called "Hair U R" at 9am. Joy had four women in front of me, not including the young lady sitting in her chair. I signed my name in the book and walked over, spoke to Joy and sat down. When 10:30am rolled around and I still hadn't been shampooed. I decided to go up to one of the nail techs and asked if she could squeeze me in. She said sure and that she was available right now. While I'm sitting; getting my nails done, someone tapped me on the shoulder. I turn around and it was my cousin Keisha. Keisha was what the guys in the neighborhood would call a *hood rat*. She was nineteen; had a two-year-old son name Jason. *Of course she named him after his father, that's what hood rats do.* Her baby's daddy was locked up in Bellamy Creek Correctional Facility for possession of a firearm and possession of an illegal substance. He had more than five grams of cocaine in his possession. Keisha stood about 5'4" inches, her body measurement are 36, 24, 36. She had a bad ass body, but her face was just average. She wouldn't stand out in a crowd with just her face alone. She was receiving money from the state. She didn't have a job. She would go dance at some of the local strip clubs when she needed extra money. She stayed fly and kept her hair and nails done. She didn't want to go to college. Getting a high school diploma was good enough for her. All she wanted to do was get high and get fucked. This is the definition of a hood rat. She was a lower level Simone. While Simone got all the big figga niggas, Keisha got all the nickel and dime ass niggas from the neighborhood.

"What's up girl?"

"Nothing, chilling, waiting to get my hair done," I said.

"Joy doing your hair?" she asked.

"Yeah."

"So, who is doing your hair?" I asked her.

"Dee."

"That's cool."

"So, what you got up for tonight?"

"Well, Jamal is coming in town from Atlanta. So we gonna chill."

"That's what up," she said, "Y'all should come to the club tonight."

"I'm good on that, maybe I'll come up there one night with Simone."

Keisha made an ugly face and said, "That's what's up."

"So, when are we gonna hang out cuz? We ain't kicked it in a while."

"Well, we can kick it next weekend."

"Cool." I gave her a hug then she walked off to get her hair shampooed. Three more hours went by and I was finally out of the hair salon looking better than ever. I got my hair cut in layers and my hair was extra bouncy. I got home around 2:30pm and took a bath, and tried to find something cute and sexy to put on. I figure, I'll kill some time while waiting on Jamal to call. So I started reading this new book call *Me and My Boyfriend* by Keisha Irvin. I've been dying to read. An hour went by and my phone rang.

"Hello," I said.

"What's good, Ma?"

"Nothing much, just chilling. May I ask who do you want to speak to?"

"You don't know my voice by now?"

I thought for a second, than replied, "Keith."

"Yeah."

"Damn, if you're not calling from a block number, you're calling from different numbers."

He chuckled. "Girl, you are a trip."

"Yeah I know, so how is your day going so far?" I asked.

"Good, now that I'm talking to you."

"That's what's up."

"I want to see you tonight."

"I can't. I have plans. One of my college friends is in town this weekend, so I'm gonna hang out and kick it."

"My bad, I forgot you told me already you had plans the other night." I wasn't about to tell Keith that my ex-boyfriend was in town and that I was gonna hang out with him. Keith probably won't call me anymore if I told him that. So I told him a friend, it wasn't a lie.

"We'll get at me later."

"O.k., be safe out there."

"What made you say that?"

"I always tell people that. It's just something I say. You never know what might happen so I say be safe."

"O.k., baby girl you be safe as well."

It seemed like right after I got off the phone with Keith, Jamal called. He called to tell me he would be at my house by 8:00pm- no later than 8:30pm. He had some friends and family members that he needed to see. Jamal knew his way around Detroit. He use to come to Detroit with me on holiday, plus he has family members and friends who live here as well.

Jamal didn't show up until 9:30pm. To say, I had an attitude would be an understatement. He called me from his cell phone.

"Come on outside baby."

"This is the bullshit that I be talking about; you can't ever get any place on time."

"Just bring your ass outside."

When I walked outside, Jamal was sitting in a red 2006 Cadillac STS. I signal for him to pop the trunk so I could put my overnight bag in there. As I closed the trunk, I notice he had a customize license plate that read *J Dog. I thought to myself he is so country.* The inside of the car was fully loaded with the wood grain, a navigation screen, and a DVD player.

"Damn nigga, what you doing? I know you can't afford this car on a teacher's salary."

"You know, I do a little something on the side."

"Like what?" I said.

"I tell you over dinner. So, where do you want to eat at?"

"It doesn't matter to me. It's too late to go to the movies so anywhere is cool with me."

"Well, I want to go to J Alexander. That's where all my boy's been talking about when I told them, we were going out to eat."

"That's what's up. Do you know where one at?"

"Yes." I wanted to tell him to go to the one in Somerset Mall so I could get some gear, but the mall was closing in thirty minutes, so I gave him the directions to the one in Novi.

We got to the restaurant in about fifteen minutes. I was glad that there wasn't a wait because I was hungry. The hostess seated us in a minute later. Our waitress came over to the table to take our order. Jamal ordered a steak- medium well done with a bake potato, and a house salad. I order the roasted chicken with loaded mashed potatoes. The waitress asked us would we like something to drink. Immediately I said, "Yes."

I ordered an Apple Martini with Ciroc, and Jamal ordered a Grey Goose and Cranberry juice. Soon as the waitress left, I started in on Jamal.

"So how can you afford that car? What are you really doing? Are you still teaching school?"

"Damn baby, you can't even tell me how much you miss me, all you want to know is how I'm getting money."

"Yep," I said.

"Well one of my boys down south that I get my weed from, propositioned me about going into business with him."

"What kind of business?" I asked.

"What do you think? He needed someone to go in with him to cop a couple pounds of weed with him."

As we were talking, the waitress brought our drinks. Jamal stopped talking until the waitress left and then he resumed the conversation.

"I've known dude for a minute, even before I went off to school. He said his last partner got caught in Texas and he really didn't trust anyone else. Dude got some fire ass weed. I cop from him all the time for my personal use."

"So now you want to be a drug dealer?"

"No, it's just weed."

"Weed is drugs."

"Whatever, Tomika."

"Whatever then, so do you still teach?"

"Yeah,... I just go in half with him on the weed. He sells it and I get my money back with a little profit. But my cousin got a hook up here in the D, so I just brought six pounds up here for him."

Our food came. We ordered some more drinks and ate our food, and continue to talk about his business venture and my new job. Jamal told me that he was happy for me and that if I need anything he would help me out. We left the restaurant two hours later and headed for a hotel. I wanted to go get a room that was close to my house, so we went to the Double Tree off of Southfield and Ford Road.

Jamal handed me three hundred dollars to get the room, while he ran over to the store to get something to drink and a blunt. I told him don't forget to grab some condoms. He looked at me like I was crazy. He dropped me off in front of the hotel and pulled off. I retrieved my overnight bag, went to the front desk, and asked for a suite. The guy at the front desk said that a suite was going to be two hundred and sixty nine dollars with tax, but he could give it to me for a hundred and fifty dollars if I was paying cash. Black people are always trying to get over. After paying for the room, I still have a hundred and fifty dollars to put in my pocket. The room was nice it had a mini kitchen, a queen size bed, a love seat, and a huge Jacuzzi in the corner of the room. I went in the bathroom to freshen up a bit. It was no need for me keeping on my clothes. We both know what we came here for.

When I got out the bathroom, I turned the T.V. on and purchased one of those x-rated movies. I knew Jamal would like that, he's such a freak. Not long after that, Jamal call my cell phone to get the room number. When I opened the door, Jamal had a big smile on his face. I was wearing one of the lingerie outfits that I recently bought. It was a pink and black, satin and lace set- all Jamal could say was, "*Damn!*"

He started kissing all over my neck and breasts. I had to tell him to close the door. When he got in the room and notice that I had a nasty movie on, his dick got hard instantly.

"You want something to drink?" he asked.

"Yeah."

He fixed us both a shot of Grey Goose. We sat on the bed and took our shots. He then started rubbing and sucking on my breasts. My pussy was getting so hot and wet, I didn't want any more foreplay. I was ready for some dick. He took my bra off and then he proceeded to kiss on my stomach and down to my navel. When he got to my navel, he pushed me up closer to the headboard so he could prop my legs up. When he got my legs up, he entered my pussy with his middle finger.

"Damn baby your pussy so tight and wet."

"Shit nigga, I haven't had any dick since the last time I fucked you."

"Whatever, you ain't got to lie to a nigga."

"Straight up."

"We'll see when I get up in it."

Jamal snatched off my panties and start licking on my pussy. Just when I thought I couldn't take it anymore, I came. I came so hard that my cum skirted out of my pussy. Jamal looked at me and smiled as he wiped his mouth, "I'm gonna give you a chance to recuperate." He was taking off his clothes when he said that.

When he got down to his boxers, I had to take a deep breath. I had forgotten how big his dick was. Jamal's dick was about 8 to 8 ½ inch long, but his width was the problem. His dick looked like a tree trunk. He got on top of me and tried to enter me without a condom.

"Hold up partner, what's up with that?"

"Come on Ma, you know I don't like to use them things."

"Well I guess you not gonna be getting any pussy."

"This some bullshit."

"Call it whatever you want to but if you don't put a condom on, it's a wrap."

He thought about it for a minute then he reach over and pulled an XL Magnum out of his pants pocket. When he stuck his dick in me I wanted to scream, but after a couple of minutes the pain became pleasure. Jamal made me cum two more times that night. I was so tired and my pussy was sore as hell. I quickly went off to sleep. Jamal got up and rolled him a blunt and watched some more porn movies.   Around 4 o'clock in the morning, Jamal woke me up with his dick poking at my butt.

"You ready for round three?" he said.

"Boy, I'm sore as hell."

"Well, I'm horny as hell."

As I lay on my side, Jamal went and started kissing all down my back and down to my butt cheeks. Then he spread my butt cheeks open and started licking my ass hole. I was going crazy. After I came twice, he put on a condom and started hitting it from the side. We got up, got dressed, and went to the Original House of Pancakes to grab something to eat. Jamal had to leave out early because he had to go to work in the morning. He dropped me off and handed me five hundred dollars. I looked and asked him, "What's this for?"

"Just some money to have in your pocket."

"Thanks."

"You got it."

"Well, I had a good time last night and I guess I'll see you later. Call me when you make it to Atlanta."

"I will. Next time I come to Detroit, can we hook up again?"

"For sure."

"Call me if you need anything."

"I will."

I gave him a kiss on his cheek. He pulled off and I went in the house, showered and went to sleep. I was glad that my mother wasn't home.

Chapter Five

Gotta Get That Money

Yesterday was a trip. I can't believe Jamal laid it down on me like that. I finally got out of the bed around 3 o'clock in the afternoon. I had cut my cell phone off last night because I didn't want any interruptions. I turned my phone on when I woke up and I had four voice messages;

-The first one was from Simone,

"What's up bitch? I know, Jamal fine ass blew that back out last night. Call me when you wake up, one." I just laughed at her freaked out ass.

-The next message was from Jamal,

"Hey baby, I must of put it on you if you're still sleep, but anyway, I'm just headed into Tennessee. So I'll call you when I get in Atlanta."

-The next message was from Keisha,

"Bitch! You and Jamal should have come to the club last night it was off the hook, your girl Simone was there."

-The last message was the one that put a smile on my face, it was from Keith.

"What's up Ma? I guess you had a long night cause you didn't come to church. Holla at me when you can."

I wanted to call Keith back so bad, but I had a slight hangover, and my legs and pussy was sore as hell. I also wanted to get my clothes together for work tomorrow since I had to get up early. Later on in the evening, my mother came home and tripped out on me for not coming home last night.

"What the fuck is wrong with you? Why didn't you bring your ass home last night?"

"It got too late so I just spent the night over Simone's house."

"That's bullshit and you know it. You were with Jamal or some nigga."

"I was with Jamal earlier, and then I had him drop me off at Simone's house."

"Look, I'm no damn fool, your ass is not about to be running in and out of my house all times of the night. You start your job tomorrow. You need to concentrate on that and leave them nothing ass niggas alone. By the way, I saw that slick ass nigga at church today, he asked me where you where."

"What did you say?"

"I told him you were at home sleep and that you couldn't get up because you hung out all night."

"Mommy, why did you say that?"

"Because it's the truth."

"Whatever," I said.

I called Keith around 8:00pm. The phone rang three times before he answered it.

"Hello."

"Can I speak to Keith?"

"This is he."

"What's going on?"

"Nothing, I missed you at church today. I heard you had a long night."

"I guess you could say that, so what's up with you now?" I asked.

"Nothing, about to grab something to eat."

"O.k., I guess. I'll talk to you later on."

"Or, you could come with me and we can get something to eat together."

"That's what's up."

"Give me about thirty minutes and I'll be there," he said.

"O.k., you remember where I stay?"

"Yeah."

"Call me when you get outside," I said.

It was the middle of July and it was hot, so I decided to put on a cute sundress that my mother bought me from the Limited. The dress was beige and white with spaghetti strings. I had some really cute beige sandals and a mushroom purse that set the dress off just right. I took a quick shower, lotion my body with some Victoria Secret lotion, sprayed some Donna Karan Cashmere Mist perfume on, and threw on my clothes, comb my hair out, put some lip liner on and I was ready to go. I walked downstairs and my mother was in the living room watching T.V.

"Where are you about to go now?"

"I'm going to get something to eat with Keith."

"That nigga from church?"

"Yep, that's him."

"Girl, you need to quit. I'm telling you, he's nothing but trouble. Going to church every Sunday like he isn't out here doing wrong."

"What are you talking about?"

"That nigga is as slick as grease. I don't trust him. All he wants to do is use you up."

"Mommy, you said that about everybody. You don't like anyone I hang out with."

"Well you hang out with losers."

"I hear that."

"So, where are you going?" she asked.

"To get something to eat."

"Well, bring me back something to eat. So I can take it to lunch."

"Alright."

Keith arrived at my house approximately at 8:45pm. He rang the doorbell. I could have sworn, I told him to call me when he got outside. My mother answered the door.

"Hello Miss Smith, is Tomika home?"

"Yes, hold on for one second." My mother didn't let Keith in. She yelled for me to come out of the living room.

"Tomika, Keith is here for you."

"O.k." I said. Then I grabbed my purse and headed out the door.

When I got to the porch, my mother said, "Don't come home late tonight, you have to get up early in the morning for work."

"I won't," I said. I was so embarrassed she said that to me in front of Keith but I just brushed it off. We decided to grab something to eat at Outback Steak House. Keith and I ended up going to Outback Steak House on Middle Belt and Ninety-Six. I didn't want to order a strong alcohol beverage because I had to get up early in the morning so I opted for a frozen strawberry daiquiri. Keith had a double shot of Remy.

"You love your dark liquor," I tease him.

"Yeah, I need something strong to take the stress away."

"What stress do you have?" I asked, after the waitress took our order.

"I wouldn't know where to begin."

"Try at the beginning."

"Well, I'm having trouble with some of my tenants that's all."

"I hope things get better for you," I said with a smile on my face.

"Thank you, you're not like most women that would keep inquiring about my problems."

"If you wanted to tell me more, you would have. I don't want to know anything about you that you don't want me to know," I said.

"That's real," Keith said. "So, what did you get into yesterday, where you couldn't get up to come to church today?"

"Nothing much, just went out drinking with a friend from out of town."

"I hope you were not out cheating on me," Keith said with a sneaky smile on his face.

As I was about to say something, the waitress came back with our food. I had an eight-ounce sirloin steak medium well done with a loaded baked potato. Keith had salmon, with mixed vegetables, a bake potato with butter, sour cream and cheese. We enjoyed our food and talked some more about *his so called businesses*. I knew Keith was doing more than selling houses, especially after what Simone said about him. I figured I'll call Simone tomorrow and get some more info on Keith but until then, I was having a wonderful time. I called the waitress over to our table so I could place my mother's order. I told her to put it on a separate bill but Keith wasn't having that at all. So as we waited for my mother's order to come up, we ordered some more drinks. Keith had ordered another double shot of Remy and a Budweiser. I ordered another Strawberry Daiquiri.

We began our conversation back up and I asked Keith did he have any kids. He said yes, that he had two little girls; one was five years old and the other was seven years old. I did the math in my head real quick and concluded that he had his first child when he was twenty-one years old and the second when he was twenty-three years old.

"Do both girls have the same mother?" I asked.

"Yes, they do, why did you ask that?"

"Because there are a lot of men out here that have four and five children with different mothers, and the kids will be about six months to a year apart. I just wanted to see how you where cut."

"Well, I'm cut from a different cloth than most of these niggas out here, and just to let you know, I take care of mine."

"I hear that," I said. "So are you still with your daughter's mother?" I asked.

"I see you don't listen. I told you a couple days ago when I was over your house that I didn't have a woman."

"Yeah, you're right," I said, trying to play it off. I could see that Keith was becoming annoyed by my comments so I change the subject.

I didn't get home until 11:30pm that night. Just like I expected, my mother was pissed.

"Girl I told your ass before you left to be home early. You know you have to get up at least by 5:30am to make it to work on time, and the first impression is everything. I don't think you're serious about this job. But just to put something on your mind starting next month, you're going to have to give me five hundred dollars a month to stay here."

I could not believe the shit that my mother was talking. I said, "Yeah- whatever," and went up stairs to take a shower. 5:30am came too quick for me. I was in the middle of an x-rated dream of Keith and I having sex, but before anything could happen, my alarm clock went off. I got up, took a shower, brushed my teeth, washed my face, and put my clothes on. Since the weather was still hot and the dress attire was casual, I decided to wear a black business like Capri outfit from the Limited. I pulled my hair up into a bun like I wore it for my interview. I sprayed on some perfume and I was headed out the door.

I arrived at work at 6:45am. I grabbed me two donuts and an orange juice from the store in the main lobby of the building and headed up to the fifth floor where hopefully a successful career would start.

Chapter Six

Straight Up

A couple of months past and everything was going good in my life. Keith and I were hanging out almost every weekend together, *when he's available*. We even started going to church together. My work life was going good, even though I felt that I was overworked and underpaid. My boss, Mrs. Moore had me doing everything from getting coffee, to picking up her dry cleaning. I felt more like an errand girl instead of an assistant associate producer. I couldn't complain because I learned a lot from her. After my first week working there, she told me to call her by her first name, which is Jennifer. I also met some people at work that would prove to be true friends in the end, and some to be evil human beings. For instance, my first week working at the station, I met a young man named Michael Adams. He was an intern at the station. He attended Wayne State University. He was a junior and his major was communications, and his plan was to be a news reporter when he graduated college.

Michael and I basically had the same job at the station. The only difference was that I was getting paid for my services. We became real close due to the fact that we had to work side by side every day. Michael was cute, in a nerdy kind of way. He was light skinned *which I don't like*. He had a nice grade of hair, medium height about 5'8". He dressed like a young college student, Polo shirts and pants, Lacoste shirts, and pants. If I was in college and liked light skinned brothers, I would definitely be on his head, but all I could think about was Keith.

I talked to Michael about Keith and he talked about his girlfriend. His girlfriend was a senior in high school and he has been with her for two years now. I thought that he was too old to be dating a girl in high school, but I couldn't talk. Keith was six years older than me. Michael was cool. We had our own private joke that we would share with each other about other people at work; especially the newscasters, they were so phony.

There was this older black lady that has been doing the news before I was born. Everyone loved her, the fans that is. She would have thousands of fan mail a day. You would have thought she was a sweet older lady, but truth be told she was a BITCH! She would run Michael and me on errands all day for her assistants, her kids, and her dogs. I would always complain to Jennifer about it for the simple fact that she had her own personal assistant, but she would rather for us to do it. Jennifer would always say to me, "This is the type of people you will have to endure when you become a producer one day, so you might as well learn how to tolerate it now."

I would just smile and say, "O.k.," Michael on the other hand would put the work off on another intern; another person that I met while working at the news station was a young lady named Danielle. Danielle was a thick brown-skinned chick, around my age. She wore her hair braided to the back and she dressed like a boy. She was a pretty girl. Danielle work in the mailroom, everyone knew she was a lesbian. Other co-workers *females for example*, would treat her funny or wouldn't hold too long of a conversation with her. I didn't act funny toward her. Shit, she was cool with me. I got to know Danielle because I had to go to the mailroom and get all the mail for the newscasters, so they would have their mail on their desk before they came in for work.

Michael and Danielle made up my work crew. We would all go to lunch together when our schedule permitted, and we would even go out for drinks at this bar called Goldmine every

Thursday. It's an after work affair, all drinks where half off on Thursday plus the bar was right around the corner from where we worked. Sometimes Jennifer would join us but I could tell that she felt uncomfortable around Danielle. But I just brushed it off, Danielle was my girl.

It was Friday, September 12th, 2006. My birthday was next month and I wanted to do something nice on my birthday. So, I had plans to meet Simone at her house so we could make arrangements for all my friends to hang out together. We had plans to grab something to eat at Red Lobster. It felt good to be able to go out to eat and not worry about money. I was putting half of my check up every week in my savings account, and I even started paying on my student loans. My mother had a change of heart about me helping out with the bills. She wanted me to get my finances and myself together before I started helping her out. My mother saw how committed I was to my new job, so she bought me a couple outfits from Ann Taylor and Express.

I hadn't talked to Keith too much this past week due to the fact that he was always going out of town on business. He would say that he had to see about some property in Cleveland, Ohio, Atlanta, Georgia, and Charlotte, North Carolina. Before he would go out of town, he would always ask me if I need anything. I always told him no. Sometimes I would want to say yeah, but I didn't want him to think that I was a gold digger.

I arrived at Simone's house around 6:30pm. It was a usually hot day for this time of year. I had stayed at work an extra hour to help Michael out with some of his homework, then I headed to Simone's house. I was wearing a cute Kenneth Cole Capri set that I purchased from Marshalls. I'm a bargain shopper and a damn good one I might add. My whole outfit, from the shoes to the accessories cost me ninety dollars.

I called Simone as I was walking up to her door to let her know that I was outside. When I walked inside the apartment Simone's friend Sheretta was sitting on the couch drinking a strawberry daiquiri.

"Hi, Tomika," Sheretta said.

"What's up girl? What you doing here?" I asked.

"Shit, Simone, told me that you and she were going out to eat so I asked her could I come along, if that's cool."

"Girl you know, you good. Y'all ready to go?" I said.

"That's what up," Sheretta said.

When we got to Red Lobster, it was a forty-minute wait. We decided to sit at the bar and have a couple drinks. When we got to our second round of Apple Martini's, our names were called to be seated at a table. As we were ordering our food, Keith called me.

"What's up hot girl?" Keith said.

"Nothing much, chilling at Red Lobster with a couple of my girls."

"Who, that girl Simone?"

"Yeah, her and this girl name Sheretta."

"How long are you going to be there?"

"I don't know, we are ordering our food now. Why what's up?"

"I wanted to see you tonight. I know you don't have to work tomorrow and I wanted you to chill with me."

"That's sounds like a plan. I just have to stop at home first."

"Ok, just call me when you're leaving your house. So I can give you directions to my house."

"That's what's up."

When I got off the phone with Keith, I told Simone and Sheretta what he just said. Out of all the times Keith and I hung out, we never went to his house. We either went out to eat and then to the movies, or just chilled at my house. Simone and I were curious to where Keith lived at.

"Girl, you finally going to get some dick from that nigga," Simone said.

"I know right."

"How long you been talking to ole boy?" Sheretta asked.

"Just for a couple of months," I said.

"And you haven't had sex yet?"

"I'm not a freak like you hoes." We all started laughing.

"No, for real, he never came at me like that, and I don't want to play myself."

"I feel you, but damn, when was the last time you had sex?" Simone asked.

"When Jamal came to visit in July."

"You're a good one," Sheretta said.

"I know right. When I leave here, I'm going to go home and put on one of those sexy lingerie sets that he bought from Victoria Secret and get me some tonight, you feel me?"

"Whatever," Simone said.

"For real, it's on tonight."

After we finished eating, we headed back to Simone's house so that I could get my car. We didn't even discuss plans for my birthday. We were too busy talking about Keith all the while we were at the restaurant.

While Simone drove me to my car, I told her I just wanted to have dinner with all my friends, and then we could go to a couple of clubs and chill. So we agreed to do just that. I hit the freeway like a mad woman.

I wanted to take a quick shower and lotion my body down good so I wouldn't have any ashy spots on my body. I wanted Keith to see my body flawless. I decided to wear a pair of Joe Jeans the Honey style which had a couple of cuts in the front, a black short sleeve shirt with rhinestones on it with some black Nine West sandals with rhinestones on the heel.

I was looking cool and sexy with my black rhinestone bracelets and rhinestone necklaces on my arm. I had my black and silver Kenneth Cole purse.

The time now was 10:00pm. I called Keith to get directions to his house. I arrived at Keith's house at 10:40pm. Keith lived in a condo in Bloomfield Hills, Michigan. There was a security guard at the gate. I had to show him my ID. He then called Keith to let him know that he had a guest waiting. Keith told him that he was expecting me and to let me pass. When I arrived at Keith's house, my mouth dropped as I walked in. His walls were painted beige, which had African Arts gracing almost every wall. All the pictures had a wooden frame with beige color matting around them. His dining room furniture was beige as well. He had a marble table with four leather chairs *of course they were beige* with a marble vase centerpiece with beautiful color flowers in it. His kitchen had stainless steel appliances in it; the kitchen color scheme was black and silver- I assume due to the stainless steel appliances.

Keith's living room was something else, it was breathtaking, he had to have had a woman to help him decorate it. He had a leather living room set that was a sandy brown color with a marble and glass coffee table in the center of it all, with two marble end tables with marble lamps on each one of them. And to set it off, he has a marble life-size statue of a man and a woman embracing both of which were naked. I was out done when I saw that.

"You have a beautiful house," I said.

"Well thank you, but you haven't seen all of it. Let me show you the basement then I will take you upstairs."

"That sounds like a plan."

When we got down to the basement, it started to look more like a bachelor's pad. He had black leather sofa, a sixty something inch screen TV, a pool table, two small TV's mounted up over by his bar area and all types of Play Station and XBOX games off to the side. In the bar area he had all types of liquor, from Patron to Remy Martin. He even had my drink of choice Ciroc. He had a full size refrigerator with all types of juices; mixes to make fruity and frozen drinks and beer.

"Do you want something to drink before we go upstairs to see the rest of the house?"

"Yes, thank you," I said.

"What would you like?"

"I would like Ciroc and Cranberry Juice."

As Keith made our drinks, I went over to the pool table and started racking the balls up.

"So I see you're interested in pool."

"Yeah."

"Do you want to play a game or two?" Keith asked.

"As long as you don't act like a big baby when you lose."

"I see you got jokes. Well put your money where your mouth is," Keith said while handing me my drink.

"O.k."

"Let's bet a hundred dollars a game."

"You got me fucked up. I don't have money like that."

"So what do you want to bet?" Keith asked.

"How about ten dollars a game?"

"That's cool."

About two hours later and two more drinks later, I owed Keith forty dollars. I had handed Keith two twenty dollar bills.

"Yo, you good Ma. I was just playing with you."

"You, good one. Because if it was me, I would want my money."

"I see," Keith said.

"You hungry? Because I'm starving right about now," Keith said.

"Yeah, I could eat something."

"What do you want to eat?" Keith asked me.

"It doesn't matter."

"Well, I got a taste for some pizza."

"That's cool with me."

"Well you know, I don't eat pork."

"I know so what are we going to get on the pizza?" I asked.

"Turkey pepperoni, green pepper, onions, and turkey sausages."

"That's sounds good, but what pizza place put turkey meat on their pizza?" I asked.

"Its a little mom and pop's pizza place out here that does, and they deliver; they stay open until two in the morning."

"I wouldn't think anything around here stays open after midnight. I guess hood shit goes on no matter where you live at."

"Yeah, you're right, but what did I tell you about your mouth?"

"I'm working on it," I said.

Keith ordered the pizza and while we were waiting for it to arrive, he showed me the rest of his house. He had two bedrooms upstairs. I found it unusual that his laundry room was upstairs- center, in between both bedrooms, which was different. Keith's bedroom was indescribable. His bedroom was painted white with a black bedroom set that was trimmed with white. His head board was black with white leather in the center of it, and the foot board was the same. He even had black leather around his dresser and mirror. He had two large black and white pictures that cover one entire wall. His lamps that stood on the nightstands were black and white as well, and he even went as far as to have a black and white picture of the movie poster of Scarface over his headboard, and to set the room off he had a forty-two inch plasma television mounted on the wall with a DVD player attached to it. I thought to myself, *this boy is a mess.*

His other room was set up as an office, this was the only normal room in the house besides the bathrooms. The room had a black leather futon, a twenty-inch silver Sony computer screen, a black computer deck with a black leather chair to match, a couple of framed posters of Robert De Niro, Redd Foxx, Richard Pryor and Al Pacino.

Keith's bathroom upstairs had a whirlpool bathtub and a shower that was separated from one another. His bathroom was decorated in black and white, and it was directly across from his bedroom. The other bathroom was located on the first floor right off of the front door and the kitchen. It was a half bathroom with just a toilet and sink.

The pizza arrived just as we were coming back downstairs. We took the pizza downstairs to the basement. He turns on the television and we watched Def Comedy Jam, ate pizza, and had a couple of beers. I was surprised to see how good the pizza was. I'm a pork lover to the heart, but actually I couldn't even tell the difference. When we finished eating, the time was 2:30am. I was tired and buzzing, I didn't feel like driving forty minutes to get home.

"You good Ma?" Keith asked me.

"Yeah, I'm just a little buzzed, and I really don't want to take that drive all the way home by myself."

"You good, why don't you just stay here for the night?"

"You don't mind?" I asked him.

"I said you was good. You can sleep in my room."

"Where are you gonna sleep at?" I asked.

"I'll sleep in the other room or in the basement."

"You don't have to do that, you can sleep with me," I said.

"Ok, since that's settled, let's go up stairs so I can get you something to sleep in." We cleaned up the basement before we headed upstairs. Since we used plastic cups, we didn't have any dishes to wash.

Keith cut all the lights off in the basement and in the living and dining room. He left both the lamps on that were on the end tables, then we went up stairs. I just knew it was about to be on. To my dismay, Keith handed me an extra tall white tee to put on;

not wanting him to think that I was a dirty chick, I asked him for a bath towel because I wanted to take a shower. He gave me everything that I needed, and he even handed me a fresh bar of soap.

"Do you have a shower cap? I don't want to get my hair wet."

"Nope."

"Why you don't have any shower caps?" I asked.

"Because I'm a man, and I don't need a shower cap to take a shower," he said.

"Fuck it." And took my clothes off to get in the shower. I at least wanted him to see me in my sexy under wear but it seems as if he wasn't even paying attention. So to get his attention I asked him did he have an extra toothbrush. He turned around to show me where to get the toothbrush out of the hallway closet.

When he saw me in my thong and bra, he was like, "Damn little Mama." But he didn't try to grab me or do anything physical to me. When I came out of the shower he was already in the bed with the TV on ESPN. While I was in the bathroom, I looked for some deodorant and lotion. All he had was baby oil and baby powder so I used that. I'm glad I didn't find anything that I didn't want to see. I was a little mad that my hair got wet in the shower, but I had a hair appointment in the afternoon anyway, so it was cool. I said my prayers and I got in bed with Keith.

Thirty minutes went by and he cut the television off and turns on the stereo. It was playing smooth jazz. I thought to myself, *he's about to make his move* but he never did, he turned on the opposite side and went to sleep. I couldn't sleep, I was so nervous about being in the bed with him. I turned to face his back so I could put my arms around him and when I did that, Keith immediately shut me down.

"What you doing? I don't like being touched when I'm going to sleep; besides I don't want you to think that I'm your man."

I had the biggest pie face in the world after he said that. I thought to myself, I just got played to the fullest. I turned back around and went to sleep.

I got up around 8:30 in the morning. I couldn't get any sleep, plus I was ready to get out of his house. I told myself after last night, I wouldn't call Keith anymore and I planned on sticking to that. As I was putting on my clothes, Keith woke up and asked me what I was doing. I told him that I was headed home. He got up out of the bed and headed to his jeans that he had on last night. He went into his pockets- I wanted to say *nigga I know you don't think, I stole some money from you*, but instead I just continue to put my clothes on. I went in the bathroom to brush my teeth, and then I walked down the stairs to grab my purse and put my heels on.

"Damn, baby girl. What's the hurry?"

"I couldn't get any sleep last night, so I'm going to go get in my own bed."

"Well, here you go." Keith handed me a hundred dollar bill.

"What's this for?" I asked.

"So you can get your hair done. I see you got it wet when you took a shower, and now it's all over your head from you sleeping."

"I'm good, I don't need the money."

"Just take it anyway." And he put it in my hand.

"I had a good time last night; call me when you get home," He said.

"Alright." Then I headed out the door. I was so pissed at how Keith played me I wanted to call Simone and tell her, but I knew she wouldn't be up.

When I got home my mother was up and cussing me out.

"Where the fuck you been at all night?" she asked.

"I was over Simone's house; Simone, Sheretta, and I. We all went out to eat then we went to a club and it got too late, so I just spent the night with her."

"I don't believe shit you're saying, you probably was with that nothing ass nigga! Look Tomika, you're not going to be coming in all hours of the night or not coming in at all without calling me and letting me know what's going on."

"I know Momma. I was tired and I didn't want to drive all the way home."

"Don't let it happen again."

"O.k." *I got to get my own place. I can't take this shit much longer*, I thought to myself.

After talking to my mother, I went to my room and went to sleep.

Chapter Seven

Shop Gossip

When I arrived at the hair salon, it was a quarter past two o'clock. I was fifteen minutes late but I said, "Fuck it, Joy has me waiting for at least two hours before she starts on my hair anyway." As usual the shop was packed.

Even though it was fall and the weather was in the low sixties- high fifties, girls in the shop still had on tight ass summer wear. My stylist Joy, she had on a Baby Phat bodysuit that was about two sizes too small and some Baby Phat boots to match. Joy's hair stay fly and she always had on some serious jewelry. She had an iced out Rolex on her wrist and an iced out tennis bracelet. Her ear game was out cold, she had five-carat diamond studded earrings on. Joy stayed fresh to death, if only she would buy clothes that fit. And let me not forget her hair, she rocked a short spike hairstyle.

As I was waiting to get my hair done, my phone rang.

"Hello."

"What's up bitch? Did you get your back banged out last night?" Simone asked.

"Hell nall, that nigga was on some other shit. He didn't even try to touch me or anything."

"So what happen?"

"Nothing, we just chilled, played pool, ate and just kicked it."

"Did you try to do something with him?" Simone asked.

"Nawl, I wasn't going to play myself, especially if he wasn't feeling me. I spent the night and we slept in the same bed, but that was about it," I said. I wasn't about to tell Simone how Keith played me when I try to put my arms around him.

"Well you should just ask him what's up with some dick, shit it's been a minute since you had some."

"I know right."

"So what you got up for tonight?" Simone asked.

"Nothing, I'm at the hair salon now. You know I'm going to be here for a minute. Why, what you got up for tonight?" I asked her.

"You know that nigga Blunt you met over my house that day we went out?"

"Yeah."

"Well he and one of his boys want to hang out tonight. I was going to ask Sheretta if she wanted to go, but Blunt asked me to invite you first. So what's up?"

"That sound like a plan, what time are you talking about hanging out, because I don't know what time I'm leaving here."

"I say between 9 and 10pm."

"That's what's up, where are we gonna meet at?"

"They're going to pick us up at my house."

"Well can you come get me around 8 o'clock?" I asked Simone.

"Yep."

"Alright, I'll see you then, one."

"Bye bitch."

I decided to get a manicure while I was waiting. I figured that I had two more hours to be at the shop like I predicted; an hour went by and I was seated in my stylist chair.

"So what's been up with you?" Joy asked.

"Nothing much. Just chilling and working, that's about it."

"I hear you're fucking with that big nigga they call Monster."

"What, who told you that?" I asked Joy.

"Simone, she came and got a sew-in a couple days ago, and we were talking about niggas and somehow ole boy's name came up. She told me that you were kicking with him."

I didn't want everyone knowing my business, especially not these hoes at the shop because once they hear something, they run with it, even if it's not the truth. I definitely didn't want my business in the streets and I didn't want Keith to hear something and think that I ran my mouth. "I'm not kicking with him at all. We just cool. I met him at the mall and we talked a couple of times, but that's just about it."

"Girl that's too bad, that nigga's money runs long."

"Girl, what you talking about?" I asked her.

"You didn't know he's getting that bread?" she said.

"No I didn't know, but I guess I know now," I said. *I can't forget to ask Keith why they call him Monster, note to myself.*

I quickly changed the subject. I felt uncomfortable about discussing Keith with Joy and I knew she gossiped a lot. She asked me what I was doing tonight, and I told her me and Simone was hanging out with some niggas Simone knew.

"I know they must have money, because that's all Simone messes with," Joy said.

"I know that's right," I said.

Thirty minutes later, I was out of the hair salon and looking good. I had Joy spiral curl my hair all over, and pull them out so my hair would be full and curly. The temperature had dropped outside and it was in the upper forties. I had to go home and find something to put on, because if I knew Simone she was going to be fresh to death. I had a few hours to kill. So I decided to go to the mall and find a cute sweater or blazer to wear tonight. I got home just in time to freshen up a bit and to change clothes. I decided to wear a pair of black Joe jeans with a black wife beater and a black and gray short sleeve blazer that I bought at the mall. All my accessories match my clothes, my boots and purse were black and I wore a black and grey pea coat that I got from Old Navy. As soon as I was putting my lip gloss on, Simone was calling me, telling me that she was pulling up.

When I got in Simone's car, all I could smell was weed. She was smoking a joint and listening to Keisha Cole song *Love*.

"What's up doe?" I asked as I was getting into the car.

"Shit, getting fucked up, you mind driving back to my house. I'm fucked up and I don't want to chance it with the police because Jefferson is off the hook with police officers."

"Alright."

As usual, Simone was looking on point. She had on some knee high black Gucci boots, some black legging, a black and white Donna Karan sweater that hanged off one of her shoulders, a short black Donna Karan black leather jacket, and a dog ass black Gucci purse that matched her boots. I had to admit Simone stayed fresh to death. Not to hate, but if I was fucking with all the niggas she did, I would stay on point as well. But she's my girl and I can't hate; get money mommy.

"Bitch you know you killing them, right?" I asked Simone.

"Whatever, you looking good too," Simone said.

"I hope ole boy isn't ugly, have you seen him before?" I asked while pulling out of my driveway.

"I think so, but Blunt got so many boys I don't even know. He don't sound ugly," Simone said.

"It's not like I'm going to fuck him or something like that, so fuck it. I just want to have a good time and kick it."

"Bitch if the money's right, you better fuck that nigga." Simone said while laughing.

"You ain't nothing but a big hoe," I said.

"No, a big paid hoe," Simone said.

"Oh, my bad."

While driving to Simone's house, I got so much play from the niggas that were downtown driving around trying to find something to get into. I knew it all wasn't for me, it was the car I was driving; Simone's BMW.

I guess niggas can be groupies just like females when it comes to material things. I guess because they see me driving a BMW, they think I got money. Pull over baby girl, or what's up for tonight, where you going, were just some of the comments I hear as I was driving to Simone's house. Simone was high as a kite and she didn't pay the guys any mind. When we got to Simone's house, I decided to make myself a drink to get prepared for the night. Simone and I sat and talked about Keith and this new basketball player she was dating that played for the Chicago Bulls, name Michael Richardson.

A half an hour later, Simone's doorbell rang and it was Blunt and his boy. Blunt looked good as hell. He had on a pair of dark denim Sean John jeans with a red and white Sean John shirt, a black, red and white Sean John warm-up jacket, and some black and red Prada boots on. Like before when I saw him, his jewelry was on point. His boy looked nice as well, he had on a green and white LRG outfit on with some green and white Air Force Ones. He had a nice iced out watch, one two-carat diamond earring on.

"What's up? This is my man Eric," Blunt said. Simone and I both said hi in unison. Eric stood about 5'9" inches. He had a nice hair cut and lineup. One could tell that he kept his self up. He was caramel complexioned.

We all got into Eric's truck, which was a black Range Rover supercharged; sitting on some fat ass rims. I sat up front with Eric while Simone and Blunt sat in the back. Soon as Eric started up the truck, Blunt lit up a blunt and he and Simone started to smoke.

"Do you smoke weed?" Eric asked me.

"No, do you?" I asked.

"Every now and then, but not like that nigga back there."

"Yeah, I feel you, so where are we going?"

"I thought we would go play some pool, then grab something to eat and check out a club or two."

"That's what's up," I said.

"Well, y'all didn't ask us what we thought about the plan," Simone said with much attitude.

"What do you want to do?" Eric asked her.

"I want to go get something to eat first."

"Me too," Blunt said.

"Alright, where do y'all want to go?"

"It doesn't matter to me," I said.

"Well I would like to go the J Alexander," Simone said.

"O.k., that's where we're headed," Eric said.

On the way to the restaurant, Eric and I had small talk. I learned that he was twenty-six years old, he didn't have any children and that he had a condo in Southfield, Michigan where he lives by himself.

I asked him did he have a girlfriend. He said, "No just friends."

"I respect that."

He asked me similar questions, I could tell he wasn't feeling the fact that I lived with my mother, but after I explained my situation, he understood.

It was a wait at the restaurant, so we all sat at the bar and ordered some drinks. Simone and Blunt was so high that they were feeling all on each other.

"Excuse me, I have to go the restroom. I'll be back," Eric said,

"Hold up man, I gotta go to," Blunt said.

"Girl, that nigga is fine, and he got the waves going on in his hair. He don't have any kids and I can tell he got some money. You better get on him."

"Bitch you ain't shit, but a gold digger," I said.

"I ain't saying she's a gold digger but she ain't fucking with no broke nigga," Simone said singing a Kanye West song, Gold Digger.

"Whatever, I don't think he's feeling me like that, but he seems cool."

"You need to get him to feel you like that. You got to start getting money out here. I know you want to get out of your mother's house."

Now Simone knew she hit a nerve by saying that I did need to get out of my mother's house, but not by tricking. But to shut her up, I agreed with what she said.

Dinner went well. We all had a good time. After dinner, we went to a sports bar in Birmingham, Michigan and played some pool. After that, we went to a strip bar called Bare Backs on the eastside. When we pull up to the bar it was about 1:00 in the morning, the parking lot was full with expensive cars. Simone whispered in my ear, "Ain't nothing but money in here, and I'm with this nigga." I just laughed at her silly ass. I was feeling good. I had a nice buzz and I was ready for whatever.

All night I was checking my phone to see if Keith called and he didn't. Blunt paid for everyone to get inside the club. When we walked in, all I could smell was ass. Them hoes were getting down and dirty for that money. It was cats in there making it rain. Eric went to the bar to get us some drinks. While he was doing that, Blunt was trying to find us a table due to the fact that it was so packed.

We didn't have any luck finding a table, there were two VIP booths up front by the stage, so Blunt asked one of the waitresses how much the booth was. She told him five hundred dollars. He counted out five one hundred dollar bills and handed them to her. She proceeded to direct us to a VIP table.

"We can't be sitting in VIP and not popping bottles," Blunt said.

"Excuse me baby girl, let me get a bottle of Grey Goose and a bottle of Moet black label," Blunt said to a waitress.

We stayed at the club for about two hours. Blunt and Eric made it rain before we headed out. Eric was so drunk that he couldn't drive. Blunt and Simone was too high to drive, so I took the keys since I was the only one sober enough to drive. It took me about an hour to get to Simone's house, because I did the speed limit.

"So, I guess, I'm crashing over here tonight," I said to no one in particular.

"We all are chilling here tonight," Blunt said.

"Tomika, you and Eric can sleep on the futon in the other room, or one of y'all can sleep on the couch, and the other one can sleep on the futon." I just looked at her like she was crazy.

"Do you have an extra scarf so I can use to wrap my hair up?" I asked her.

"Yeah, in the bathroom."

"Wherever you want to sleep at is okay with me," Eric said.

"I'm going to sleep on the Futon. You can sleep with me if you want to. I just have a habit of sleeping with the TV on."

"Me too," Eric said.

I woke up the next afternoon around 1pm. Eric and I didn't get much sleep because we were up talking and laughing at Simone and Blunt having sex. They were so loud it sounded like he was killing her. Simone kept calling out his name and telling him it hurts and to hit it harder. After I jumped in the shower and brushed my teeth, I got my cell phone to call my mother, but I figured she was already at church, but I was greeted with two voice messages. First message was received at 10am Sunday morning, lasting 45 seconds.

"I don't know what the fuck is wrong with you, but I've told you about leaving this house and not calling and letting me know

where you're at. Get your ass home as soon as you get this message."

I already knew my mother was going to trip, but the next message caught me off guard. The operator stated that the call was left at 1:15pm, lasting 30 seconds.

"I guess you're not attending church anymore, call me when you get a chance."

The last message was from Keith, he called while I was in the shower. I'm glad I didn't answer with all the noise Simone and Blunt was making, he would have thought Simone and I had a threesome or something. We all decided to go to breakfast.

After breakfast, Eric dropped me off at home and we exchange phone numbers. He told me to call him as soon as I got a chance. He seemed alright, *I'll keep him in mind,* I told myself, because while we were sleeping, he rubbed against me and his dick was hard and BIG!

Chapter Eight

That's What's Up

The past weekend was a trip. Simone is a fool. I wish I could be so up front with guys. My mother was tripping on me so tough, I knew it was time for me to get out of there. My money wasn't right but I would just have to make something happen.

When I arrived at work, Michael was already at his desk getting busy on some research that we had to gather for an upcoming news broadcast on children with Autism.

"What's up?" I said to Michael as I walked over to set my things down on my desk.

"Nothing much, trying to get some work done before Jennifer gets here. You know she's going to have a lot of shit for us today."

"I know right."

"So what did you get into this weekend?" Michael asked.

"I hung out with my girl Simone and I kicked it with Keith."

"What? Did he try to get some?" Michael asked.

"Boy, if you don't stop playing, he was acting like he didn't even want me to touch him," I said to Michael.

"Whatcha mean? What did he do?"

"He didn't try anything, not even a hug or a kiss. And to top that off, I spent Friday night at his house because we were drinking and I didn't want to drive all the way home. So we slept in the same bed. I put my arms around him and he flipped out, talking about he don't like being touched when he's sleeping."

"Hell nawl, he said that shit for real?" Michael asked.

"That's not all, he said that he didn't want me to think that I was his girlfriend."

"Ole boy straight hoed you."

"I know right?!" I said.

"So what's up with you and him now?" Michael asked.

"I don't know. I haven't talked to him since Saturday morning when I left his house. He called me Saturday but I didn't answer my phone."

"You're playing hard to get?"

"Nope, I'm just not in the mood to deal with his bullshit, I don't know what to say to him. I'm gonna call him today," I said.

"Well you need to ask him what's up with some dick. Because it looks like you need some."

"Whatever nigga."

"But on the real, you need to see where you stand with him," Michael said.

"What's up bitch?" Simone said when I answered my phone.

"Nothing- working, what's up with you?" I asked her.

"At home waiting for this nigga to come over and give me some money for my rent."

"You's a hoe, hoe." I said quoting Ludicrous the rapper. "Bitch, I'm a good one. Anyway, what's up with you and your boy Keith?" Simone asked.

"Girl, I can't call it. I want to know why he's acting like he doesn't want to be bothered with me one minute, then the next he's all in."

"Well you need to just step to him about it, and you need to cut into him about some money, especially if he's acting funny style."

"Everything is about money with you," I said.

"You got that right. Niggas ain't shit, so I want to get paid for my time and heartache. They playing me for pussy and I'm playing them for cash."

"I heard that," I said.

"You should have been a dancer with that state of mind."

"If my ass wasn't so flat, I would have," Simone said. And we both burst out laughing.

"I gotta go, this nigga is buzzing my apartment. But on the real, you need to talk to ole boy and see what's up. If not, you gonna have to start getting this money."

"Yeah, you right, so who's that at your door?

"This guy name John Blake. He plays for the Lions."

"Girl use a condom, one."

"Alright, I'll holla at you later on."

After talking to Michael and Simone about Keith and me not having sex yet, I decided to give Keith a call. I asked him to meet me for lunch, he agreed. I wanted to ask him what did he want from me or rather yet, what does he think I want from him, and why hasn't he came at me about getting some pussy.

I was running late, because I had some extra work assignments given to me at the last minute before my lunch break. I was dressed very professional and I wanted Keith to see me in something other than (street clothes) jeans. I arrived at *The Eatery* about 12:45pm. When I walked in the restaurant I noticed Keith sitting in a booth talking on his cell phone, I walked up to the booth to sit down.

"Damn, I thought you would never get here," Keith said.

"I texted you, to let you know that I was running late. Did you have somewhere else to be?"

"No, but you can chill with the smart mouth."

"Boy, what's wrong with you today?"

"Nothing, just waiting on you. So how was your weekend? I haven't heard from you since Saturday morning."

"It was fine. I hung out with my girl Simone and a couple of her friends."

"Is that so, your girl seems like she's out there. Every party I go to or an event that one of my boys are having, she's always there," Keith said.

"What that mean?" I asked.

"That your girl is out there, I hope you're not out there like that."

"Just so you know, I'm nothing like her, but she's not a hoe."

"Whatever. So is that why you weren't at church, because you were hanging with your girl?" Keith asked.

"Yes, but why are we even talking about her? I came here to talk about us and to see what's up with us," I said.

"What do you mean what's up with us? We chilling, having a good time I thought," Keith said.

A waitress approached and took our order, as usual Keith order a shot of Remy and a Corona beer. After the waitress left, I continued our conversation, "I know we chilling, hanging out, but I want to know why we haven't had sex yet, it's been about three months." Keith cut me off before I could finish my statement.

"Baby girl, I'm not pressed about sex. I can get pussy when I can't eat," Keith said.

"What do you mean about that?" I asked.

"I mean I can get pussy anytime and anywhere I want it. I like you. I would rather get to know you first before we do anything serious. I don't want you to fall in love with me or go crazy if we have sex to soon," Keith said before he started laughing; then I joined in with the laughing. Keith is just too full of himself, I thought.

"O.k., I understand that. I just want you to know that I like you and I would like for us to be more than just friends, but if it doesn't happen, I won't be mad."

"I like you too, baby girl. I just got a lot going on right now, but when things calm down, it's gonna be cool for us, alright?" Keith said.

"Alright," I said.

Our food came out. We ate and had lighthearted exchanges while eating our food. Keith paid for our food and walked me to my car. I felt kind of embarrassed to be getting in an older model car while he was going to hop in a big body BMW.

"I had a nice lunch, maybe we can do this again in the near future," I said.

"For sure. And by the way, you look real nice today."

"Thank you."

# # # # #

"So how did your lunch go with Keith?" Michael asked.

"It was cool. I didn't get a specific answer to why we haven't had sex yet."

"What did he say exactly?"

"He told me he can get pussy, when he can't eat."

Michael just busted out laughing.

"What's so funny?" I asked.

"That nigga's a pimp. He ran some cold ass game on you."

"Whatever."

"You know that he's fucking somebody else, that's why he said that to you," Michael said.

"Well I don't care. He knows how I feel about him. So it is what it is."

I felt stupid for telling Michael what Keith said, I just know not to tell Simone because if Michael said that he was playing me, I don't know what Simone might think.

Chapter Nine

I Want to Sex You Up

Eric had called me in the middle of the week asking did I want to hang out, just the two of us. I said, "O.k." Since I hadn't heard from Keith since we went to lunch on Monday. Eric and I made plans to go out to the movies and out to eat on Saturday after my hair appointment. Simone called me as well in the middle of the week wanting to hang out. I told her Eric and I had plans. She was happy that I wasn't sitting at home waiting for Keith to call or come by.

"Girl, I'm glad you're taking my advice and starting to hang out with other niggas with money besides Keith. So where are you and Eric going this weekend?" Simone asked.

"We're going to catch a movie and grab something to eat."

"Are you going to give him some?" She asked.

"Girl, I just met him last week."

"So, what does that mean?"

"Girl you are a trip, but I'll see you at the Salon on Saturday," I said.

"That's what up. What time is your appointment?" She asked me.

"Mine is at 11am, why?"

"I just wanted to make sure you'll still be there when I get there."

"Alright, one."

"One."

Eric picked me up at 8:30pm. I liked that he was on time. I wasn't hungry because I had grabbed a bite to eat, while I was at the hair salon. So we decided to go to the movies first, he took me to the Emagine Movie Theatre. The movie theater serves alcohol beverages there, so of course I ordered a Strawberry Daiquiri and Eric ordered a beer. We bought a large popcorn and headed into the theater to see *Talladega Nights: The Ballad of Ricky Bobby.* We were laughing so hard in the movie theatre that the usher had to tell us to be quiet. After the movie, we went to Red Lobster for dinner. I got home around midnight. Eric walked me to my door and gave me a hug and a peck on my lips. I really had a good time with Eric, maybe he would help me get over Keith.

While I was out with Eric, Keith called me twice; each time we were in the movie theater, and I didn't want to be rude and answer. I decided that I would return his phone call when I got home.

After taking a shower and calling Simone to let her know how the date went with me and Eric, I decide to call Keith.

"What's up Ma? I see you finally decided to return my phone call huh?" Keith said.

"I was at the movies and I didn't want to be rude and talk, so what's up with you?" I asked.

"Nothing much, chilling at home. I wanted to see you tonight but I guess you're in for the night," he said.

"What did you have in mind for us to do?" I asked.

"I wanted to chill and watch a movie or two. I got some new releases that are at the movies on DVD."

"O.k., you want to watch them tonight or do you want me to come over tomorrow?" I asked him.

"I would like for you to come over tonight, if it's not too late."

"It's cool, give me about forty-five minutes and I'll be over there."

"Alright, I'll see you then. Oh, by the way, who did you go to the movies with? And what movie did you go see?" he asked.

I wondered to myself why would he ask me those questions at the end of our conversation, but I went along with him and answered them.

"I went to the movies with my friend and we saw *Talladega Nights: The Ballad of Ricky Bobby*, why you asked?"

"I just wanted to see if I had a movie over here that you already seen tonight."

I got to Keith's house in less than thirty minutes. I was in a rush to see his fine black ass. Keith answered the door wearing light denim Evisu jeans on, and a white and red Evisu tee shirt on. He was looking good as a motherfucker. It looked as if he had a fresh haircut. At that moment he reminded me of that fine ass man, Idris Elba, that played Stringer Bell on the TV show **The Wire**. I removed my coat and shoes. He hung my coat up in the hallway closet and then I proceeded to follow him downstairs to the basement.

"Are you hungry? Do you want something to drink?"

"No, I'm good right now."

"When the movie starts, I don't want you to be asking for nothing," he said.

"What's all the attitude about?" I asked him.

"I'm just saying, I don't like to do a lot of running around when I watch a movie. I like to chill and watch the whole movie with no interruptions."

"I hear that. Since you're acting all funny style, may I have a bottle of water and a glass of Ciroc with Cranberry Juice?"

"Yes, you may."

While he was getting the beverages, I was looking through the DVD's that he had laying on the table. The movies that he had were, **Idlewild, 16 Blocks, When A Stranger Calls,**

Black Christmas, and Saw 3. I took it upon myself to put in ***Saw 3.***

Keith came back with the drinks and some chips and salsa. We got halfway through the movie when he started to rub my head.

"Your hair looks really nice," he said.

"Thanks, I got it done today."

"You get it done for your date tonight?"

"No, you know I keep my hair done."

"Yeah, whatever."

Keith started rubbing on my thighs and legs, my pussy was throbbing so hard, that I thought it was going to jump out of my pants. He moves his hands from my thighs to my breasts. He then try to unfasten my bra with not much luck, and two minutes later after beginning to become aggravated, I took off my bra for him. Keith than proceeded to suck, nibble, and rub my breast. His touch felt like a light feather against my body. I pulled his head up and begin kissing him in the mouth. We kissed for a couple of minutes, and then his hands roamed my body some more. He whispered, "Let's go up to my room."

"O.k., but are you sure you want to do this? Let you tell it, you can get pussy when you can't eat," I said, referring back to our last conversation when we met for lunch.

"Girl, be quiet and come on."

As soon as we enter the room, our clothes came off. I can't remember who took whose clothes off first. I just know they came off.

Keith stood in the middle of his bedroom with only a pair of socks and some boxer on. His dick was sticking straight up in the air. I could only estimate that his dick was about six and a half to seven inches. His dick wasn't that long and compared to Jamal's it was actually short, but it was thick. I wanted to grab it and put it in my mouth since I hadn't sucked dick in a while, and his was so pretty. Keith's dick was caramel color, which was lighter than the rest of his body; it was all the same color. Unlike most guys, I know whose dicks were two to three different colors. I wasn't going to play myself and give him head our first time, but if he chose to do me I would do him, *fair exchange ain't no robbery.*

Keith turned on the stereo and the raspy, smoothing voice of Anthony Hamilton filled the room. I laid down on my back in Keith's bed while he continued to explore my body. His mouth moved from the top of my head to the bottom of my ankles. When he got to my navel, my body began to shiver and the thought of what ecstasy I was going to experience next. Much to my disappointment, his mouth, nor tongue never entered nor touched my cat trap. He kissed my inner thighs, but not once did he explorer my treasure box. I never had foreplay that felt so good, the only thing that would make it better would be some head, but he wasn't budging and I wasn't either.

*Could it be your nice silky tone that make me want you girl, distance night and love on the phone as I touch myself...*Anthony Hamilton was saying as Keith reach under the bed and retrieved some condoms.

I can't believe that he had some Magnums. He could have gone with some Lifestyles, his dick isn't that big. But anyway, when he enters me, a tear slipped from my eye; it felt so good, his dick fit my pussy like a glove.

"Baby, your pussy is so good. Your shit is wet as hell, I'm gonna come quick." He didn't lie either, the first time we had sex he came in about fifteen to twenty minutes. But he made up for it, because we did it two more times after that. Keith fucked me in every position imaginable for the next two hours.

When I got up to use the bathroom and to wash up, the clock read 4:15 in the morning. I got dressed and said goodbye and headed home. He asked me was he going to see me at church. I told him if I get up.

"After what you did to me, I need to go to church and ask for forgiveness," I said trying to be funny, but I guess he wasn't amused.

"You better get your butt up," Keith said. Then he got up and walked me to the door. He kissed me on my forehead.

"I had a good time last night, I hope we can do it again real soon," Keith said with a smirk and then he said, "Call me when you make it home."

I was so tired when I arrived at church with my mother. She gave me an evil look this morning when I walked downstairs with my purse in hand ready to go to church.

"Where are you about to go?" she asked.

"To church with you," I said.

"So now you want to go to church, you haven't been in the last three Sundays. What makes today so special?"

"I go to church when I get up on time, and today I'm up. So I want to go to church. Is it a problem, because I can drive myself?"

"Don't get smart, before I smack the shit out of your ass."

"Whatever," I mumbled under my breath.

As soon as I saw Keith, I got my second wind. He just made my day. I sat in the pew thinking about the wild night Keith and I shared last night, knowing that I shouldn't be having these thoughts in church. It seemed as if the pastor knew what I was thinking, because the title of his sermon was *Lust & Temptation.*

When church was over, Keith came up to my mother and myself and spoke, and asked if we wanted to go out for an early dinner. My mother was hesitant for a minute, but I quickly accepted for the both of us. We meet up with Keith at Chili's. I was hoping that my mother would start to like Keith after this dinner, but I was wrong. I couldn't wait to go. Not because their encounter wasn't going good, but I wanted to call Simone and let her know that I got some, and also I couldn't wait for work tomorrow so I could tell Michael as well.

Chapter Ten

Go Shortie, It's Your Birthday

Go Shortie, it's your birthday. We gonna party like it's your birthday, and we don't give a fuck because it your birthday! Fifty Cent was blazing in the background as I was getting dressed, so I would be ready on time to hang out with my girls for my birthday. Simone's freak ass had hired some male dancers to come to her house and strip for us, then we were gonna go to Morton's Steak House for dinner, and then we were gonna end the night at this club called **The Avenue**. I had no idea what to wear for the night since it was an unusual hot autumn day and the temperature was about 64 degrees.

It was October 9, 2006. I turned twenty-three years old and I was happy. I thought life couldn't get any better. I had a good man in my life, my work life was going good *although it could be better* and I had good people in my life.

"Girl turn down that god damn music." My mother yelled from her bedroom downstairs.

"It's my birthday, I don't know why you tripping."

"I don't give a fuck what day it is. Turn down that shit now!"

I was so glad that I was spending the night at Simone's house. I was in no mood to hear my mother's mouth about me staying out all night. I did as I was told and turned the music down and proceeded to get dress. I decided to wear a long brown, short sleeve, Donna Karan turtleneck dress with a black

A S A P u b l i s h i n g C o m p a n y

and white belt, and a pair of Kenneth Cole knee high brown boots. My accessories were simple. I had on my diamond earrings, a silver necklace with a rhinestone shaped heart attached to it, and the two-carat diamond platinum tennis bracelet that Keith gave me the day before for my birthday gift.

Keith had to go to Ohio to take care of some business, so tonight it was just gonna be me and my girls. Keith had a dozen pink roses sent to my job the day before with a note attached saying;

Sorry I can't be here with you for your birthday but I hope my gifts make up for my absent. Enjoy yourself and stay out of trouble.
Keith

I didn't know what gifts he was talking about. I tried to call him but I kept getting his voicemail so I continue with my day. When I got home there was a big, gift-wrapped box sitting on the dining room table with a card on top of it with my name on it. The card read;

Happy Birthday, See you when I get back.

I opened the box up expecting to see a purse, some boots, or something big, but instead I found twenty-three hundred dollar bills on top of a long gold box. When I opened the box up there was a platinum two-carat diamond tennis bracelet, my mouth just dropped opened. I couldn't believe Keith had got me all of this for my birthday. I knew from that moment on that I would never leave him, but I was also scared because Simone and Joy were telling me that Keith was the big dope man in the Detroit area.

Simone arrived at my house at 6:27pm. She was late as usual. Our reservations were for 7:00pm, and we still had to go get Keisha. I decided that I didn't want to see no dirty dick niggas stripping, so we canceled that.

Sheretta and her girl MarKita were going to meet us there. Michael said that he didn't want to go because there were going to be too many *hoes* there as he put it, so he took me to lunch the day before. Danielle was going to meet us at the club later that night. She told me to call her when we left Morton's. She said, she didn't want to hang out with all my friends. She didn't want to feel awkward around my girls because she was gay, and didn't know how they would react. I told her she didn't have anything to worry about, that they were all cool. I know that Simone had done a couple of threesomes. So she has got down with a girl before, and with Keisha's job profession, she would do anything for some money *just like Simone, so I know she got down before.*

After everything was said and done, we got to the club around midnight. Danielle already had a table reserved for us, so we didn't have to stand around looking stupid. Simone ordered two bottles of Moet Rose. She felt like a baller that night. We laughed, drank, and had a good time. Blunt and Eric show up about an hour later and ordered another bottle of Moet and shots of Patron for all of us. We all were so drunk that the manager of the club had to come put us out. We didn't want to leave, we all were just kicking it and talking shit to each other. Everyone decided to go back to Simone's house and get high. Since I rode with Simone, I didn't have to worry about driving. Blunt and Eric decided to follow Simone and I home. When we got to Simone's house, Blunt rolled up a blunt and Simone, Danielle, Keisha and Blunt started a smoking session.

"Girl hit the blunt it's your birthday," Simone said.

"Whatever, you know I don't get down like that, just keep doing you."

"You're such a lame."

"I'll be that, I'm just gonna stick to drinking. Does anyone want a shot of Patron while, I'm up?" I asked.

"Yeah," They all said simultaneously.

After they all finished smoking Eric asked, "So what are you going to do for the rest of the night?"

"You mean the rest of the morning?" I asked.

"You know what I mean," he said.

"Nothing, chill until I fall to sleep, I guess."

"So you're staying over here tonight?"

"Yeah."

"Well, I'm gonna chill with you. Is that ok?" Eric asked.

"You good, I guess we need to get the futon out," I said while laughing.

Simone drunk and high ass started talking out of the side of her mouth, "Y'all nigga's need to put some money on the floor and we all can get down." I looked at her like she had lost her damn mind.

"What do you mean by that?" I asked.

"Bitch, you know what I mean. We all can fuck each other for some bread."

"You know, I'm not even cut like that. I can't believe that you put me out here like that."

"I'm sorry, Miss Goody to shoes," Simone said.

"It's not even like that. I'm just not going to put myself out there like that." Eric saw that our conversation was beginning to escalate, so he jumped in on the conversation.

"Y'all need to chill out. You know that your girl was just playing with you, it's your birthday. Chill, let's have some more shots."

"Yeah, you right. I took it the wrong way," I said. Simone came up to me and gave me a hug.

"You know, I was just playing girl."

I know how Simone gets down and I know she was not playing, and from the way Blunt was looking at me, he wanted it to go down. I shook that mess out of my mind and continued to have three more shots with Eric. Everybody started leaving the house around 4am. I thanked everyone for hanging out with me.

We ended up getting in bed at five in the morning. I was so tired, I didn't even bother turning the TV on or wrapping my hair up. I had brought a wife beater and some shorts to wear to sleep in since I thought it was going to just be Simone and me there. While we lay in bed, Eric started to run game on me.

"You know, you were looking good tonight, right?"

"Thanks."

"I mean it, Simone said that you had someone that you were talking to, but if I was that nigga, I wouldn't leave you alone looking that good all by yourself. A nigga like me might come and snatch you up."

"I don't think that he has anything to worry about," I said.

"Straight up, you dissing me like that boo?"

"What boy, I'm just saying, I'm not married to anyone so it is what it is. I don't have a man, I just got friends."

"That's what's up," he said.

I lay with my back facing Eric. He had his arms wrapped around my waist. An half-an-hour or so later, which I thought he would be sleep, Eric started kissing on my shoulders and down to the spine of my back. It was feeling so good that I didn't want to stop him. I guess he thought he was being slick, but I was so drunk and horny, I wanted something to go down. Plus, he was looking good as hell his-self tonight with his Black Locoste sweater, black Chino pants, and black Gucci boots on. He dressed so preppie to me, and I liked it. He wasn't looking like a thug, but like a young rich, educated black man and that turned me on.

Eric eased his hand down in my panties, while still kissing on my back. When he got his hand to my clit, I knew he was surprise to see how wet I was. He started rubbing on my clit and moving his fingers in and out of my pussy. It was feeling so good that I started to moan.

"You like that. Don't you?" He whispered in my ear.

"Yeah, don't stop," I said.

Then he turned me over so that I was now lying on my back. He roughly but smoothly took off my shorts and panties and pulled my wife beater off. He started to suck on my breast, taking his time with each one of them; making sure that he spent equal time on them both. Then he cupped both of them together and started licking them at the same time. That shit was turning me on. He moved from my breast to my navel, and from my navel to the spot of no return. He teased me with slow and long licks on my clitoris, and then he moved around to my lips and finally landed inside of my pussy. He was sucking and slurping so loudly, I knew Simone and Blunt heard it all. It felt so good that I couldn't contain myself. And when I came, I yelled his name.

"Damn, Eric why are you doing this to me?" I asked him in the heat of the moment.

"You like this shit don't you? I bet your man can't eat pussy like this. Can he?" This nigga just ruined the mood for me. Why did he have to say that stupid shit? I hadn't even thought about Keith until he said that stupid shit. Even though Keith and I weren't a couple; we didn't even have an understanding. I still felt guilty about fucking Eric. I wanted to stop but it was feeling so good, and I didn't know what Keith was doing. He was in another state, probably fucking and sucking too, so I just went with the flow.

"I don't have a man but if I did, I don't think he could eat pussy as good as you," I said to Eric.

"Well, I bet no nigga you been with can eat pussy as good as me."

"Nigga shut the fuck up with that bullshit. You'll fuck up a good nut. You know and I know that you can eat pussy, so enough with that shit."

Eric started laughing, "You know, you got a smart mouth."

"Are we gonna talk the rest of the night? Or are we gonna fuck?" I asked.

"I got something to shut you up with," Eric said, and he wasn't lying. He was rubbing his dick; getting it extra hard. And when he pulled down his boxers, my mouth dropped. Seeing the size of his penis for sure shut me up.

"Cat got your tongue now. I thought you would be quiet." He reached down into his pants pocket to get a condom. When he pulled out a XL Magnum, I knew that I was in trouble. I wanted to tell him that I was scared. But as much shit as I was talking, I couldn't go out like that, so I took it like a champ.

Eric shoves his dick into me so hard that I let out a scream, "Damn, nigga take it easy! You know you're working with a monster."

"I want you to talk all that shit that you were talking earlier," he said.

"Look, you're not about to beast fuck me, you need to chill with all that rough shit."

"Just lay back and take the dick."

"Nigga, ease the fuck up."

After a couple of minutes going back and forth, Eric finally eases up. His foreplay was so tender and nice, but his sex was rough and hard. He took long deep strokes, not once did he want me to get on top. He wanted to stay in control.

"This pussy is so wet and good. I can stay in this pussy all night," Eric said. It felt like he was ripping my insides out. I wanted to tell him to stop, but I put myself in this situation. I was just hoping that he would hurry up and bust a nut.

Twenty minutes has past already, then at last, he turned me over and start hitting it doggy style. The pain got unbearable and I yelled out, "Don't go deep!" Then he came.

He got up to go to the bathroom to wash up. I notice that Simone was coming out of her room laughing, "Girl, I can't believe you fucked ole boy, I thought you was in love with Keith."

"Whatever, I'm trying to be like you."

"If you trying to be like me, you would have got paid before. He smelled the pussy," she said.

"I hear that."

"Well let me get back to this nigga, he wants to fuck me in the ass. I told him he got to pay me at least two fifty."

"Girl you a hot mess, goodnight," I said.

"Goodnight hoe, make sure you clean my futon off and spray some Lysol on it," Simone said.

Eric came out of the bathroom with his boxer on while Simone was walking back to her room. She looked down at his boxers and said, "I know why you were moaning and groaning."

"Bye, bitch," I said.

Eric had a warm rag in his hand and washed me up. We talked for a minute, then fell to sleep. I got up the next afternoon and headed to Somerset Mall with the girls to spend some of the money Keith gave me for my birthday.

Chapter Eleven

This Christmas

The month of December wasn't a good one for my mother and me. She was on my head so much about all the time that I was spending with Keith. Ever since we first had sex, we have been inseparable. That is except for the times when he's out of town on business or hanging out with his friends, but for the most part we were together the majority of my time. If I wasn't at work or hanging with the girls, I was at Keith's house. The only time my mother would see me was on Sunday morning, when we would go to church together, but afterwards I would leave church with Keith. The week before Christmas things had gotten so bad between my mother and me. We had an all out argument about me not coming home on the weekends.

"If you think that you're going to be spending the night out and coming in anytime you think, than we have a problem," She said.

"I'm a grown woman. I can do what I want to do," I said.

"You can't do shit when you don't pay any bills. If you stay out one more time without calling, you can just pack your shit and get the fuck out!"

"Are you for real?"

"As real as a hundred dollar bill," she said.

My mother had plans for us to spend Christmas with our immediate family; that meant my sister and her family- my mother, Keisha, her son, her mother and brother. I was looking forward to seeing my sister and her family, but being bothered with Keisha and her ghetto fabulous people was another story. My sister moved out to Houston when she was nineteen years old. She got pregnant at eighteen years old, had a baby at nineteen and got married to a military man, her high school sweetheart, Douglas Deon Weaver. My sister has two children a boy named Marcus Deon Weaver that is eight years old, and a little girl named Brooklyn Tamara Weaver age six.

My mother looks at my sister whose name is Tiffany Maria Weaver, as the perfect child. She got married, went to college. Now she's a second grade teacher and has the perfect family. I always got along with my sister even with the five year age gap. We still hung tight up until she got pregnant, and her life started to revolve around Douglas and her kids, but I couldn't wait to see them.

Later that night, I went out to dinner with Keith. I had told him about the conversation, well rather the argument that my mother and I had.

"Baby, don't worry about it. Things will get better between the two of you, just give it time. But let me ask you this, do you want to have your own place? Or are you happy living with your mother?" he asked.

"I would love to have my own place, it's just that I'm not financially ready. I don't want to put myself in debt. Right now, I would like a new car instead of my own place. I know what you're about to say, that's real ghetto. To get a car before you get an apartment, but I have a place to live. I just have to abide by her rules."

"If you like it, I love it. But how much money do you think you would need to get your own apartment?"

"I don't know. I would need to furnish the apartment and pay the monthly bills. I guess around five thousand dollars," I said.

Following dinner, I went over Keith's house but I didn't stay to long because I wanted to keep the peace with my mother. So we had a quickie and I left.

Ever since my birthday, Keith hadn't been spending money on me like I thought he would. I thought my birthday was just the beginning; I presume that I would be getting cashed out. Guess I was wrong, but I never once asked him for anything. Since I didn't have to pay any bills at home, my money went on clothes and into my saving account.

Christmas came in no time. I didn't have any time off at work since I was one of the new people hired in. I had to work on Christmas, my mother had prepared a big dinner; honey baked ham, barbeque ribs and chicken, candy yams, macaroni and cheese, collard greens, potato salad, a fresh garden salad, green beans and potatoes, sweet potato pies, lemon meringue pie, upside down cake, and a double chocolate cake. She was so happy that my sister was in town that she went all out.

I had to be at work later that night at 8:00pm to help with the scheduling with the eleven o'clock news. Simone and I had made plans for her to come over my house and have dinner with my family since she wanted to see my sister and we were going to exchange gifts. Keith also was going to stop by and exchange gifts as well. He told me that he was going to drive to Cleveland to visit his daughters.

The time was three in the afternoon. Keisha and her son walked in the door looking and smelling good. Jason looked so cute with a Sean John winter coat on with the fur around the hood, and matching hat and gloves. When she took his coat off, he had on a black and red Sean John outfit with some black Timberland boats. He was just too much. Keisha had on some True Religion jeans with a gorgeous red and yellow sweater, with some cute black boots to match with an imitation yellow Gucci purse.

Everyone started coming over a little after four o'clock. Simone called and said that she was just going to drop my gift off and leave since Blunt had invited her over to his mother's house for dinner. When my sister and her family pull up in the drive way, Simone and Blunt followed right behind them in a brand new, Black 750Li Sedan. She was in the passenger side, just smiling. Simone jumped out and ran to my sister Tiffany, not even noticing Douglas or the kids.

"What's up bitch?" Simone said to Tiffany.

"Girl, I see you still got a foul ass mouth. I miss your ass. So what's up with you? I see you still getting money." Tiffany said while looking at the car and watching Blunt's fine ass getting out of the car.

"And you know it bitch."

"Girl watch your mouth in front of the kids."

"My bad. Blunt can you get the bags out of the trunk for me thanks."

"Damn, y'all can come in. I want to see my niece and nephew, before I have to go to work. Bring y'all asses in the house." I said.

"Girl if you don't stop all that cussing, I'm gonna kick your ass," my mother said while walking up to the door.

Everybody came in the house. We all sat around, gossiping, eating, and just catching up on everything.

"I'm sorry, but I have to go. My friend and I are going over his mother's house for dinner," Simone said.

"Yeah, but if I would have known that there would be this much food over here, we would have made plans to come over here," Blunt said jokingly, and everyone laughed.

"Girl, get my gift so we can exchange gifts before I leave," Simone said to me.

"Bring your butt upstairs, it's in my closet," I said.

"I don't feel like taking off my boots."

"Girl bring your ass."

When we got to my room, Simone sat on my bed and said, "Hurry up. I want to meet my man's family."

"Bitch, next week you'll have a new man, and when have you ever had a real boyfriend? Are you done getting money?" I asked.

"Hell nawl, it's just that Blunt been spending money and time with me. He's the only nigga, that invited me out to meet his family for the holidays, and that lets me know that he's feeling me."

"I hear that," I said. I went in my closet and pulled out Simone's gift. She was so surprise at how beautiful the gift wrapping was.

"Girl, what's in here? It better be a purse," she said teasingly.

"Whatever hoe, I ain't one of these trick ass niggas."

"Thank you girl, these boots are fly, and you know I got the perfect outfit to wear with them."

"If you don't, you gonna go out and buy one," I said.

"I know right."

I had bought Simone some black knee high Kenneth Cole boots with silver zippers hanging off the side of each boot. She handed me my gift, it was in a Macy's bag.

"Damn bitch, I couldn't get my shit gift wrapped?"

"Like you said, you're not one of these niggas' I fuck with." Simone had bought me some Seven Jean and a cute t-shirt to wear with the pants, the outfit was cute. We hugged each other then headed down the stairs.

"Girl, what did Blunt get you?" I asked.

"He bought me a Gucci purse and a pair of sun glasses to match."

"That's what's up. What about your other tricks?" I asked while laughing.

"Shit, I got money and gift cards, no one took the time out to go shop for me, like Blunt."

"Girl, you on ole boy's head, it might be a wrap for them other niggas."

"Not right know, Blunt's money ain't long enough."

"So what did Keith get you for Christmas?" Simone asked.

"I don't know, he hasn't come over yet. I told him that I have to be at work by eight tonight. He said, he would drop by before I go to work because he is leaving for Ohio to visit his kids."

Everyone said their goodbyes to Simone and Blunt. We all started to exchange gifts ourselves. When all was said and done, I ended up with two pair of slacks, two sweaters, a pair of boots and three gifts cards.

Time was whining down, it was five o'clock so I told everyone that I was gonna lay down for a minute before I have to go to work. My sister and her family were staying with us, so I would see them later anyway.

"Goodnight, I'll see you in the morning because Douglas, the kids and I are going over his parents house in a minute." Tiffany said.

"O.k. see you when I see you," I said.

I had a slight attitude because it was five o'clock and I hadn't heard from Keith. I wasn't going to call him, I didn't want him to think that I was pressed or on his head. I figured he forgot about me and headed to Cleveland to see his kids. I'll just call him tomorrow.

Before I could lay my head down good, my sister started knocking on my door.

"Yeah, what's up?" I asked.

"Girl you got some fine ass nigga down here, wanting to see you," she said.

"Ok, tell him I'll be down in a minute."

"Where you meet him at?" Tiffany asked.

"At church," I said.

"How long have you known him?" She asked.

"Bitch, what's up with these twenty one questions? I got to get dressed," I said.

"Fuck you, I'll go let him know you'll be down in a minute."

"Thank you," I said with much attitude. I hurried up and put my work clothes on because by this time it was a quarter to six, and I had to be at work at eight. When I finally came down stairs, I noticed that Tiffany's friend Ebony was sitting in the living room, eating and talking to my mother. I said hi to her and scanned the house for Keith. I found him in the kitchen playing with my niece.

"Merry Christmas," I said.

"Same to you."

"I thought you weren't going to make it."

"I had to take care of a couple loose ends before I get on the road. Speaking of which, don't you have to go to work in a few?" Keith asked.

"Yeah, but first I would like my Christmas gift."

"Straight up little momma, I didn't even get you nothing." I was pissed when he said that, but I kept my cool.

"Well, I got you something, but it's in my car. Let me go get it." I ran to the living room closet, grabbed my coat and retrieve his gift out of the trunk of my car. When I got back in the kitchen, Keith was sitting on the barstool drinking some cranberry juice.

"Damn, you need to work out if you're out of breath already," he said.

"Whatever, here's your gift," I said. "Thanks, the gift wrapping is beautiful. Do you want me to open it now or wait?" Keith asked.

"You can open it now, it's up to you," I said.

"I'll open the gift up now, but I'll wait to read the card later."

"O.k."

"First, let me give you your gift."

"I thought you didn't have anything for me."

"I lied." Keith handed me a card.

When I opened the card up it was a cashier check for the amount of five thousand dollars. I didn't even pay attention to what the card said. I was too busy looking at the check.

"You can close your mouth," Keith said.

"I can't help it, I never seen this much money or rather this check amount in my life. What's this for?" I asked.

"I remember you saying that you wanted to get your own place, but you didn't have enough money. So this should help you out a bit."

"Yeah, but I don't know the first place to look."

"Well if you would have read the card, you would have seen that I got you an apartment."

He was right- the card read;

Merry Christmas, I hope that this money would be enough for you to furnish your new apartment. We can go take a look at it when I get back on Monday. Hope you don't mind me taking the liberty to purchase your apartment.

Love, Keith
"2006"

I just couldn't believe it. I was finally moving out of my mother's house. I couldn't wait to call Simone and my best college friend Tory to let them know about my Christmas gifts.

"Now it's your turn to open your gift up."

When he looked in the box he started to smile, I had bought him a pair of brown Bally loafers.

"Thanks, you didn't have to spend this much money on me," Keith said.

"Boy what? I should be saying the same thing to you."

"Well, baby girl I have to go. I'll call you when I touch down."

"O.k., be careful. Don't drive too fast and tell your kids I say hi."

"Alright, one."

"Thanks, I love the gifts and I love you." I said.

He didn't even say anything. We had never ever said the *love* word to each other, so I must have taken him by surprise, because all he said was ok. Keith left and I went up stairs to get dressed for work, while I was getting dressed my sister came in my room.

"Girl, does he have an older brother by the name of Derrick?" She asked.

"I don't know. All I know is that he has two brother's; one older and one younger. Why you ask?"

"Because Ebony said that she knows his family, and that his older brother is in prison for murder and has been in there for the past eight years."

"How does she know all of this?" I asked.

"Her girl, Ashley use to mess with his older brother. You remember Ashley, don't you? She came by sometimes with Ebony."

"Yeah, so what's the big deal?"

"Girl, Ebony said that nigga was crazy. He used to whoop Ashley's ass all the time. She said that the whole family is crazy, and that they don't give a fuck; they are heavy in the street."

"Girl, you know how they gossip. I don't believe that. Keith has a job and he is so nice and sweet. He goes to church every Sunday. She didn't say any of this in front of mommy, did she?" I asked.

"Nope, she just told me. Just be careful. He looks like he don't play no games. Anyway, what did he get you for Christmas?"

I forgot all about the check. I showed Tiffany the check and the card and she started to scream. I told her to shut the fuck up before our mother came up stairs.

"So when are you going to tell mommy?" she asked.

"I don't know, I guess after I go look at the apartment. I know she's going to be mad."

"Yeah, but you have to live your life. Shit, you're twenty-three years old, you don't have any kids, and you're doing good. Just don't let him control you and get some boundaries established. You don't want him thinking that he can control you, just take it slow."

"I will, let me get out of here. I'll see you later."

# # # # #

Monday came quick, it was the day before New Years' Eve. I still didn't tell my mother about the Christmas gift that Keith got me. I wanted to wait and make sure that it was a sure bet before I told her. Keith picked me up around two o'clock that afternoon.

"So are you ready to see the apartment I picked out for you?" he asked.

"Yeah, I hope I like it. I see you like to take control of situations."

"Whatever girl, this is my gift to you."

We left Detroit and were headed into the city of Novi, Michigan. There were a lot of condos and apartments all around. A couple of minutes later we pulled up and saw a beautiful apartment/townhouse complex.

"This is so pretty, where is my apartment at?"

"Hold your horses, we're about to get to it now."

We pulled up to the second apartment unit in the complex, we got out. Keith pulled out a pair of keys and opened the door, then we walked up to the second floor and unlocked the door and my mouth drop. The apartment was stunning. It was a two bedroom apartment with one and half bathrooms, a living room, dining room, and the kitchen was so big that I could put a small table in it. The kitchen came with all of the appliances such as; microwave, refrigerator, stove and dish washer. There was a washer and dryer off to the side of the kitchen. The master bedroom had a full bathroom with a whirlpool tub in it.

"This is nice, but I can't afford this apartment. I know it has to be at least eight hundred a month."

"I didn't ask you if you could afford it. This is a gift from me to you. I leased this apartment for a year, for you. So if we're not together in a year, there will be no hard feelings."

"Like I said earlier, you like to take control of situations."

"Whatever. When do you want to move in? The lease starts January 1, 2007."

"New Years Day. Isn't that nice? I guess, when I get a bedroom set and a television for my bedroom. Then I'll be ready to move in."

"You can start tomorrow and do all of that," Keith said.

"I guess you got everything figured out. Now all I have to do is tell my mother I'm moving out."

For the next few weeks, I shopped at Wal-Mart, Target, and Art Van to furnish my apartment. Simone helped me pick out pictures and place settings for the apartment. Simone has great taste. She even picked out my dining room set. When I told her how much money Keith gave me to furnish the apartment, she started to scream.

"Girl I never got that much money at one time from one nigga, ever. You must got some bomb as pussy," she said.

"I don't know. All I know is he got that bread and he gives it to me."

With the money Keith gave me, I bought a bedroom set, two plasma T.V.'s, two T.V. stands, and some dishes and silverware. Everything else I had to put in layaway because I didn't have enough money.

When Keith came over one day and asked why I didn't have a living room set, I told him that I had one in layaway I was going to get it out when I get some more money. After I said that, he said that he would have another check for me that should cover everything else. Indeed it did. By the end of January, my apartment was fully furnished and Keith was spending every weekend with me.

Chapter Twelve

Moving On Up

I can't believe that Keith got me an apartment for Christmas, I really love him. When I told my mother I was moving out, she just looked at me and said that I'm a damn fool if I'm gonna let some man control my life.

"Momma how is he controlling my life? All he did was lease me an apartment for a year. It's not like he bought it for me nor has a key to the apartment. It has two sets and I have both of them. He didn't even ask for the keys to the apartment."

"Yeah, not now but he will. I just don't trust him. He's evil," My mother said.

"Well it is what it is. I can't stay here anymore with all your rules, I'm a grown woman. I can't be having a curfew, so it's better that I move out," I said.

"It's not your own when a nigga buys it for you."

"Whatever," I said.

"Play the fool if you want to but don't come back here when that nigga put you out."

"Don't worry I won't." With that said, I grabbed the rest of my clothes, walked out the front door and never looked back.

My mothers' and I relationship was strained for the next couple of months, but eventually she came around and respected my decision to move out. Keith and my mother were amiable to one another, but you could tell that Keith left a sour taste in my mother's mouth. Oh well he's my man, not hers.

The first month on my own was scary. I had always lived with someone. When I was in college, I had a roommate. When I got an apartment my senior year in college, I had a roommate. I never fully been on my own until now. To tell the truth, I didn't like it. Every noise that I heard, I would panic and call Keith or Simone. Simone would come over or call me crazy and talk to me on the phone until I calmed down. Keith on the other hand would laugh and tell me to stop acting like a little girl. So I had to toughen up. I don't know why I would worry. I lived in a nice complex and the community that I was in was well kept. The apartment complex had two security cars driving around twenty four hours a day. On top of that, the residents of the apartment complex had twenty-four hour access to the maintenance department, and the security company that they hired to secure my apartment compound.

I thought that since I have my own place that I would be spending more nights with Keith than I had before. But in all actuality, we spent less time together. Keith and I still hung out the majority of the weekends and we would go to church together, or I would go with my mother and see him there. But as far as him spending the night, he would come over and spend the night once a week and it would be on the weekends.

Simone said that Keith just got me an apartment so he could keep an eye on me. Even though he never asked for keys to my place, I gave him a set. I thought that it was only right, due to the fact that he pays the rent. I didn't tell Simone or my mother, but when Keith came over he never called first. He would just come over. He would knock first, but he never waited for me to ask who it was before he came in. I wanted to ask him why he even bothered to knock if he was just gonna come right in anyway.

Keith started to make more and more unwanted comments about my relationship with Simone. Every time I went out, he would ask me,

"Are you going with that hoe slut Simone?" or "I hope you not out tricking like that hoe Simone." Keith rarely used profanity unless he was in fact pissed off, so I know he meant what he said about Simone. He really hated her. I've watch enough T.V. and read enough books to know that when a guy hates a girl that much, he must have fucked her before or something to that extent. I think that something went down between the two of them.

It was a Friday night and I had a long week, Valentine's Day was in two weeks and I wanted to hang out. Michael, Danielle, and I stop at the bar for a drink but the both of them had plans for the night so they left. I wasn't going to sit at the bar by myself, so I left as well. I called Keith about three times and he didn't answer the phone. I didn't leave him a voice message because I felt you should only leave a message when it's important or an emergency. I then called Simone but she said she had plans for the night with Michael.

"Girl who is Michael?" I asked.

"The guy that plays for the Chicago Bulls, they're playing the Pistons tonight and we're going to hook up after the game. I got an extra ticket. Do you want to meet me at the game?" Simone asked.

"Nawl, I don't feel like driving that far out tonight. I wanted to go out to a club or something."

"Girl call Keith."

"I did, he's not answering his phone," I said.

"Well than call Eric," she said.

"I can't invite him over, what if Keith comes over?"

"Doesn't he call first? But anyway go over his house or meet him somewhere," Simone said.

"I would feel bad doing that, knowing that I'm with Keith."

"Are you with Keith? You haven't told me that was your man, so is he your man?" Simone asked.

"He's not my man, but he is someone that I'm kicking it with and I wouldn't feel right hanging with Eric."

"You just scared that you might fuck Eric. Keith is not your man, so you can do what you want to do, but let me get off this phone and get runway ready." Simone said.

We both laughed and I hung up the phone.

I tried calling Keith again, this time his phone went straight to voicemail, so I decided to leave him a message saying,

"What's up baby? I was calling to see if you wanted to hang out tonight, but I guess you're busy. So I'm going to go out with Simone. I'll talk to you later. Be safe, one."

I knew that message would get to him because he didn't care for Simone. I decided to call my mother and see if she wanted to go out to eat she said, "Yeah." I headed out the house.

An hour later while we were at the restaurant my phone started to vibrate. I looked at it and it was Keith, I decided not to answer. I would just call him after I dropped my mother off at home. I put my phone in my purse and went on with my dinner.

When I pulled out of my mother's driveway, I grab my phone to call Keith back. I had five missed calls and two voice messages, one from Sheretta (Simone's girl) and the other four from Keith. I checked my message before I called anyone back.

The first message was from Sheretta.

"What's up? Girl Simone called me and said that you wanted to go out. Call me, when you get a chance and let me know what's up."

The next one was from Keith.

"I've been calling your ass for the past hour where the fuck are you?" I knew he would be mad, but not like that. I decided to call him first, but I didn't get an answer.

On my way home I called Sheretta.

"What's up bitch?" she said when she answered the phone.

"Shit, just left my mother's house. We went out to eat at Texas Road House," I said.

"That's what's up, Simone said that you wanted to go out."

"I did earlier, but I didn't have anyone to go out with. So I just kicked it with my momma."

"What you about to get into now?" Sheretta asked.

"Nothing, pulling up to my apartment now. Why you asked? You want to do something?" I asked.

"Yeah, I'm bored. I want to go downtown to one of the casinos or something," Sheretta said.

"Well let me change clothes and I can meet you over Simone's house. I can park my car and ride with you."

"That's what's up," Sheretta said. While she was continuing to talk, I was unlocking my door. I got in the house, cut the lights on and screamed.

"What's wrong bitch?" Sheretta asked.

"Nothing girl, Keith just scared the shit out of me that's all. Let me call you right back," I said.

"Whatever, I know you're not doing nothing now. Just holla at me tomorrow," she said.

"O.k., one," I said.

"Damn, you scared the shit out of me. Why were you in here sitting with the lights off?" I asked Keith.

"I was waiting on your ass. Why you didn't answer your god damn phone?" Keith asked.

"Because I didn't hear it," I said.

"Whatever, don't play with me girl. When I call you, you better answer my call. I don't give a fuck where you're at, you better pick up the god damn phone," Keith said.

"Nigga please, who are you?"

"What, I'm the nigga that's paying these bills up in here."

"You mean bill, you only pay one bill up in here," I said.

"It don't matter how many bills I paid, I'm in charge."

"What? You not even my man. You don't run shit up in here. Know your position."

"Girl, I will smack the shit out of you. I don't have to be your man, we got an understanding and what's understood doesn't need to be said," Keith said.

"O.k. whatever, do you want something to eat?" I asked.

"Nawl, I'm good. I'm about to go. I just wanted you to know what's up. I'll be back by tomorrow," He said, before he gave me a hug and a kiss.

I should have known then that something was off with him. Anytime a nigga sit in the dark for no reason, something's not right. And then his little smart comment, *what's understood doesn't need to be said.* What the fuck does that mean?!

Monday came fast. When I got to work, I didn't waste time telling Michael what went on with Keith and I over the weekend.

"You need to leave dude alone, it sounds like ole boy is borderline crazy."

"Yeah, you right. He does do some crazy shit at times, but I'm not going to leave him alone just yet," I said.

While I was in the middle of talking to Michael, my office phone rang. "Hello, Jennifer Moore's assistant. May I help you?"

"What's up bitch?" Simone said.

"Nothing, at work talking to Michael, what's up with you?" I asked.

"Nothing, waiting on this nigga to come by so I can get some money. I was calling to see if you wanted to go to the All Star Game in Las Vegas." she said.

"Isn't it like right after Valentine's Day?" I asked.

"Yeah, so what?" Simone said.

"I have to see what Keith got planned for us," I said.

"Bitch, you mean you have to ask him if you can go. Shit he might be there himself," Simone said.

"Yeah, you right, well let me call him and see what's up. Can I ask Keisha if she wants to go?"

"Girl, I don't care. It's money out here for everybody. I'm gonna holla at you later. Ole boy is at the door and I want to look on the internet and see if I can get us some cheap plane tickets," Simone said.

"Everything is going to cost a lot since it's only a week and a half away."

"Girl, don't worry about that I got the hook up on the rooms. We just have to pay seventy five dollars each a night," Simone said.

"Alright girl, you know it all. I guess your pussy is that good. I'll holla at you later, peace," I said.

Later that night, Keith came over to eat and spend the night with me. I cooked us some baked chicken breast, baked potatoes, and broccoli with cheese. I figured that was something quick and easy to make and I knew I couldn't mess that up.

"What's up baby girl?" Keith asked.

"Nothing, chilling. How was your day?" I asked.

"Alright, niggas act like they don't want to pay a nigga. I had to check a couple of dudes about this house on Six Mile and Evergreen. Chris and I did all the improvements to the house and now they don't want to pay." Chris was Keith's so called partner in their real-estate business, called *Detroit's Best Real-Estate Company*. Chris was a nice looking guy, he stood about 6'3 tall, a nice brown complexion with steamy dark eyes, and a nice Cesar fade. Chris always dresses like a thug. He weighs about two hundred and eighty pounds. He's a big man, but he wears his weight well.

"So, I guess you know not to mess with them anymore," I said.

"Wrong, them dumb niggas know not to fuck up our money anymore," Keith said. How could they fuck up his money if he was doing his job? This led me to believe that Keith was into some other shit as well.

"Baby, do you have anything planned for us for Valentine's Day?" I asked.

"Why you ask that for?"

"I just wanted to know because Simone and her girl invited me to go to the All Star Game with them the weekend following Valentine's Day, and I wanted to go if we didn't have any plans for the whole weekend." Keith's face turned to stone as he spoke.

"You love hanging with them freaky hoes. I think you might be cut like your girl and just playing the role for me. Why would you want to take your ass to Las Vegas? We can go for the fight in May."

"First off nigga, my girl is what she is. That don't have shit to do with me. Second of all, I haven't been anywhere since I've been back in the D. I just want to hang out with my girls and kick it for the weekend. We will leave Thursday afternoon and come back Sunday night; early Monday morning," I said.

"You know what- do what you want to do. If you want to be a freak hoe, then so be it. But I'm telling you now, if I hear anything about you or your girls acting like some hoes, I'm beating everybody's ass."

"Whatever nigga, there ain't any reason for us to be acting like hoes. Everybody got somebody. Baby, I'm happy with you. Shit if I wanted to fuck with other niggas, I would do it here. I don't need to go all the way to Vegas to fuck with a nigga," I said.

Smack!!!

Keith smacked the shit out of me.

"Bitch, don't be trying to talk that slick shit to me. I'm not the one to be fucking with. You been hanging around them hoe's too long. Don't let them be the cause of your ass getting beat."

Keith said. I didn't even respond. I just held the left side of my face and ran to my bedroom and locked the door.

Boom! Boom!

"Come open this door before I knock it down," Keith said.

"Just leave me alone and take your crazy ass home."

"Bitch, I ain't going nowhere. I pay bills up in this bitch. I'll go when I want to." Keith kept knocking on the door until I finally let him in the bedroom. I was so scared, I didn't know what he would do to me. He had the look of a demon on his face. I just stood in front of him crying.

"What the fuck, you crying for? You the one with the slick mouth. You haven't come across a real nigga to put you in check, but you done met the right one now. Clean yourself up then go out and clean up the mess in the dining room," Keith said.

I just thought to myself, *how did I get here*? Standing in front of me was the man of my dreams or so I thought. I would never guess in a million years that Keith would be treating me like this. I did as I was told.

While I was cleaning the dining room up, Keith had taken a shower, got in the bed and was watching ESPN. That was his favorite show next to watching actual football and basketball games. Simone called me as I was heading to the bathroom to take a shower as well; and call it a night.

"Hello," I said.

"What's up girl? Did you ask your man yet if you could go to Las Vegas?" She asked.

"Not yet, I'll do it in the morning. He's over here right now ready for me to put it on him," I lied.

"Let me know something by tomorrow, I got three rooms reserved for us. I figure you was gonna call your girl Tory and tell her to meet us out there," Simone said.

"Who the fuck are you on the phone with?" Keith asked as I was entering the bedroom to get my night clothes.

"Girl, what's wrong with that nigga?"

"Nothing let me call you back in the morning and let you know what's up," I said.

"O.k., one."

After I got out of the shower and got in the bed, Keith was knocked out. He had a couple glasses of Remy Martin. I guess he was tired. So I got on my knees, said my prayers and asked God to help me with Keith. I prayed everyday and attended church very often, especially since I got with Keith. But this was the first time, I asked God to help me with man problems. I love Keith and I just didn't want him to leave me. I've had men put their hands on me in the past, just not in this type of situation where it was my man.

The next morning I woke up, Keith was gone. I got up went to the bathroom to pee, brush my teeth, and get in the shower. As I was getting ready to wash my face, I notice an envelope on the sink. I opened it and it had twenty hundred dollar bills in it with a note that read:

"I'm sorry baby, I over reacted last night. I want you to go to Vegas and have fun. Here is some money to go shopping with. Let me know if you need some more, I love you."

I can't believe that he said that he love me; that put a smile on my face. I went to work and told Michael what happened with Keith, of course I left out the part where Keith hit me.

"Baby girl, you need to leave him alone, he sounds crazy."

"I know right, but I love him, and that shit kinda turned me on," I said.

"You a sick chick," Michael said.

"Whatever. Let me call Simone and let her know that it's a go."

Chapter Thirteen

Spoiled

I talked to my girl Tory in L.A and she said that she would meet us in Vegas. Keisha's hot ass was game to ride out too. So it was gonna be Simone, Sheretta, Keisha, Tory, and myself. Everything was set up. I was ready to go party. I've been to Vegas a couple times before; once with Jamal and once with my mother and sister. Valentine's Day was in two days and I still hadn't gotten Keith a gift. Ever since that incident where he slapped me, he's been extra nice to me. He told me to take the day off work for Valentine's Day so that we could spend the whole day together.

The next day when I got off work, I went to Somerset Mall and picked Keith up a pair of Gucci Moccasin shoes. I knew that Keith was going to go all out for Valentine's Day. I was hoping that he got me the new Gucci purse that I seen at the Gucci store in Somerset, when I got his shoes. I told him about the Gucci purse and he said he would get me something that I would love. His comment was, "You act like you have to have some name brand shit to be the shit. You the shit in my eyes, but I'll get you something name brand if that's what you like."

Valentine's Day started off with me waking up to some scandalous head. Ever since Keith and I have been together he has never given me head, I almost came instantly, just feeling his lips on my pussy. After I came for the third time, I figure it was my turn to return the favor. I got on top of Keith, tenderly placing his dick in my mouth, going all the way down to his shaft and working my mouth up and down slowly until his dick was fully erect. This was the first time that I've given Keith a blow job, so I wanted him to enjoy it, and I didn't want him to cum to quick.

"Damn, baby this head is scandalous," Keith said.

I didn't pay him any mind, I continue with the blow job. Once his dick was hard, I moved faster up to the head and just drenched it with saliva and continue sucking the head of his dick until he came in my mouth. After the unbelievable foreplay, we had some incredible sex. While we were having sex, the condom broke. I was scared not about becoming pregnant but about catching a STD. We always used condoms that had spermicide within the lubricant. When the condom broke, I jump up went to the bathroom to urinate and to jump in the shower. Keith got in the shower with me.

After we got dressed, we headed out to eat breakfast. I didn't feel like cooking and Keith didn't press the issue. We decided to exchange gifts when we got back from breakfast. As we were walking out of the door, I saw a black Ranger Rover Sport in one of the parking spaces with a big red bow on it. I had no idea the truck was for me. As I was walking to Keith's truck, I stated, "That is so nice. I have never seen anything like that. That's some shit you see in the movies. I wonder, who up in here Valentine's gift that is?"

"That's your gift," Keith said.

"Stop playing. Shit if that was my shit, you would have said something."

"For real, that's you baby girl," Keith said while holding the keys up in the air. I grabbed the keys and ran to the truck. The interior was Cashmere with the wood grain trim. The truck was fully loaded. I was speechless, then seated on the passenger side was the Gucci purse that I asked for. I started crying and thanking my man. I wanted to give him his gift now, so we headed back to the apartment and I gave him his gift. I told him to take off his clothes and just put on his shoes so I could give him some more head. Needless to say, we stay in the house sucking and fucking all day. Later that night we exchanged Valentine's Day cards, ordered pizza and chilled for the night.

Keith had to leave for a minute to go handle some business so that he could be able to go to the All Star Game and stay for the whole weekend, or at least that's what he told me. I wasted no time after he left to first call my sister, then Simone, Keisha, Michael. And last but not least, my mother to let them know about my wonderful Valentine's Day presents. Everyone was happy for me except for my mother.

"Girl, that nigga owns you now. He already got you that apartment, now you got him buying you cars. He knows now that he has control over you," My mother said.

"No he doesn't. He is just leasing the truck. I have to pay my own car insurance. He just wants to make sure that I have a reliable source of transportation," I said.

"Girl you are so stupid. That nigga is using you."

"How is he using me?" I asked?

"All I'm saying is that nigga is no good and I know he's going to hurt you. Just leave him alone before it's too late."

"Whatever. Happy Valentine's day," I said.

"Same here. Love you and Tomika, be careful."

I love you too Mommy."

I had some last minute packing to do since we all would be leaving tomorrow afternoon for Vegas, so I chilled, packed my clothes and made me a couple of frozen Strawberry Daiquiris. Keith called me later that night, well actually Thursday morning because it was 1:30am when he called, talking about some stuff came up and he was heading home as we spoke. He told me to have a safe trip and to call him as soon as I touchdown.

"I'll see you when I get there. Don't be on no bullshit because I don't want to have to bust no heads when I get there," Keith said.

"Whatever, man. I had a lovely day today. Please don't ruin it. I love you and will call you when I get there."

"Love you too. How are you getting to the airport?" "Simone's gonna drive," I said.

"O.k. baby girl. I love you, see you tomorrow."

"O.k. one."

Keith was coming to Las Vegas with his partner Chris and his boy Mike. They were set to arrive in Vegas first thing Thursday morning.

Chapter Fourteen

All Star Weekend

We arrived in Las Vegas at 4:45pm. Our hotel which was the MGM Grand was already off the hook with ballers from all over. Sheretta and I decided to share a room because we knew that Simone would be getting her grind on, and we both didn't want to be in a room with different men running in and out all times of the day. My girl, Tory was going to fly in on Friday due to the fact that she couldn't get off work on Thursday. I decide to stick her in the room with Keisha. Since Keisha wasn't legal yet, I figured Tory would keep her company when she couldn't hang with the big dogs. Tory wasn't a party girl, she was a quiet down to earth west coast girl. She was medium built, weighed about one hundred thirty pounds. She has a butterscotch complexion with light brown shoulder length hair. Tory has a nice shape, but you could never tell because she doesn't wear skimpy clothes revealing her shape. That left Simone alone in the room.

"Fuck y'all hoes! I don't care if y'all don't want to be in the room with me. I'm gonna be getting money this weekend."

"We know," I said to Simone as we headed up to the service desk to check in. We all checked in and headed to our rooms. All three rooms were on the same floor, which was the twenty third floor.

We all decided to take a nap and freshen up before we headed out to see what was popping in Las Vegas. Simone had gotten all of us passes to get in the Magic Johnson Ballard Tournament on Friday night, thanks to John Blake; the guy who plays for the Lions. She also got all of us tickets to the actual All Star Game. I don't care what anyone says about Simone, that bitch is about money and she gets it. If you don't have any dough, do not look her way.

After I unpacked and got out of the shower, I checked my cell phone. I had three missed calls all from Keith. I had my phone on silent while I was on the plane, and forgot to change it when I got to the hotel. I decided to call Keith before I checked my messages.

"Hello, what's up baby," I asked.

"Why the fuck you ain't been answering your phone? I left you two messages and you're just now calling me back," Keith said. I couldn't believe he was talking to me like that.

"What? You must have me confused," I said.

"Bitch, don't play with me. Where the fuck have you been? When I call you, you better answer the fucking phone."

"Nigga fuck you, who the fuck you think you talking to? You a bitch!"

Sheretta was lying on her bed watching TV, when she heard me arguing on the phone. She turned around to face me and mouthed the words "Who is that?"

I mouthed back, "Keith."

"Did you just call me a bitch?" Keith asked.

"Look, I don't have time to argue with you. You are fucking crazy. I had my phone on silent because I was on the plane and I just remembered to turn the ringer back on. So what is your fucking problem?" I asked him.

"I was worried about you. I haven't heard from you since last night and I figured you should be in Vegas by now. I called you as soon as I touched down. I figured you would do the same," Keith said.

"Whatever, you are on some bullshit right now and I don't want to talk to you anymore, so goodbye." I hung up the phone and started to tell Sheretta what had just happened.

Right in the middle of my sentence, my phone started to ring, and of course it was Keith.

"Hello."

"Look, I'm sorry for tripping on you like that. I just have a lot on my mind and I took it out on you. I know how your freak ass friend gets down, and I just don't like you hanging out with her, especially in Vegas. "But that's no reason for you to call me a bitch."

"I said I was sorry. Look, I apologize for calling you out your name."

You know I didn't mean it. Do you forgive me?" Keith asked.

"Yeah, I guess," I said.

"So what do you have up for tonight? Are you coming to see me?" Keith asked.

"I'm gonna go shopping and sightseeing, then we all are gonna go to Smith & Wollensky for dinner. I didn't think you wanted to see me tonight."

"I want to see you all the time. So call me, when you get back from dinner. I'm staying at Caesars Palace, room 614. Alright baby?"

"Alright."

After I got off the phone with Keith for the second time, I explain to Sheretta what went down with Keith and me. Consequent to giving her all the details, I checked my voice messages; the first one that Keith left was polite, and the second one was off the hook.

"I don't know what the fuck you doing but you need to answer your fucking phone. You out there with them hoes, acting like you done lost your damn mind. You better call me back right now."

I erased the messages and just shook my head, "what have I gotten myself into?" I thought. Simone called our room around 7:00pm and asked us were we ready to go shopping. I told her to give us about thirty minutes. She said that she was gonna call Keisha and Tory and tell them to get dressed.

We all met downstairs in the lobby at 7:30pm. Everyone was dressed causal but sexy, even Tory. Tory had on some skintight Seven jeans with a snug fitted t-shirt, some brown Nine West pumps, a cute short brown wool pea jacket and a Louis Vuitton purse winter 2006 collection. Since it was February it was still a little chilly in Vegas. It was about 62 degrees. Simone has on some Gucci jeans; extra skin tight, but I will say this, the jeans made her look like she had an ass, with a Gucci halter top, a Gucci sweater that stop at the middle of her back and only cover her arms. Simone was doing it real big with some black and gray knee-high Gucci boots with the purse to match, and to top it off, she had on some black Gucci sun glasses setting on top of her freshly done short sub-metric jet black sew-in, the girl was fresh to death. Sheretta, was a little less flashy with the name brand as Simone. She had on some black knee-high Jessica Simpson boots with some black leggie and a black Guess Sweater dress, short black leather jacket that was similar to Simone's sweater, and a big black leather Kenneth Cole purse. Keisha's ghetto ass pull it together and class herself up with some black Seven jeans, a black button up BeBe shirt, some black boots and a red Gucci purse. I set it off with some skin tight light blue Rock & Republic jeans, a light blue V neck sweater that showed a lot of my cleavage, some different color blue ankle boots and a blue and gray Gucci purse. We were sex in the city, Detroit style.

When we got to the restaurant, we all ate steaks and drank Apple Martinis. After dinner everyone decided to go their separate ways. I was going to meet Keith so I text him while I was having my third and last martini, letting him know that I was on my way. Sheretta and Tory decided to come with me to Keith's hotel to gamble a bit and to check out the Forum shops located in the lower level of Caesars Palace. Keisha and Simone being the hoes that they are decide to go back to the hotel and go to a party at one of the clubs inside the hotel that a guy from St. Louis was having. Simone and Keisha both said that the guy looked like his paper ran long and they were going to find out. We all said our goodbyes and headed our separate ways. When I arrived at Keith's room, he answered the door with just a towel on.

"Damn baby, you look good," I said.

"Get your fast ass in here," Keith said.

"What's wrong with you?" I asked.

"Nothing, you just be on some bullshit. You were supposed to be here almost an hour ago. What the fuck you been doing? Fucking with some nigga, I knew you was going to be out here hoeing, especially since you're here with your freak ass friends."

"Nigga, I'm tired of you talking shit about me and my girls. Ain't nobody a freak. You need to just chill the fuck out. Why are you tripping on me about some petty shit?" I asked.

"Because you be on some bullshit, but it's cool. Just don't let me catch you doing something. What you got up for tonight?" Keith asked.

"I thought I would chill with you, for the night. Why, do you have plans?" I asked.

"Not right now, but later me and my niggas are going out to a couple of parties."

"O.k. I guess, I'll leave now then."

"Bitch, you bet not move. Sit your ass down and chill. You just want to take your hot ass out with your freak ass girls."

"Whatever," I said. Keith had this devilish look in his eyes that scared the shit out of me. So I just sat down on the couch and ask him to fix me a drink. I listened to him talk shit for another thirty minutes before he shut up and calmed down.

"Baby, you make me so mad sometimes. I think that you are out to play me and I can't have that shit. I'll kill a motherfucker before they play me. I got too much to lose out here. I'm not for any games," Keith said.

"What are you talking about? I haven't done anything to disrespect you. All I want to do is love you. You think that everyone is out to get you, for what I don't know. I just want to be your girl, chill with you and have a good time."

Keith grabbed me by my arm and lifted me up and starting kissing me all in the mouth and on my neck. He started taking off my clothes. One thing lead to another, and we were on his bed having the greatest sex ever with all the arguing and making up. Keith didn't put on a condom and I didn't stress the issue either.

I got back to the hotel around 3:00am in the morning. Keith wanted me to spend the night but I didn't have my head scarf, and I wasn't going to be in Vegas for the next couple of days with a bad hairdo.

As I was walking up to the very crowded hotel, I saw Keisha and Simone talking to some guys in the lobby.

"What's up Whitcha," Keisha asked.

"Nothing, chilling. Coming back from Keith's room. What y'all up to?" I asked.

"Slow motion, trying to get up on some money," Simone said.

"Well, I'm about to head up to the room. You guys hear from Sheretta and Tory?" I asked.

"Tory in the room sleep with her lame ass and Sheretta somewhere in here gambling. We just saw her about an hour ago," Keisha said.

"Alright, I'll get at y'all tomorrow. Simone, what time is the pool tournament tomorrow? Because I want to sleep all day."

"It starts at 8:00pm."

"O.k., call me if something comes up. I'll be in my room."

"It looks like Keith fucked the shit out of you," Simone said as I walked to the elevator.

"Hold that elevator," a man's voice said as I entered the elevator. I pressed the open door button, as the man ran to get in.

"Would you please press sixteen for me, please? Thanks for holding the elevator," The man said.

"No problem," I said. The man stood about 5ft 8inch. He was dressed conservatively. He had on some black and white Prada loafers with some black slacks and a black, white, and gray polo style shirt. He looked very distinguished. He had a bald head with a salt and pepper goatee, which you could tell he was too young to have. He looked around thirty-three years old.

"So where are you from?" He asked.

"Detroit."

"It seems like everyone here is from Detroit."

"I know right, well this is my floor. You have a nice time here," I said.

"I will baby girl. Oh, by the way, what's your name?" he asked.

"My name is Tomika."

"Nice to meet you Tomika. My name is Reggie, but everyone calls me Red."

"O.k., Red have a good night, I mean morning."

We both laughed as I walked out of the elevator.

I slept half the day away, when I woke up it was 1pm. Simone was still in her bed sleep, so I got up and called Keith. We didn't talk long because he was at the Wynn Casino gambling. After I got off the phone with him, I jumped in the shower. When I was getting out of the shower, Sheretta was on the phone with Simone.

"Bitch, I don't feel like it. I'm tired. She's right here. O.k. hold on." Sheretta held out the receiver for me to grab it. I whispered, "What she want?"

"Somebody to go to this nigga's room with her," Sheretta said.

"I don't feel like going either, what's up?" I said as I grab the phone.

"Nothing, I need you to roll with me somewhere."

"And where might that be?"

"This baller, I know wants me to come to his room and I want to bring someone just to make sure everything is straight," Simone said.

"What about Keisha?" I asked.

"That bitch is booed up with some nigga she met this morning. Please girl, all you got to do is chill while I see what's up; if he wants to trick or whatever."

"Girl, I can't. What if I miss Keith's call or something?" I said.

"You can talk if Keith calls and wants to hang, then leave. I just want you to know what he looks like and where I'm at. Please Tomika. You know I don't never ask you for anything."

"Whatever."

Simone talked me into going to the NBA player's hotel room with her. He had a suite at the Bellagio. When we got to his suite, it was loud music coming from his room. Simone knocked on his door for about five minutes until I suggest that she call him and let him know that she was outside. After the third ring, he picked up.

"What's up baby? I've been knocking on the door for ten minutes now. What's up with that?" Simone asked him, a couple seconds later the door opened up.

"What's up? Baby doll, you look good as hell," he said while waving us in the room.

"Who's your friend"? he asked.

"This is my girl Tomika. Tomika, this is Brian. He plays for the Pistons," she said introducing us to one another.

We said, what's up to each other and I proceeded to sit on the couch. I was so amazed at the suite, I couldn't keep my mouth close. There were about five, 40" or more inch flat screen televisions all over the living and dining area. The kitchen had marble floor and there was a marble top island in the middle of it.

As I was checking out my surroundings, I smelled a foul odor that was coming for the back. I assumed it was from one of the bathrooms. I figured, he was shitting before we got here and he was in a hurry and forgot to spray some air freshener.

"Girl, chill right here for a minute. I'm about to go to the back with him," Simone said.

"You good Ma, do you need anything?" Brian asked me.

"Yeah can you give me the remote control so I can watch T.V.? Also do you have anything to drink?" I asked.

"Yeah, its pop, water, beer, champagne, and liquor in the refrigerator, help yourself." As he was talking, he handed me the remote control.

I flipped through a couple of channels; watching movies on HBO and Showtime. I could have sworn, I heard another man's voice in the room. I shook it off and went to the kitchen. Opening the refrigerator up, all I saw was bottles and bottles of Moet and Cristal champagne all unopened except for one bottle of Cristal, which was one cup from being empty. I don't drink out of open bottles so I decided to open a bottle of Moet, *black label of course.* After finding a cup that I thought was clean enough, I washed it out five times in scolding hot water. I poured me a cup of Moet and brought the bottle in the living room with me. About thirty minutes and a half of bottle later, Simone came walking out of one of the back rooms with a smile of her face.

"What's up? Girl, why you got that stupid smile on your face?" I asked.

"Shit, trying to make some major paper. Is you down to make some money?" Simone asked.

"Girl, what are you talking about? Didn't you and ole boy already fuck? Shit you was gone for an half hour," I said.

"No, we all were back there talking."

"What you mean we all, who else is back there?" I asked.

"Him and his boy, they want to have sex."

"Bitch, is you out of your mind? I'm not fucking no nigga. You are straight up crazy."

"Bitch, they don't want you to fuck, they just want you to watch them fuck me. I already told Brian you weren't cut like that. So what's up? You down?" Simone asked.

I couldn't believe this bitch, she would do anything for a buck. When we get back to our hotel, I'm going to have a talk with her.

"Girl, I'm good, you do you. I'll wait out here for you. I don't want to leave you in a room with two niggas. If something happens to you, I would be blaming myself, but you're on some bullshit for this one. How money hungry can you be?" I asked her.

"Bitch these nigga's is going to give me five thousand dollar for them both to fuck me, shit that's called hitting a lick. I didn't come down here to the All Star Weekend for nothing. I'm about my money. Five thousand will set me straight for the whole weekend. I can go back and chill with John for the rest of the weekend."

"Like I said, do you. I'll be waiting for you right here."

"They want you to watch. They'll pay you two thousand dollars just to sit and watch; that kind of shit turns his boy on. He got major figures too. He plays for the Miami Heat. You know you could use the money, and you don't have to do anything at all. I promise, just watch.

I can't believe that Simone got me in this bullshit, but she was right, I could use the money, and if any one of them niggas try to touch me or do some foul shit it's gonna be a wrap. So I said, "Fuck it." Made me a drink, *this was gonna call for some Remy VSOP,* a double shot of cognac and followed Simone into the back bedroom that she had just came out of.

When I walked in the bedroom, it smelled like straight up ass. I thought to myself, these niggas been up in here fucking each other.

"Damn, y'all need to spray some air freshener up in here," I said.

"Chill girl," Simone said.

"There's some Lysol in the bathroom," Brian said.

I went to the bathroom, got the air freshener and sprayed the room for about a minute.

"I see you got jokes," the guy who plays for the Miami Heat said.

"It's not that. It stinks in here, for real. I don't know how y'all get down," I said. Brian cut the tension by getting down to business.

"I'm gonna need for both of y'all to hand me your cell phones."

"What type of shit is this?" I asked.

"We can't take any risk of this shit getting out. You might have a camera or video camera on your phone, and record all of this and we can't take any chances. I'm not going out like that, I'm paying a lot of money to y'all and I would like to feel safe."

"Whatever," I said.

"Let's just get started," Simone said.

Simone got in the bed with both of them and started sucking the guy who plays for the Miami Heat's dick. She got in the doggy style position, therefore Brian was behind her and old boy was lying on his back underneath her. That girl was getting down and dirty as Brian started fingering her pussy.

"You like this bitch?" Brian said.

Simone couldn't talk because she had a dick in her mouth, but she shook her head yeah and started moaning. Brian was staring at me all the while he was fingering and rubbing Simone's pussy.

Simone was sucking the shit out of ole boy's dick. She was licking his balls, spitting on his dick and jacking him off with her hands all at the same time. My girl was a head doctor for real. Brian was getting so horny watching Simone suck his boy off, that he told her it was his turn to get some head. Simone turned around and started sucking Brian's dick, while ole boy got behind her. He grabbed some KY Jelly from underneath the bed and stuck his dick in her ass. I couldn't believe it, he didn't put a condom on or nothing, but that wasn't the bad part, my girl didn't even flinch. She just took the dick in her ass like a porn star. I can't lie this shit was getting me hot, but not hot of enough to join in. Simone must have been reading my mind, because she took Brian's dick out of her mouth and said, "Girl, you want to join in and get one of these good ass dicks?"

"I'm good. I'm just enjoying the show," I said. I had to play the part, it was stacks on the line. Both guys has some nice size dicks, but for them not to be concern about using a condom, I knew that something wasn't right. Ole boy nutting all over Simone's ass, then he told her to get his dick back hard again. Simone turned back over to face his dick and started sucking his dick again, while Brian put on a Magnum condom and went up in Simone's asshole.

"Damn bitch, who ass is this?" Brian asked.

"It's yours when you up in it," Simone said. I wanted to laugh so hard when she said that shit. Ole boy's dick got back hard, so he then too decided to put a condom on and went up in Simone's pussy. I just thought to myself, *that's a bad bitch, that hoe was taking two dicks up in her at the same time.*

After the fuck session was over with, we got our money and cell phones back and headed to the Forum Shop. Simone bought her a Ferragamo purse and heels to match. I didn't see anything that I liked for myself, so I picked Keith up a pair of Ferragamo gym shoes and wallet to match.

When we got back to our hotel, it was time to get ready to go to the Ballard Tournament. Keith hadn't called me all day so I decided to call him.

"Hello."

"What's up baby girl?"

"Nothing, missing you. What have you been up to all day?" I asked.

"Shit, gambling; winning and losing money. What about you?"

"Shopping, about to get ready to go to the Ballard Tournament," I said.

"O.k., be careful, and call me when you get there, and when you leave."

"I will. Love you," I said.

"Same here." Click the phone went dead.

When we arrive to the tournament around 9pm, it was off the hook. Everybody who was anybody was there, Young Jeezy, Jim Jones, Gabrielle Union, Vivica A. Fox just to name a few. Keisha and Simone were happier than a fag with a bag of dicks. We all were up to par, so fitting in wasn't an issue. Sheretta, Tory and I went straight to the bar and ordered a couple of martinis, while Simone and Keisha went their separate ways trying to find their future baby daddy.

It was a nice environment, and we were having a good time drinking and talking to a couple of guys here and there. Tory met a guy that was from California, so she left and got a table and chilled with him. That just left me and my roommate for the weekend. Sheretta and I hanging by ourselves, looking like some wallflowers. As we were talking about people who were there and all the famous people that were hooking up with one another, but acting like they can't stand the person when they're in front of the camera, someone tapped me on the shoulder. The way that Sheretta was smiling, I knew it was Keith. As I was turning around, I said, "Hey baby." To my surprise it was Red.

"I like that," he said.

"Do you call everybody baby? Especially the people you just met?"

"No, I thought that you were someone else," I said.

"Who was the lucky person that you thought I was?" he asked.

"I thought you were my man-friend." I didn't want to say boyfriend because I didn't want to sound childish and I didn't want to say man, in front of Sheretta, after the way Keith acted yesterday. Then again, Keith never really said that he was my man.

"Well can I buy you and your girl a drink before your man friend comes and take you away?" Red said.

"That would be nice, but I'm not expecting my man friend to come in here tonight."

"That's good to know because you are looking good tonight, and I want to enjoy you all to myself." Red said.

I just smiled. Sheretta got her drink and said, "I think, I'm going to go mingle and leave you two alone. Thanks for the drink and nice to meet you."

"Likewise. Well, I really do have you to myself now," Red said.

I spent the rest of the evening talking to Red. Come to find out that he lives in Detroit, well not Detroit, he lives in Troy Michigan. He told me that he owns a couple of car washes in Detroit and that he is originally from Chicago. He's been in Michigan for the last eight years. I didn't notice the time but it was getting late.

Simone came over to us and asked, "Are you ready to go? Because we want to hit some more casinos, and clubs while everyone is out partying. I heard that the Playboy Club is supposed to be off the hook tonight and I wanted to go over to the Palms Casino and see what's up."

"I don't want to go, I'm gonna call it a night. Who all going with you?" I asked.

"Everybody."

"Even Tory?"

"Yep, you acting like an old woman. We came here to party, stop being so lame."

"Whatever, y'all have fun. I'm gonna catch a cab back to the hotel," I said.

Red cut in as I was talking to Simone, "The cab lines are going to be off the hook, it's the All Star Weekend. I got a car, I can give you a ride back. I'm heading that way as well."

"He's right, we're going to ride with these niggas that Tory's nigga is with," Simone said.

"Alright, I'll see y'all later, be safe."

"O.k., call me when you get to the room and by the way, who is this that you're with; just in case we have to look for you?" Simone said.

"This is Red. Red this is my best friend Simone. I'm sorry for being so rude."

"So Red, are you going to take good care of my girl? Don't try anything crazy, I don't want to have to hurt you," Simone said while trying to flirt with Red on the sly.

I didn't mind because I was buzzing and thinking about getting in the bed.

"Your girl is in good hands, I'll get her back safe and sound," Red said.

While I was riding back to the hotel with Red, I got a text from Keith that read:

Where the fuck you at? The tournament was over with twenty minutes ago. You need to be on your way back

to the room or you need to call in and let me know what's up. NOW.

All I could do is shake my head. I text him back saying:

On my way to the hotel right now. Damn, give me a chance to call or text you.

He texted me back:

Call me now.

I waited till I got to the hotel room to call Keith. I wanted him to see that I was calling from my hotel room. Red rode the elevator with me and walked me to my hotel room and asked if he could see me again before we head back to Detroit.

"I would like that, but I have a friend. I don't think he would appreciate me going out with another man."

"I can respect that baby girl. But I'm digging you right now. So if I get another chance to hang with you, I'm gonna take it," Red said.

"I hear that. You have a goodnight and stay out of trouble." I said.

"If you get bored call me. I'm in room 1656.

"O.k. I will."

"Just in case, the room is under my name, Reggie Ford."

# # # # #

"What the fuck took you so long to call me?" Keith said when he answered his phone.

"I miss you too boo," I said.

"Don't play with me, Tomika. I'm not in the mood. Why didn't you call me when you left out?"

"You told me to call you when I got back in the room and that's what I did."

"You know what? When I see you, I'm going to smack the shit out of you. You hanging out, thinking you don't got no fucking nigga out here. Trying to be like them hoes you hang with. But I'm going to show you better than I can tell you."

"First off, you said you were not my man. That our situation is what it is." Keith started yelling and going crazy after I made that comment.

"Bitch, you know what I meant by that. You my woman, stop playing these games with me. When I tell you to do something you do it. You better be glad it's late out because I would make your ass catch a cab to my hotel. Anyway, keep your ass in the hotel room. Tomorrow, I don't want to see or hear that you been hanging at any party."

"Are you serious, that's what we came down here for, to hang out and party and go to the All Star Game? How you gonna tell me I can't go out?"

"Do what you want to do, but be prepared for the consequences," Keith said before he hung up the phone.

I was getting sick of Keith. I loved him true enough, but this bi-polar attitude had to give. I decided to take my mind off Keith by calling Red. We talked on the phone for hours. The only reason we got off the phone was because Sheretta came in. Since I was still up she wanted to tell me everything that happened that night/morning.

Later that day Keith called me and apologized for his behavior last night. He said that he lost a lot of money and had a little too much to drink, and that he needed to talk to me. I wasn't around when he needed me. He said that he was just talking shit when he said that I couldn't go anywhere tonight. He asked what parties did we plan on going to tonight. I said that I didn't know, that Simone knew all the hot spots. He just asked me to call him and let him know where I was going to be at later. We talked for a couple more minutes, then Keith said he was going shopping and that he wanted to see me later tonight. I told him we could hook up when we both left the clubs or parties, and that we should go out for brunch on Sunday.

"That's what up baby. I must be missing you, that's why I'm tripping so much," Keith said.

"Alright, let me get back to sleep. I love you," I said.

Simone called us and told us that there's going to be a party at our hotel; some guy from Chicago was throwing it. We all met down in the lobby at 10:00pm. Keisha looked like she'd been getting high all day.

"What's up with you?" I asked her.

"Shit, enjoying my time in Vegas. I got to come here more often, the niggas show you much love," Keisha said.

"Girl, that's because it's the All Star Weekend. Niggas ain't like this on the regular," Simone said.

"Right, but I did meet some nice dude that's from L.A., so I'll be keeping in touch with them when I get back home," Tory said.

"Anyway, let's hit the party," I said. I didn't tell any of them how Keith has been tripping on me lately. I just didn't feel like hearing their mouths on the situation.

We got up in the club and come to find out the nigga that was giving the party was Red. As we were looking for somewhere to sit, Red came up to us. "Y'all ladies can come sit up in VIP with me and my boys if y'all want to."

"Hell yeah, we want to," Keisha said. She can be so ghetto sometimes; we all just looked at her.

"O.k., follow me," Red said.

As we were walking to the VIP area I asked Red, "Why didn't you tell me that you were giving a party tonight, we talked for hours and you didn't even mention it?"

"Well it's not just my party, it my boys too. And I thought if I told you, you probably wouldn't come because your man might be here or let me rephrase that, your man friend," Red said.

"Why would you think that my man would be here and that I wouldn't come?" I said.

"Because your man is here, and I know how he can be. I wanted you to enjoy yourself."

"How do you know who my man is?"

"I know everything," Red said. I just left it alone and followed him. When we got to our seats my mouth dropped. Keith was sitting there with Mike and Chris. There were two women sitting next to them, but they looked like they were in their own little world, they were so high.

"I want whatever they were smoking," Keisha said.

"Me too," Simone said.

Keisha and Simone sat by the two females; getting acquainted with them and trying to smoke for free.

"What's up baby girl?" Keith said, as I made my way to sit by him.

"Nothing, hanging with my girls. I didn't know that you would be here," I said.

"Mike knows the niggas that's giving the party, so he wanted to stop by and kick it for a minute," Keith said.

"Oh, o.k.," I said.

"I see your freak ass girl and cousin don't miss a beat, their names been ringing out here all ready."

"Baby, please don't start. We came here to have a good time."

"I'm just saying they're some hoes. You know your girl came on Chris last night."

"And, what happened?" I asked.

"He let her suck his dick, but he said he didn't fuck because he didn't have a condom. He told me that your freaky ass girl wanted to fuck without a condom."

ASA Publishing Company

"Look baby that's her. We all know how she gets down. It is what it is," I said.

"Yeah you right about that but what about the saying, birds of a feather flock together? Let me find out that you get down like that, I'm gonna fuck you up," Keith said.

"Baby let's not start this again, you know that I'm not like that. Let's just have a good time. By the way, I bought you something. When we leave here, let's go back to my room," I said.

"Cool, I've been wondering how you been getting by. You haven't asked me for any money since we been here."

"I got my own money baby, you know that I only asked you for something when I need it," I said.

"Yeah right," Keith said.

We drank and partied all night. Keith even got on the dance floor with me. These are the times when I love being with Keith, when he was just chilling. While we were dancing, I could feel Red looking at me. When we got back to our seats, Red came over and asked us were we having a good time.

"Yeah, this party is off the hook," Keisha said.

"Do you want to dance?" Red asked her.

"That's what's up," Keisha said as they headed for the dance floor. Simone gave me a look, like what the fuck is that nigga doing? I already know he was trying to make me mad, but I was here having a good time with my baby. Keith and I left early and went to my room so that I could give him his gift and a quickie before Sheretta came up to the room.

As I was giving him head, he started talking crazy, "Tomika if I find out that you're cheating on me, I'm gonna kill you. I love you and I'm not gonna be played like a fool," Keith said.

"Nigga, what are you talking about? I'm trying to give you some head and you talking crazy."

"I just want you to know the real."

"I know the real," I said. I stopped with the oral sex. He got up grabbed me hard and started kissing me, then he laid me down and entered me again without a condom. This was starting to be a bad habit.

We all were sick from drinking and partying, that we didn't go to the All Star Game. Well not all of us, Keisha and Tory did. Tory didn't over do it like we did, so she was good to go. Keisha on the other hand wasn't going to miss meeting any NBA player or other kinds of baller with money. Simone came down with Sheretta to my room to talk about last night.

"First off, what about your boy Red last night? He was so sick that you were with Monster, that he tried to make you jealous by asking your cousin to dance."

"I know right, and first off his name is Keith."

"Bitch everybody and the streets call him Monster."

"No they don't, I haven't heard anyone but you call him that, and you don't say it to his face."

"Whatever bitch, so what's up with you and Red?" Simone asked.

"Nothing, we just cool. We talked on the phone that's all."

"So he got your number?" Sheretta asked.

"No, I called his room and we talked like that."

"So he knows what room you stay in?" Simone said.

"Yeah," I said.

While we were talking, Sheretta thought that we need to start packing so that we would be on time to catch our flight that leaves out at 9:00am in the morning. So we talked and packed.

"Since we didn't go to the game, you know that we need to hit the parties tonight," Simone said.

"I'm down with that," I said.

As we were talking the room phone rang.

"Hello," Sheretta said.

"How you doing? Can I speak to Tomika?"

"Hold on for a second." Sheretta handed me the phone, I already knew who it was.

"Hello."

"What's going on with you?" Red asked.

"Nothing chilling, why aren't you at the game?"

"I didn't come down for the game, I came down to party and hang out. I wasn't gonna pay all that money to go to the game," Red said.

"I hear that, we had tickets but we were so tired from last night that we're just sitting here chilling," I said.

"Well how about I take you out to a late lunch?"

"I can't do that, what if my man finds out? Then it's gonna be trouble for me," I said.

"Well how about you come up to my room and we order room service?"

"I don't know about that either?"

"Your man not gonna find out," Red said.

"O.k., let me put some clothes on. I'll be up in about an hour."

"Girl, what is he talking about?" Sheretta asked.

"He wants me to come up there and get something to eat," I said.

"Are you gonna go?" Sheretta asked.

"I don't know, I told him I would be up there but I don't know."

"Girl, take your scary butt up there, you be acting like Keith the only nigga on earth. You don't know what he's out here doing," Simone said.

"Yeah, let me get ready to go up there. Shit, I'm hungry anyway. What are y'all gonna do?"

"Shit, go shopping and see what's popping. I'll call you if we get into something before you get back," Simone said.

"That's what's up. If Keith calls the room, tell him that I'm still sleep," I told Sheretta. Before I headed in the shower I told them Red's room number just in case they don't hear from me.

Red's room was neat. I was surprised because he told me that he and his boy shared a room. His boy was always out gambling and that he told him not to come back to the room for a couple of hours so that we could be alone. We ordered two T-bone steaks with bake potatoes and salad. Red also order a bottle of Moet and orange juice. I was having a good time; we cracked jokes on each other and watched movies. Just when I was getting a little too comfortable, Keith called my cell phone.

"Hello," I said.

"What's up baby?"

"Nothing, watching a movie. What's up with you?" I asked.

"Just chilling, what time does your plane leave in the morning?" Keith asked.

"9:00am, why you asked?" I said.

"I wanted to see if we had time to do anything before we leave. Are you dressed?"

"No, why what's up?"

"I want to take you on a gondola ride at the Venetian Hotel and grab something to eat," Keith said.

"O.k., give me about an hour and I'll be ready."

"I'll be there at 6:30pm."

"Well I guess you have to go now," Red said.

"Yeah, thanks a lot for lunch. I guess I'll see you around. Have a safe trip back."

"Yeah, same here. Can I at least get a hug?" Red hugged me so tight, it felt so good and he smelled so good.

"Damn what kind of cologne you got on? It smells good as hell," I said.

"It's a secret. I get a lot of compliments on it though."

"Alright, I'll see you around," I said.

"That you will," Red said.

Keith took me on a romantic date. We took a ride on the gondola, and then we went to eat at the Pinot Brasserie restaurant. My last night in Las Vegas was wonderful, and to think that I was going to mess our relationship up by doing something with Red. I needed to stop listening to Simone and follow my own heart.

Chapter Fifteen

Dirty South

August the 10th, 2007, the day that I'm suppose to meet Keith's mother, was just two days away. Keith and our relationship has been going strong for the last couple of months. I know that I am mainly responsible for it. I know that he doesn't like for me to hang out a lot, so I've been hanging out at home mostly and having my girls come chill at my house. I did party hard one time while Keith was in Las Vegas, from May 5th to the 7th, during the Floyd May Weather and Oscar DeLaHoya fight. Keith's mother lived in Atlanta, Georgia. Well that's the nearest city; she stayed in the suburbs outside of Atlanta called Acworth. The weather in Detroit was already in the mid 90's, so I could just imagine how hot it was going to be in Georgia. We were only staying for three days and two nights, but I wanted to be prepared. I had to bring two dresses for clubbing, an outfit for church, and about three chill outfits for shopping and lounging around.

We arrived in Atlanta at 1pm. We went to Enterprise to rent a car. I just knew that we were going to be riding in a Caddie or a truck, something that let people know my man had money, but instead Keith had me rent a Ford Taurus. The ride from the airport to Keith's mothers' house was about forty-five minutes. While we were driving to his mother's house, I asked Keith why did he rent a Taurus.

"I don't want us to be to flashy on the way back to Detroit," he said.

"What, I thought that we would be flying back since we flew down here," I said.

"That's what you get for assuming," Keith said.

"Why are we driving back?"

"Because I have a lot of stuff to bring back, and I'm sure that you're going to be shopping. That's going to be too much luggage to carry on the plane," Keith said.

"Whatever, you on some real bullshit. That's about a thirteen hour drive. I don't want to be driving for all that time."

"You're not going to be, all you have to do is drive us out of Ohio. I'll do most of the driving, just chill," Keith said.

I left the issue alone, we were getting along good and I didn't want to trip over driving back, it was no big deal. I wanted to enjoy my time here and make a good impression on Keith's mother.

"Hello, Ms. Jackson," I said when she opened the door.

"Child, you can call me Brenda. I look too good for someone to call me Ms. Jackson," she said then laughed.

"O.k.," I said.

"What's up beautiful?" Keith said while reaching towards her for a hug.

"Same ole, same ole. Did you bring me something?"

"I figured that I would just take you shopping because I know that Tomika is gonna want to shop, so I figure I'll kill two birds with one stone. Matter of fact, you two can go shopping tomorrow, while I'm out taking care of business," Keith said.

"That sounds like a plan," Brenda said. Keith mother's house was beautiful to say the least. She had a spiral staircase, the house was a tri-level with three and a half bathrooms, four bedrooms, a laundry room off of the kitchen and a finished basement. Three bedrooms were upstairs with a bathroom in the master bedroom. One bedroom downstairs which she said was the guestroom and that we would be sleeping there, and a half bathroom in the basement.

"Y'all go and take showers and get dressed. I want us all to go out to eat tonight," Brenda said.

We went out to Houston's Steakhouse for dinner. We rode in Brenda's CLS550 Coupe. Now this is the way I'm use to getting around. I really liked Keith's mother. She was down to earth. Even though she had money, she treated everyone she came in contact with the same way.

After dinner Keith and I changed clothes so we could hit some clubs, *of course we drove Brenda's car.* We partied so hard that we didn't wake-up until noon the next day. Brenda left us breakfast in the microwave with a note on the counter. The note said that she wanted to take us to the Georgia Aquarium. Keith said that he wasn't going to be able to go, he had some business to take care of, but that I should go and get better acquainted with his mother, then we could go shopping later since we were leaving early Monday morning.

Keith handed me six thousand dollars with instructions to give his mother half. He took the Taurus and headed out after eating and taking a shower.

Brenda and I wore out the malls. We went to Northlake Mall, the Underground shopping area and Lenox Mall. Brenda could shop and she liked to buy high-end clothes. She had bought items from Macy's, Neiman Marcus, Bally and Saks Fifth Avenue. I bought a couple pair of shoes from Saks and some shirts at Forever 21. I had too many clothes already and I didn't want to overdo it. Christmas was coming up and I wanted to be able to shop big then.

We got back to the house 7pm that night. Keith was already home.

"It looks like y'all bought the mall out." he said.

"Not me, just your mother," I said.

"What can I say, I like to shop. So did you take care of what you needed to take care of while we were gone?" Brenda said to Keith.

"Yep, now I'm about to take my lady out to eat. Come on baby, go get dressed so that we can grab some food and go out to some of the strip clubs down here."

"O.k.," I said.

"So mama can't hang out with y'all tonight?" Brenda said jokingly.

Keith took me to Justin's restaurant where we got soul food and had a couple martinis, and then we headed to Stroker's. We went to Magic City, there the women dance hard for five and ten dollar lap dances. I can't believe that they get naked for five dollars. That shit wouldn't go down in Detroit. Detroit girls about that bread, they charge ten to thirty dollars a lap dance and they don't even get naked. Keith said that he was meeting some of his boys in Magic City. We ordered a couple shots of Patron and chilled. I paid for two lap dances for Keith while we were waiting. When Keith's boys did arrive, Keith asked me to go to the bar and order a couple of gold bottles of Ace of Spades. I figured he just wanted to get a rise out of me for a minute because the bar was off the hook, and it was going to take a minute for me to get back.

As the bartender was taking my order, someone called out my name. I turned around and it was Jamal standing there looking as good as ever. The bartender stated that it would be about ten minutes before the waitress would be able to bring the bottles to our booth because of how crowded it was in the club. I looked over at the booth and noticed that Keith was still holding a conversation with his associates. So I figured that I would talk to Jamal for a minute at the bar.

"So, what brings you down to the dirty south?" Jamal asked.

"I'm down here with my man. We came to visit his mother and decided to hang out while we were down here," I said.

"That's what's up, where is your man at?" I pointed over to where Keith was sitting at. "That's your man with the white short sleeve shirt on?" Jamal asked.

"Yeah, you look like you know him or something," I said.

"No, it's not that, he's over there talking to my cousin that's all. I don't think y'all came down here just to visit his mother."

"Why you said that?"

"Because my cousin is getting money down here; anyone who fucks with him is getting money too, and selling them thangs," Jamal said.

"Boy you swear you are a thug."

"Whatever Ma, you want something to drink?"

"Yeah, get me an Apple Martini with Ciroc Vodka," I said. As I was reaching for my drink I notice that Keith was done talking, so I headed back to our booth.

"It was nice seeing you again. You are looking real good, don't be a stranger. Next time you in the D, holla at me," I said.

"Same here, I can't believe you're in my city and you didn't holla at me or my moms," Jamal said.

"I'll call you when I get back home," I said.

Keith had a crazy look on his face when I got back to the table. He whispered in my ear "Who the fuck was you over there talking to? You know, you a very disrespectful bitch! You better be glad that we are in this club, because I would have smacked the shit out of you!"

"What the fuck is wrong with you? That's an ole friend from college, he live here in Atlanta," I said.

"I don't care who the fuck it is, you were talking to him too long."

"Whatever." Needless to say the ride home was a quiet one.

The next morning we got up to go to church with his mother. After church, Brenda cooked us a nice home cooked meal. Keith and I still didn't say much to one another. Keith went into the guest room to take a nap since we were leaving out at 3 o'clock in the morning.

"Child don't pay him no mind, whatever it is that's bothering him, he'll get over it. I think that he just got a lot of stress right now," Brenda said.

The ride back home was pleasant and quiet. We stopped a couple of times for gas and to grab something to snack on. When we got to Ohio, Keith stopped at a Waffle House so that we could sit down and eat, and I could take over the wheel.

When we finished eating Keith said to me, "Be careful driving, and do the speed limit because I have dope in the car, and in Ohio they will give you twenty to thirty years for having the stuff that I got in the car."

"What the fuck? Nigga you got me on some transportation shit, I can't believe this shit. Everybody told me that you weren't any good and that you sold drugs, but I didn't believe it. Why you didn't tell me this shit before we left Atlanta?"

"I didn't want you to get scared on me. It will be cool. You only got five and a half hours to drive. Just do you. We good, I don't have anything in the car so just relax."

I can't believe this nigga is playing me like this. I didn't want to start a fight out here so I decide to go with the flow. I said a little prayer that we make it home safe. Because after this, I wasn't going to fuck with Keith anymore.

We made it home with no problems. Keith had me drop him and the car off at a house off of Livernois and Six Mile. There were a couple of thug looking guys standing around the house. I was a little scared at first until I saw Chris come out of the house.

"Hey, how was the drive?" Chris asked.

"It was straight, we made it here," Keith said.

"Hey, can you do me a favor and take baby girl home for me?" Keith said.

"No problem, let me get my keys."

"Thanks," Keith said. I got in the passenger side of Chris's Ranger Rover, while Keith placed my suitcases in the truck. He walked up to the passenger side window, "I love you and thanks. I knew you were my ride or die chick," He said while laughing. I didn't find anything funny.

"Whatever, I don't think that we should be together anymore, you put me in a fucked up situation. I could have gone to prison because of this shit, just leave me alone."

"Whatever, I'll be over there tonight to make it up to you."

"For real, I'm straight on you, you do you and I'm gonna do me."

"Look, don't get your ass kicked out here. I'm gonna give you time to cool off, but don't do anything stupid. I'll call you in a couple days."

"Yeah alright, by the way, where did you have the stuff at?" I asked.

"In the tire."

Chris got in the truck. "Alright nigga," Chris said then we pulled off.

As soon as I got home, I got on my knees and thank God for getting me home safe. I called Simone and told her all the details of the weekend in Atlanta.

"Girl, I told you he was selling drugs, your ass didn't want to believe it," Simone said.

"I kind of figured that was what he was doing, but every time I talked to him he was always at his place of business," I said.

"Whatever, that's probably a front. He might be selling drugs out of there."

"I'm not fucking with him anymore. I told him to leave me alone."

"What did he say when you told him that?" Simone asked.

"Shit, he just told me not to do stupid shit, and that he would holla at me in a couple days."

"Girl you not gonna leave that nigga alone."

"Let you tell it, I am. He put my freedom and life at risk. I'm good on him," I said.

"That's what your mouth says, what you doing now?"

"Nothing. Why? What's up?" I asked.

"I'm about to come over. Start making the drinks, I'll be there in about an hour," Simone said.

Two weeks past and I hadn't heard from Keith. I was glad of that, but in a way, a part of me wanted him to call or come over, but he never showed.

It was Friday night, Michael and Danielle were coming over my house after work for some drinks and to just hangout. Work has been so busy these last couple of weeks with all the crime that's been going on in the State of Michigan, we've been working twelve hour days. Michael was bringing the drink which was a fifth of Ciroc, some Cranberry juice, and beer. I was supplying the food. I picked up some Chinese food. Danielle was bringing the movies. We sat around getting fucked up watching Friday after Next, and Katt Williams stand up.

"So, what are y'all about to get into?" Michael asked.

"Nothing, you act like you're about to go or something," Danielle said to him.

"Yeah I am, my girl just texted me, she wants me to come over."

"Damn, nigga you pussy whipped. I thought you were a playa, you just a punk," Danielle said.

"Watch your mouth. Just because you a girl don't mean that I won't whoop that ass," Michael said in a joking way.

"For real, though. You are acting pussy whipped; we suppose to be over here chilling," I said.

"I'll get at y'all hoes later," Michael said as he headed for the door.

"So I guess it's just you and me," I said to Danielle.

Danielle and I finished the rest of the Ciroc. Time just flew by. We were talking about love and relationships, she was telling me about all the women she had and how she never had sex with a man. While we were talking, she asked me did I mind if she took an ecstasy pill, I told her that I didn't care. It was getting late and I knew that Danielle was in no shape to drive home. She was cool until the ecstasy pill took effect. She looked like she had smoked about three blunts.

"Tomika, can I ask you something?" Danielle said.

"Yeah, what's up?" I said.

"Have you ever done a threesome?"

"Girl, no. I don't like to share, and plus, I'm not eating no other bitch's pussy!"

"I feel you, but you don't have to eat any pussy? You could just let the girl eat your pussy," Danielle said.

"I'm good with letting niggas eat my pussy," I said.

"Don't knock it until you try it."

"Whatever. Help me get this place clean so I can put some sheets down, so you can sleep on the couch. You too fucked up to drive home tonight, sleep that shit off."

"Girl you know you look good as hell to me," Danielle said.

"Whatever. Take your drunk ass on with that stupid shit."

"I'm for real, I know Michael thinks the same thing. You know he wants to fuck you."

"Girl you drunk, I'm about to take a shower and get into bed. I'll holla at you later," I said. I got her bedding ready so she can go to sleep in the living room, then I proceeded to take a shower and get in the bed.

I woke up around 3am in the morning to see Danielle trying to remove my panties. I didn't lock my door because I was so use to Keith coming over, and I didn't like hearing his mouth about my room door being lock.

"What the fuck are you doing? Get the fuck out here!" I said while trying to pull my panties back up, but Danielle had a death grip on them. I don't know how she managed to get my shorts off without me waking up.

"You know you want this. I can tell, just let me taste it."

"Bitch, get the fuck off me."

By now Danielle had my panties half way off, one of my legs were out. She grabbed a beer bottle from the side of my bed. She must have brought it in the room with her. She took a swig then proceeded to pour the beer on my pussy. I was trying to get loose from her, but she had my left leg in her hand and she wasn't fazed by me kicking her with my right leg.

"Stop fighting it, you gonna like it. I bet I make you cum like you never came before," Danielle said.

"Why are you doing this to me? I thought we were girls, you know I'm not gay."

"I just want to taste your pussy, just let me taste your pussy," Danielle said.

She started licking around my clitoris, sticking her tongue in and out my pussy, then she moved her tongue up, right on the top of my clit and was slowly sucking it until it swelled up. I can't even lie it was feeling good. She stayed at the spot until I came, and I did come hard. When she got up, nut was all over her mouth. I got up and started swinging on her. I got her one good time in the eye. She pushed me down to the floor and said, "Tomika, I don't want to hurt you. Just let me go home. I'm sorry for what I did. I just had to taste it."

"You dike bitch, get the fuck out of my house before I call the police on your ass. You better hope that I don't catch your ass in the streets with my girls, it's gonna be a wrap."

Danielle left, but she kept texting me that day saying that she was sorry and leaving me voice messages.

I was so ashamed. I can't believe I let a girl take the pussy. I couldn't go back to sleep after she left. I stayed up thinking about what I could have done to prevent it from happening. I called Simone to tell her what had happened, but her voice message came on, so I left her a message;

"Bitch call me, you're never gonna guess what happen to me last night, well this morning rather. Take the dick out your mouth and call me, one!"

The next person that popped into my mind to tell what had went down last night, was my cousin Keisha.

"What's up?" Keisha said.

"Nothing, I got to tell you what happen to me last night."

"And what's that?"

"Girl, you know my co-worker Danielle."

"Yeah, what about her? Isn't she gay?" Keisha said.

"Yeah."

"Bitch, don't tell me you gave her some head or you let her give you some head."

"No bitch, the bitch took the pussy from me," I said.

"How you let a female take some pussy from you?" Keisha asked.

I had told Keisha everything that happened last night. She laughed a couple of times, and after I finished with my story the dumb bitch gonna ask me did I like it?

"Bitch what type of questions is that to ask? I just told you, I got violated."

"So, what are you going to do? Do you want to go whoop her ass or what?" Keisha asked.

"Nall, I already socked her ass in the eye. I'm gonna get that bitch fired from work," I said.

"That's how you do that shit, but was the head from a girl different from a man?"

"No, not to me," I said.

"So tell the truth did you like it? Was it good? Let me know something," Keisha said.

"You a nasty bitch, you don't have any compassion for me. You just want to know if the head was good. To tell you the truth it was good, I came hard as hell," I said.

"I knew it. You a dike now," Keisha said while laughing.

"Fuck you, and don't run your big mouth and tell anybody."

"I won't, let me go. I got to get little man ready so we can go see his father," Keisha said.

"O.k., one."

Later on that night, Simone called me back and I told her what happened.

"Bitch, that bitch ain't shit. The bitch shouldn't have just ate it like that, if she knew you wasn't down for that shit. But fuck it, you know how many bitches out here I've let give me some head?" Simone said.

"No, and I don't want to know. You know you are a freak for real, so have you gave a girl head before?" I asked.

"Yeah, I ate one bitch out. I was doing a threesome about two years ago, that wasn't my cup of tea but ole girl gave me the best head I've ever had."

"I hate to say it too, but ole girl's head game was on point. But she disrespected me to the fullest, so you know that I got to get her back."

"I feel you girl, so have you talked to your boy yet?"

"Nope, he hasn't called or came by since we got back," I said.

"He's probably putting you on punishment for going off on him."

"I don't know what he's doing, and I don't care."

"I feel you, I'll get back at you later," Simone said.

Keith walked in my bedroom room at 11:15pm later that night. I was in the bed watching *I Love New York*.

"What's up with you? Are you good now? Your little hissy over with?" Keith said.

"Nigga you put my freedom and life at risk. That lets me know that you don't give a fuck about me," I said.

"What the fuck you talking about? We made it home alright. Your freedom wasn't at risk if anything would have happened, I would have taken the rap."

"Whatever, that's what you say now. Look, I don't want to be with you because it's obvious that you don't give a fuck about me. Because if you did, you would not have put me in that situation," I said.

"You know what, I'm tired of hearing this bullshit. Do what you want to do and get your head cracked. You want to complain because a nigga had you bring back some work that wasn't even in the car? How the fuck you think this apartment is being paid for? How the fuck you think you driving that truck? You about the stupidest female I know. I know your girl done told you how I get down in these streets. I handle my business and make sure everybody that's in my life is taken care of. So miss me with that bullshit you talking," Keith said.

"You need to miss me with that shit as well. You did some hoe ass shit…"

Smack!!!

Keith smacked the shit out of me. I couldn't even finish my sentence.

"Fuck with me if you want. You not gonna be talking slick to me and trying to disrespect me. I don't know what type of hoe ass nigga you've dealt with in the past, but I'm not the one," Keith said.

While he was talking, I was just sitting up in my bed crying. I just don't know how Keith keeps changing on me. One minute he's cool and calm, the next he's crazy.

"Why don't you just leave me alone and get out of here."

"I'm not going nowhere! I paid rent up in here for you to live, so you get the fuck out."

"O.k.," I replied. I got up and started to grab some clothes out of my closet to put on.

"Bitch, you ain't going nowhere! Get your ass back in the bed before I fuck you up in here." From the tone of his voice and the way he was looking, I knew he wasn't playing, so I did as I was told.

"You got anything to drink?" Keith asked.

"I got some water, pop, and beer," I said.

"You don't have any alcohol?"

"Nope."

"Well grab me a beer, I'm about to jump in the shower," Keith said.

I got his beer and got back in bed and continued to watch T.V. I wasn't going to feed into his craziness tonight. Keith got out the shower, put a wife beater and some boxers on and got in the bed with me.

"Baby, you know a nigga love you, why don't you chill and just roll with a nigga? Everything I'm out here doing is to better our lives, you understand."

"How is selling drugs bettering our lives? You was doing this shit before you met me, so I'm not even in the plan."

"Baby, I don't want to argue anymore, just chill and roll with me. I promise, I won't do anything stupid to you anymore. I love you girl," Keith said.

I decided not to argue anymore. I just wanted to get some sleep. I needed to get up and go to church the next morning. I figured that was the reason Keith came over; so that we could go to church together. As I was falling to sleep, Keith started rubbing on my legs and squeezing my breast. He kissed and sucked my breast, then my stomach, then my pussy; he sucked my clit slow. He took his time exploring every inch of my pussy from the tip to the slit. I didn't want to give in to sex, but the head was feeling too good.

"Baby, your pussy taste so good," Keith said.

"I know," I replied. Keith ate my pussy until I came, which was a half an hour later.

When we got up the next morning, Keith asked me did I need anything because he was going to Ohio to visit his daughters and take care of some things.

"I knew it, you just came over to get some pussy and make up because you about to be gone for a minute. You know what? Keith I'm straight on you, just leave."

"Don't start this shit this morning, we gonna chill and have a good day. I'll be gone for about a week. I want to spend some time with my kids. That's why I'm really going to Ohio."

"Whatever, just go," I said.

When I got home from church my mother called me.

"Hello," I said.

"Hey, how have you been doing? I didn't really get to talk to you earlier," she said.

"I know, I rode with Keith and had something to take care of."

"Well how have you been? Because you looked like you were tired. That nigga ain't stressing you out is he? You just don't look the same."

"I'm good Mommy, I've just been working twelve hours a day at work."

"Well do you want me to come over and cook you something to eat?" she asked.

"You know I do."

"O.k., I'll be over there in an hour. Go to the store and buy something for me to cook."

My mother came over and cooked me some barbeque neck bones, greens, macaroni and cheese, and some candy yams. After we ate, we sat down and had a heart to heart conversation about what's been going on since I've move out, and how she felt about the whole situation with Keith.

Chapter Sixteen

Here We Go Again

September 14th, 2007, a day I'll never forget. Simone called me in a frenzy of excitement. I didn't even get to say hello good before she started to talk.

"Girl, we got to go out tonight. I heard **The Spot** is supposed to be off the hook. Nigga with that chow gonna be up in there."

"For real," I said.

"What's so special about tonight?" I asked.

"This big nigga is having a going away party. He has to turn himself in Monday to the FED's. This is his last weekend of freedom, and it's gonna be off the hook. All the big dogs gonna be there."

"Who is the guy?" I asked.

"This nigga's name Mark Jackson. I used to fuck with him back in the day when he was getting money for real," Simone said.

"Your man Keith might be there to buy the bar out," She said, and then she laughed.

"What's so funny?" I said with a slight attitude.

"Nothing, I was just thinking. What would you do if you ran into Keith?"

"I wouldn't do anything. I would speak and keep it moving. I haven't talked to him in a week and a half. I haven't returned any of his phone calls or his texts. I'm still pissed at him. I'm not gonna be on his head."

"Whatever, just make sure you're ready at 10 o'clock," she said before she hung up.

I knew that if Simone said be ready at ten, what she really meant was be ready by eleven. I had time to try on and put something cute together to wear. I hadn't talked to Keith since that Sunday morning. I neglected to tell Simone all of the threats that Keith have been leaving me on the phone. I figured he was still out of town, seeing as he hasn't paid me a visit.

I didn't want to do anything but I knew my girl wanted to hang, and I wanted to go just in case Keith was there since he's in the game, and Simone said all the major niggas would be there. I wanted to wear something sexy and tight, so he could see all this thickness that he's missing. I decided to wear some dark blue stretch Rock Republican Jeans with some Caesar Paciotti high heels, and a red lace tank top to match my shoes. My accessories were an oversized red and black Kenneth Cole bag, a gold necklace and some gold bangle bracelets. I had just got my hair done early that day in a Mohawk. I just knew I was doing them big time. Niggas was gonna be on my head for sure tonight. I must admit every since I've been with Keith, I've upgraded a lot. I went from carrying purses from Forever 21 to buying purses from the Gucci Store, no more knock-offs for me.

Simone arrived at 11:15pm and we headed downtown. Simone was looking fly as hell with a fuck me dress on with some Gucci boots on with the purse to match. When we got to the bar it was off the hook, it was a line to get in, but as usual, Simone had the hook up and her boy got us in. As soon as we walked in, we spotted Blunt and Eric.

"What up, baby girl?" Blunt said to Simone.

"Nothing, we just came here to have a couple of drinks and chill for a minute," Simone said.

"That's what's up. What y'all drinking on?" Blunt asked. Simone orders both of us double shots of Patron.

"Hey, baby girl, long time no see. You forgot about a nigga or something?" Eric asked me as I was grabbing my drink from Simone.

"No, I just been busying with work and everything," I said.

"I hear you got a man now."

"Not exactly," I said.

"So, what's up? I want to hit that again. I know you want some of this good dick that you been missing."

I could tell that Eric was high because he was talking sideways to me.

"I don't know about all that, but it was good seeing you. Simone lets go find somewhere to sit," I said.

We were in *The Spot* for about forty-five minutes getting lit off shots of Patron when Red walked up to me.

"It must be meant for you to give me your number so that I can take you out. Because everywhere I'm at, I see you," Red said.

"Maybe it's just a coincidence," I said.

"Call it what you want, but you're going to give me your number before the night is out, so we can go get some breakfast or lunch tomorrow."

"So forget the fact that I have a man."

"If you really wanted to be with your man, you wouldn't be here.

You'd be somewhere with your man or he'll be here with you. With all these thirsty ass niggas up in here, I'm sure your man wouldn't want you here all alone."

"You are something else, but I'm not alone. I'm with my girl Simone," I said.

"I know, I got to go but I'll be back for that number. Y'all drinks are on me for the rest of the night," Red said.

"Thanks," Simone and I said at the same time. Simone couldn't really network the way she wanted to because Blunt was on her head, and she was really digging him. She said, She didn't want to disrespect him in his face, but my girl did get some numbers and give her number out on the sly tip.

We were chilling and having a good time when Blunt and Eric came and sat down with us. "I didn't mean any disrespect earlier," Eric said to me.

"You cool, I know you are a little tipsy, it's all good," I said.

"What are y'all doing when y'all leave here?" Eric asked.

"Nothing, going back to Simone's crib and chill."

Simone gave me that look, she knew that I was lying to Eric, but she didn't say anything. I just wasn't in the mood to be bothered with him, especially after he was talking sideways to me earlier.

"Damn, baby you weren't going to invite me back to your place tonight, figuring that I just paid your rent for the month," Blunt said to Simone.

"It ain't even like that, you didn't give me a chance to ask nigga, slow your roll. You know I want you to come over and get in this pussy," Simone said.

"Well that's what's up, we'll all go to your crib when the bar closes," Eric said.

"Let's just see how the night plays out," Simone said. I was glad that she said that, I did not want to be stuck with Eric not tonight- the dick was straight but he ain't got shit on Keith.

I was having small talk with Eric when I noticed he had the same fragrance that Red had on in Vegas.

"You smell good, what type of cologne do you have on?" I asked him.

"Yeah this that new shit, it's called *GIRL*. You can only buy it in select cities. I got this when I was at Neiman Marcus in Chicago, it's not sold here in Michigan yet."

"It smells so good a friend of mine had some on but wouldn't tell me where he got it from."

"He must got that money because a bottle of this cologne cost a thousand dollars," Eric said.

"Is that so, well we know you getting money?" I said.

"Yeah we getting money by any means necessary," Blunt said jumping in on our conversations.

Simone nudged me as we were sitting down and whispered in my ear, "There go your boy." I looked up and saw Keith, my heart dropped. I got up so that I could walk over to him, I didn't want him to think that I was with Eric and Blunt. As soon as I got up, Keith walked up to me and choked the shit out of me. I didn't know what to do, and I couldn't say anything because he had a death grip on me.

"Bitch, what the fuck you doing up in here? All in niggas faces smiling and laughing. Do you know I will fuck you up in here?!"

"Man chill out, ole girl and her having a good time," Blunt said to him.

"Look nigga, this ain't got shit to do with you. Sit your ass back down before you get fucked up too."

"Nigga who the fuck you talking to?! I'm not a bitch, you can't whoop my ass," Blunt said.

Next thing you know, Keith let me go and punched Blunt dead in his eye. Blunt hit the ground hard, then Eric socked Keith in the jaw, but it didn't faze Keith. Him and Eric was going at it head up. Keith was really getting the best of Eric, but Eric was backing down. Next thing I knew, everybody ran over to get Eric and Blunt up out the club.

"Don't let me see you little niggas out in the street," Keith said. I could see Red looking at me from the corner of my eyes. He was one of the guys that threw Blunt and Eric out of the bar.

"Bitch, I'm tired of you hanging out was this freak bitch. She ain't shit but a two dollar hoe."

"Wait a minute, nigga. I'm a five hundred dollar hoe, and don't put me in y'all shit. Nigga, hate the game nigga, not the player," Simone said.

"Bitch shut your disease ass up, you ain't shit but a walking STD," Keith said to Simone.

"Whatever nigga, you just mad because you can't have me."

"Bitch I can buy your nasty ass over and over, don't know no real nigga want a trashy bitch. You are a hood hoe. Bitch, you probably got AIDS," Keith said.

"Tomika, I'll be at the bar. I ain't got time for this hoe ass nigga." When Simone said that, Keith reached over to smack her, but Red grabbed his arm.

"Man you don't want to do that up in here, you already know what she's about, let that shit go," Red said.

"Yeah, you right. Now can you let my arm go nigga?"

"Oh, my bad," Red said.

"Take your hot ass home. I should fuck you up in here. I told your ass if I catch you on some bull shit, it was gonna be hell to pay," Keith said.

"I was just hanging out with Simone. What are you tripping for?" I said.

"You know I don't like you hanging with that trick bitch. Then you all in niggas faces. All these niggas up in here know me. What does it look like for my bitch to be up in the bar or hanging in the streets all the time. Take your ass home right now," Keith said.

"I can't, I rode with Simone, and she's not ready to go right now," I said.

"Bitch you better get her ready or catch a cab, but you about to get the fuck out of here. Matter of fact, I'll take you home."

As we were walking out, I stopped to tell Simone that I was leaving and that I'll call her later. On the way to my house Keith didn't say a word. He let me out and pulled off.

Chapter Seventeen

What Baby?

Keith is crazy for real - for real. I can't believe that he played me like that in front of everybody. Then to clown them niggas like that, I know their pride has to be damaged. I wasn't going to do anything to piss him off. Even more so, I decided to just go home. I got home around one o'clock in the morning, I turned on my television, sat on the couch and rehashed all of the nights events. I was just too through, so I decided to take a shower and call it a night.

While I was headed to the bathroom, Simone called me.

"Hello."

"You alright girl?" She asked.

"Yeah, I'm just tired."

"Girl, you need to leave that nigga alone. He's crazy as hell for coming up in the club and clowning like that, and he brought his ass back up in the bar."

"I know right, but anyway I don't know what got into him. I'm sorry for him going off on you. He didn't mean it, he was just mad at me."

"That crazy ass nigga meant it, but it's cool though. So, what are you doing? You want me to come over and chill with you?"

"I'm good. I'm about to jump in the shower and go to bed. I'll holla at you in the morning, be careful," I said.

"Alright, one," Simone said.

After hanging up with Simone, I took off my clothes and underwear, turned on the shower, adjusted the shower head to medium pressure, went to the kitchen and poured me a glass of Moscato. Headed back to the bathroom, turned on the stereo and turned the volume on high while Lauryn Hill sang *It could all be so simple, but you rather make it hard.* I had the *Miseducation of Lauryn Hill* playing. I was so in the zone of relaxing, that I didn't pay too much attention to the big boom that I heard. I thought that it was the neighbors moving some furniture around or someone running up the stairs.

I was washing my face with Dove soap when someone ran into the bathroom, ripped the shower curtains open, and pulls me by my arm and said, "Bitch get the fuck out of the shower and tell me where the fucking money is!"

I was so scared that I started peeing on myself, the man that was holding me by the arm had on some black Tims, black jogging pant set, and a black Carhartt coat, with a black winter type sky mask on.

When he noticed that I had peed on myself, he started to laugh, "Damn bitch, you scared then a motha fucka. I wanted to hit that pussy, but now I'm straight."

While he was talking to me, another guy came in the bathroom with the exact same outfit the one guy that was holding me had on.

"Man, I didn't find anything in the other three rooms, did she tell you anything?"

"Na, the bitch is so scared that she peed on herself."

"I know that nigga keeps his money over here, or at least some dope. If I can't find anything, we're going to have ole girl call him over so we can make him take us to the stash."

"Man let her put some clothes on and move her to the living room," the other guy said who had just come into the bathroom.

"This bitch don't need any clothes on, she's a hoe just like her girl. We should run bustoes on her."

"Dog, we came to get some money or some dope, fuck her."

I was thankful that the other guy didn't want to rape me, but I knew the one who was holding me was going to try something. The guy that was holding me- breath smelled like Hennessey, and he reeked of weed. I had no other choice than to try to bargain with them. I tried to explain that Keith didn't keep or have any drugs or money in my house. As the sensible one was looking in my bedroom for money, he threw me a pair of shorts and a white beater to put on. I got dressed while the smelly one held a gun to my head.

"Bitch you bet not try no stupid shit or I will kill your hoe ass."

I wanted to throw up, at the smell of his breath. "Please, don't hurt me. I don't know what you're looking for, but there is no money or dope in here."

"Bitch stop lying!" The one with the bad breath said.

"I promise that I don't know what you're looking for."

"So you are not Monster's girl?" The reasonable one asked.

I could not believe this, they had me half-naked now sitting on my bed, all pissy and scared to death over some bullshit due to Keith. I played stupid.

"Who is Monster?" I asked.

Smack!!! Smack!!!

The smelly one smacked the shit out of me twice. My ears seemed to be ringing for what felt like hours, but only lasted for a couple of seconds.

"You know who he is; he's the same nigga that you got into it with at the club tonight, the same nigga that you been fucking for the last year."

I thought to myself, how does he know so much about Keith and my relationship.

"Please don't hurt me. I promise you, I don't know what you're talking about. I don't have any money here. All I have is some jewelry and about a hundred and fifty dollars in cash."

"Bitch stop lying, that nigga be cashing you out, plus I know that nigga got money. So either you tell us where he lives at or you give us the money that's in here. Or you call him up and tell him to come over here, and we'll get the money from his hoe ass ourselves," the shit breath nigga said.

I already knew how this was gonna play out, they were gonna kill me. I figured, I'll go out with a fight and play the game how it should be played. I've watched too many movies and read too many books not to know how this is going to end. So I played the game as well.

"O.k., I'll call him and tell him to come over. If I do it, do you promise me that you want hurt me?" I asked.

"Bitch, we're not playing with you. Call that nigga up!" the stanky one said,

"Baby girl, we're not gonna do anything bad to you. We just want the money. You'll be good, I promise," the nice one spoke, as he grabbed the cordless phone from the charger that was sitting on my nightstand.

He walked over and handed me the phone. As he stood in front of me with the phone, I got a whiff of his cologne and I dropped the phone and just stared at him. I immediately knew that it had to be Eric and Blunt, because the person that was in my face had that same cologne *Girl* on. I could tell that the two of them was disguising their voice, but I just didn't want to believe that this nigga was in here with a gun to my head trying to rob my man. I was so disgusted.

Eric was the sensible gunman. I knew Blunt didn't care for me that much, but to stoop this low as to be robbing me and perhaps killing me for some money, this nigga was crazy. I'm definitely going down with a fight. I guess what that nigga said at the club was true, they getting money by any means necessary. I know this had to be Blunt's idea. I know, Eric couldn't be cut like this. Keith must of really hurt their pride tonight at the club, but damn, how did they know where I live at. I played it cool as he handed me the phone again and I called Keith.

The phone rang three times before he answered.

"What the fuck you want? I told you that I'll be over there when I finish handling my business. You about the stupidest bitch I know. I'm going to beat your ass when I get there. You try to play me in front of all those hoe ass niggas up in the club. It's a wrap when I see you," Keith said.

"Yeah, I know baby, I love you too. Please come over and let's make love."

"Bitch what the fuck done got into you? I don't want to fuck your slutty ass, let alone make love to you. You just like your freak ass girl, but I'm gonna show you better than I can tell you. You done cross the line with the shit you pulled tonight."

"Baby, I'm sorry, please come over. I'll even leave the door unlock so you can come right in and I'll be in the bed with a treat for you."

"Look, I don't have time for this shit. Ain't no treat or trick you could do to make me come over. I'll be there when I get there. You should be hoping that I've calm down before I get there. Because I told you before, its rules to this game when you dealing with me. Now you got to pay the price," Keith said.

"Baby, I'm sorry. Please come over and let me make it up to you. You know I love you, I'll get up and cook you your favorite meal, some gumbo." I was trying to give him some hints without letting Eric and Blunt know what I was doing.

"Bitch you know I don't eat no gumbo. Are you drunk?"

"Baby, how long will it be before you get here? Because I don't want to leave the door unlock. How are you gonna get in if I fall asleep?"

"I'm really gonna get in the ass now. Are you so drunk that you don't know that I got a key to your house? You are a drunk stupid hoe!"

"I know baby, I love you too. Just call me when you get outside so that I can come let you in. Bye, I love you," I said. I was wishing that Keith got the hints when I said bye. He knows that I never say bye, I always say one, or talk to you later.

"What that hoe ass nigga got to say? Is he on his way over here?" Blunt asked with his shit breath.

"Yeah, he said that he'll call me when he gets outside so that I can open the door for him," I said.

"So the nigga doesn't have a key to your apartment?" Eric asked.

"Nope."

"I know he's paying all the bills up in here and he don't even have a key. I guess that nigga ain't no true gangster after all. If you was my bitch, I'd have a key to everything your hoe ass got," Blunt said. Blunt was grapping on my breast and rubbing my thighs every time Eric would step out of the room.

"You ain't nothing but a hoe. I don't know why your man was in the bar tripping over you like that. Bitches come a dime a dozen."

"You don't know shit about me. You ain't shit but a broke ass nigga, robbing females out here for money. You wish you could be that nigga," I said. Next thing I know, I was on the ground.

The nigga Blunt punched me in my face and in my stomach. A sharp pain ran across my stomach like a cramp. I just laid on the floor in the fetal position, praying that God would save me.

Thirty minutes went by after I called Keith.

"Baby girl, you alright, get up and get back on the bed. All is well, I told ole boy to stay in the front and watch for your man to come over. He's not gonna mess with you anymore."

"Why are y'all doing this? I don't got shit to do with what he does. I don't have any money," I said.

"Your man getting money, we can't get to him so we got to go through the next best thing, which is you. That nigga loves you and I saw it tonight." As Eric was talking, my phone rang. I looked on the caller ID and it was Keith.

"Is it that nigga?" Blunt came in the room and asked.

"Yeah."

"Well answer the fucking phone."

"Hello," I said.

"Tomika, what's going on? Why you want me to come there so bad for?" Keith asked.

"Because I love you and miss you, but I'm getting sleepy and I don't want you to wake me if I got to get up and open the door. So do you want me to leave it open?"

"Don't over react when I ask you these questions, but is there some body over there?" Keith asked.

"Yeah baby, I do love you, you know that," I said.

"O.k., did they say what they wanted?"

"Baby, I don't want your money. I don't care that you out there in them street selling that shit."

"So they want money and dope? Did they hurt you in anyway?" Keith asked.

"Yeah."

"How many are there that's in the house?"

"It's already, past two o'clock in the morning now."

"Baby, you doing everything right. I'm sorry I tripped on you. You know I love you to death. You my heart," Keith said.

"We gonna get out of this situation together, I'll be there in about thirty minutes. If you can try to keep them in your bedroom, stay strong baby, love you."

"I love you too," I said.

"What that hoe ass nigga say?" Blunt asked.

"He'll be over in an hour."

"So we wait," Eric said.

They were watching television in my room, while I was praying and watching my life past before my eyes. I already knew how this was going to play out, there's no way I was going to come out of this alive. Shit, I've seen *Paid in Full*. What was the irony thing about the situation, they were sitting in my room watching the TV show *Lock Up*.

An hour went by, then all hell broke loose. Keith and his boy Chris came through the room shooting. All I remember was Keith telling me to get under the bed.

The next day, I woke up in Henry Ford Hospital with my mother, aunt, Keisha, and Simone by my side.

"Hi baby how are you feeling?" My mother asked.

"My whole body is killing me especially my stomach and left leg."

"They all looked at each other, and Simone and my mother started to cry.

"Baby, I hate to be the one to tell you this, but your baby died."

"What baby?" I asked.

"The one that you were carrying. You didn't know that you were pregnant?" My mother asked.

"No," I said, as I started crying. "So that's why my stomach was hurting so much when one of them niggas kicked me in it. Why does my leg burn so badly?"

Simone spoke this time. "You got shot in the leg, right above your ankle. The good news is that the bullet went right through. The doctor said that you'll be good as new in a couple of weeks."

"Baby, the doctor said that you can be released the day after tomorrow, and I want you to come stay with me. That Keith done got you into enough trouble to last a lifetime."

"Mommy, just give me a minute to think about everything that happened. I just learned that I was pregnant and lost the baby. I need to talk to Keith. I'll call you later, and we can discuss where I'm going to be staying at."

"O.k. Well I'm gonna go home and get the house ready for you. I'll be waiting on your call, I love you," my mother said.

"I love you too."

"Now that your mother is gone, what happened that night?" Simone asked.

Keisha was all ears. I broke everything down to them without telling too much. I didn't tell them who broke in or who I thought broke in.

"Where is Keith at?" I asked.

"He's on the third floor, he got shot three times. Twice in the arm and once in the chest," Keisha said.

"What?! I got to go see him," I said.

"Girl, he's alright, just fucked up, but everything is cool. Just relax. After you talk to him, let me know if you want to chill at my house. I know you don't want to be bothered with your mother asking you a lot of questions and shit like that. I hope you not even thinking about staying with Keith," Simone said. Keisha and Simone chilled with me for a couple of hours.

While they were there, Sheretta came and stayed for a couple of minutes as well. I had Simone call my job and let my boss know what's up. She had already contacted Michael. Jennifer told Simone to tell me to take all the time that I needed. My job would be waiting on me and to also let me know that Danielle got fired; the station did a random drug time and Danielle failed it. After Danielle took advantage of me that night, that following Monday at work I told Jennifer what had happened and she said don't worry about it, Danielle would get hers. She didn't care for Danielle anyway, and when I told her that Danielle did drugs, it was a wrap.

Later that night, Keith came to my room. He was in a wheelchair and he looked bad, his arm was swollen to twice its normal size. He had IV in his hand and his face was swollen as well.

"How you doing?" Keith asked.

"From the looks of it better than you. Seriously though, I'm o.k. My stomach hurts like hell." I didn't want to bring up me losing the baby, I figure he knew already.

"Yeah, I figured that, baby. I'm sorry you lost the baby. I'm gonna get them niggas back, believe me they are dead. Do you think you know who they could have been? I have some guesses, but before I turn this city upside down, I want to get your take on it," Keith said.

"Yeah baby. I think, well I'm almost certain that it was the two niggas that you cussed out; Blunt and Eric from the club that night," I said.

"Why do you think it was them?" Keith asked.

"Because the cologne that one of the them had on, smelled just like that of Eric's. It was real distinctive, then the way that they were talking about you. The way that Blunt was treating me calling me all kinds of names. It was like they were playing good cop, bad cop, you feel me," I said.

"Baby, when the police come and ask you about what happened, don't say anything, just tell them that two guys broke in your house and that's that. What's understood doesn't need to be said. I love you and I'm sorry I got you into this mess. I'll make it up to you, I promise. My mother will be here in the morning, she's going to purchase a house for us, but I'm gonna need to put the house in your name as well as hers. Is that cool?"

"Yeah baby, you know that I'm not going back to my place right?" I said.

"Yeah, I figured that. You can stay with me if you like, but I'm not going to be home a lot. I'm gonna be out taking care of business and getting with them hoe ass niggas," Keith said.

Keith explained what happened after he and Chris got to my apartment that night. He said that one of the robbers got shot, the other jumped out of my bedroom window since my apartment wasn't to high from the ground. I could believe that. Keith also told me that Chris didn't get hurt.

"My mother wants me to stay with her, but I don't feel like hearing her mouth. Simone said that I can chill at her house until I feel comfortable going back home," I said.

"You know, I don't want you staying with that bitch, but that would be the best place for you to chill at right now. Let me go back to my room before they start tripping. I'm sorry you lost the baby, I bet it was a boy too," Keith said.

"Baby, I don't want to even think about it. You know this was the first time I've ever been pregnant," I said.

Keith just looked down, I could see his eyes watering up, as he opened the door. He looked back and said, "I got our baby killed."

The police came the next morning asking a lot of questions. I did just as Keith told me to, and said that I didn't have any idea who the man could be. One of the detectives, Detective Jonathan Blake said, "you know that Keith Jackson, your supposedly boyfriend is a very dangerous man. The police are watching him as well as the FBI. If I were you, I would remove him from my life. I know that you lost your child, but you can move on and have more children. You can't have another life, be careful dealing with him. Here's my card if you think of something that might help with the case." Detective Blake and his partner Marcus Campbell exited the room.

Chapter Eighteen

Crazy and Deranged

Two weeks after the attempted robbery I had been staying with Simone, while Keith got the house ready for us to move into. I still was shaken up a bit. I didn't want to go out anywhere. I hadn't returned to work either. I just didn't feel like facing anyone other than my family, and I was in no mood to have a lot of questions thrown at me. I just wanted to be safe and left alone.

I was so mad at Simone when she called my mother to let her know that I was out the hospital. My mother cussed me out the first day I got out of the hospital, talking all that shit about I shouldn't be with Keith and that she told me he was trouble from the get go,... and so on and so on. I wasn't feeling her at all, I wanted to say to her, *Bitch, I just lost my baby, I'm not for your bullshit.*

She wanted me to move back in with her, but my heart and pride wouldn't let me. I know, I would have to hear her put down Keith and remind me every day that I lost my baby because of him. When she came to visit me at the hospital, she was somewhat nice to me but I knew the real her would come out as soon as I left the hospital.

Simone took off the first week to chill with me, plus it was just part-time and she was screwing her boss, so it wasn't a big deal. I think the only reason she took off was to fuck niggas and not feel guilty for it, because she could use me as an excuse to get money from them.

I hear her on the phone a couple nights earlier telling some guy, that she hasn't been working for two weeks because she had to take care of a close friend, because she (which was me) got in a real bad accident, and wouldn't be able to get on my feet for awhile. The next thing I know, she was telling the guy that she need two thousand dollars to help her pay her bills and help her friend out. After she got off the phone, she told me that she was heading down to the Western Union and asked me did I need anything.

For the two weeks that I was at Simone's house, Blunt hadn't stop by once or called. That further let me know that he had something to do with the break-in, when I asked Simone what was up with Blunt, she just said that he'd been acting funny since the night at the club. She talked to him twice since that night, but wasn't shit really up with them anymore like that. While I was chilling at Simone's watching TV, Michael called me and filled me in on what was going on at work.

"Jennifer is a mess without you. Everyone is asking when are you going to be back, but you know your boy is holding you down."

"Whatever," I said. "So what's been going on?" I asked.

"Nothing much, but check this, I'll be over later to chill with you and to see what's up with your girl?"

"Boy, I already told you. You not on her level, you need that bread to holla at her. What LIL Kim said, *we fuck with for car keys and seven figga niggas.*"

"Y'all some hoes for real," he said.

"Whatever."

"But before I let you go, you have to check out the five o'clock news."

"Why?" I asked.

"Shit they found two niggas dead on the west side, one guy's dick was cut off and in his mouth.

The other guy's head was chopped off and his eyes were gouge out."

"Are you serious?" I asked.

"As a heart attack. I'll be there in time for us to watch it together, peace."

"Stay up baby boy," I said. My mind was racing after Michael said that, and a funny feeling came across my body. I was thinking that maybe the two dead bodies were the two niggas that ran up in my house and tried to rob Keith. Simone and Michael walked in the apartment at the same time.

"What up my nigga?" Michael said.

"Nothing to it."

"Damn, baby you looking like you just got off the pipe," Michael said, and we all laughed.

"So what you got up for the night?" Simone asked Michael.

"Nothing, trying to take you out tonight and get to know you better."

"Boy whatever, you couldn't handle all this," Simone said.

"Well let me try."

They went back and forth until Simone finally gave in and told Michael that he could take her out the following weekend. As we all talked shit and had some drinks, I couldn't drink because I was on antibiotics, so I just drunk juice. We lost track of time and almost forgot to watch the news. I already had the television on Channel 4 for the five o'clock news, just as Michael said. As soon as the news came on, letters came across the television saying Breaking News;

"This just in, two black men founded slain on Detroit's Westside," The newscaster said. She continues to speak, "late this afternoon, police were called to the 2300 block of Kentucky. Neighbors reported hearing a man or men screaming for what seemed like twenty to thirty minutes. Police arrived on the scene at two o'clock in the afternoon, to a gruesome murder scene.

Two unidentified black males in their mid twenties had been shot in their heads execution style. One man had his penis cut off and placed in his mouth with all of his fingers cut off, and the other male had his feet cut off, both eyes gouge out, and his head was decapitated. The police believe that this was drug related. Police have no suspect in these murders. If anyone knows anything please call your local police department.

After that news segment went off, Simone and Michael started talking like what was just said was no big deal, but I knew better. I had a strange feeling Keith had something to do with it. We all decided to play spades. We were talking shit and having a good time until the breaking news came across the television screen again.

-This just in, the two males that were murdered today have been identify as John "Blunt" Washington, and Eric Jones.-

Simone started crying hysterically. Michael went over to where she was to comfort her. All I could do was stare at the television and think that I got them killed. I shouldn't have told Keith that I thought that they might have had something to do with the break in. *What have I done.*

For the next couple of days I stayed at Keith's condo. Our house would be ready for us to move into in a week, and I couldn't take staying with Simone knowing that I was the reason for Blunt getting killed. But if they did break in, did they deserve to die? But what if Keith hadn't came to the apartment, would they have killed me? Or rape me? Wait a minute, they got what they deserved. They killed my baby, well Blunt did. Why am I feeling guilt or hurt in my soul, fuck them. What goes around comes around.

Keith and I never talked about the murders and I never thought to bring it up either. Keith had bought me a gun, it was a small nickel plated Alfa .25, with a pink grips. He said that he knew I couldn't handle a big gun. He just wanted me to feel safe when I was with him. I took a CCW class and had the gun registered. If somebody wanted to mess with me again, at least I would have something to slow them down or stop them.

Our house was breathtaking, it was built in 1997. It was forty-two square feet wide with four bedrooms, three and a half bathrooms, three car garage, a finished basement with an office. The master bathroom had a Jacuzzi in it with a separate shower. We moved to Rochester Hills, Michigan, that wasn't too far from downtown Detroit, but it felt much safer. It had twenty-four hour security cars driving by. It was a gated community where you had to stop and see a guard before you could get through. And when you got to the gate, you had to have a valid ID and the resident had to okay your arrival. Since it was a mostly white community, the police stay riding around. It took two months to furniture the house and get everything in order with the house. The neighborhood was quiet and all the neighbors kept to themselves.

I hadn't been back to work in a month and I really wasn't feeling it. I decided to enroll at Wayne State University. I decided to pursue a Master's Degree in Public Relations. After seeing and reporting all the horrible crimes that was going on in Michigan, and going through that horror myself, was enough to get into a new career path. Keith had booked us a trip to Jamaica. He said that after all the stuff we've been through, we needed a vacation. Keisha moved into my apartment since I had little over a year left on my lease, and my lease was paid up.

After the break in, I hadn't returned to the apartment. Keith and Chris moved all of my things out. My mother wasn't happy at all with me moving in with Keith. She said that she didn't trust Keith or his mother. When Keith and me got out of the hospital, Keith's mother Brenda, my mother, *and* Keith and I all went out to eat at Ruth's Chris Steakhouse.

My mother said that Brenda was a phony bitch and an old ass hoe that was only out for money, I just blew her comment off. Brenda was always nice and friendly with me and she treated my mother with respect. I know that she could feel the negative vibe that my mother was giving her at the restaurant.

Brenda stayed in town for a month to help us get the house situated since both of our names were on the house; she had to stay around so that we could get homeowners insurance. Since the house was worth three hundred and sixty thousand dollars, we decided to get the house insured for eight hundred thousand dollars. Brenda said that you should always get your house insured for double what it's worth, plus how much you put into it.

Keith and my trip to Jamaica was wonderful. We stayed at the Jamaica Inn in Ocho Rios, Jamaica. We had our own private beach. We ate at all the local restaurants and we made love on the beach every night that we were there. When we got back to Michigan, our lives' started to get back to normal, I was starting to enjoy my work again, and school was going good. My life couldn't have been better. Since we had a bigger place to stay, Keith's daughters came to visit us once a month when he wasn't busy with work. Keith never brought that street life home with him, so I felt safe and having the girls with me was an added plus. Keith's daughters were so cute and they were well mannered. I often wonder why he wasn't still with his babies' momma. Every time I brought the subject up, he would just brush me off or simply say that she was a snake and that she wasn't down for a nigga. Yeah, he could be over bearing sometimes and jealous, but underneath it all he was a nice and generous man.

Since being with Keith, money wasn't an issue with me anymore. I actually had five thousand three hundred and forty-five dollars in my saving account, and another two thousand in my checking account. Keith had a safe installed in the office in the basement. He kept about twenty thousand dollars in it. He gave me the combination and told me that I was only to go in it for emergency; for instance, if he got locked up.

Every since coming back from Jamaica, I'd been feeling sluggish and tired. I decided to make a doctor appointment. I didn't tell anyone because I did not want to worry anybody. After my check up, the doctor informed me that everything was fine, and that I was pregnant. From his guess, I was only a month or so. I was so happy to tell Keith the good news that I went to his place of business. Upon my entrance, I heard him and Chris talking…"Dog, I can't believe that this nigga gonna call me about a gig. I told him shit is tight, and all I'm fucking with is big things," Chris said.

"I know what you mean, shit I got three households to take care of, and you know I just bought a new house. Every time I turn around, my mother got her hands out for some damn money," Keith said.

"What's up with you and your boy in Ohio? Are you gonna holla at him or what?" Chris asked.

"Yeah, I'm going to holla at him, next weekend before I go pick my girls up."

"That's what's up," Chris said.

"Hey y'all," I said as I walked in their office.

"What's up Tomika?" Chris said while walking out of the office and heading to the lobby.

"Hi baby, what are you doing here?" Keith asked.

"I took the day off to go to the hospital because I wasn't feeling good."

"So what's wrong?" Keith asked.

"Nothing, I'm pregnant!" I said. Not at all happy, by this time after hearing him talking about everyone he has to take care of. Plus the fact that he's selling drugs, and the thought of me maybe getting hurt or killed really sunk in at the time that I told him I was pregnant.

"Baby are you for real? How many months? Yo, Chris come here."

"What's up dog?"

"My baby, is having a baby!"

"Congratulations!" Chris said to the both of us.

"Well I guess, I'll be going. I just dropped by to give you the news."

"Damn baby, you act like you not happy that you're carrying my child; my little man, because I know it's a boy."

"I'm not happy about the circumstances of which this baby will be coming into this world."

"Don't go there with me today, Tomika. I'm happy about this. You should be too. You know what it is, you could have left anytime after you knew how I got down. Now that you're having my baby, it's a wrap."

"What's a wrap?" I asked.

"You leaving me, you carrying my seed. All bets are off. It's certain rules to being with a man like me, and if you break them you face deadly consequences," Keith said.

"You know what, I'm getting tired of your threats and street code language. Whatever you gonna do, do it. I love you, but I can't deal with this crazy shit," I said.

While we were talking, Chris said to Keith, "Man your boy will be here in a minute to get that stuff, he just called."

"Alright, I'm finishing up now. Look baby, I got to handle some business. I'll see you at home later," Keith said.

"O.k., do you want me to cook? Or do you want to bring your babies something to eat?"

"Oh, now it's your babies."

"Yeah, I'll stop and get all of us something to eat, love you."

"You better," he said.

As I was walking out of the office, Red was coming in.

"Hi, miss lady. How have you been doing?" He asked.

"Fine, how about yourself?"

"I can't complain, and if I did no one would listen."

"So you doing business with my man?"

"I thought you didn't have a man, you had a man friend."

"You knew I had a man."

"You don't forget nothing I see, huh."

"No I don't."

"You are looking real nice today, but let me get in here, I don't want you to get in trouble with your man friend for talking to me this long," Red said.

"Whatever. Have a good day," I said, and walked to my truck.

Damn I thought to myself, this nigga looks and smells good. All that shit he was telling me about, him having his own businesses, shit that nigga sells dope too.

Later that night, Keith came home with some Outback carry-out. "Here you go baby, I got you a grilled chicken salad and loaded baked potato. Do you want to eat in the room or down here in the kitchen?" he asked.

"We can eat downstairs, I'll be down in a minute," I said.

When I got downstairs, Keith had everything on the table and even poured me a glass of lemonade. I was grateful that I didn't have to cook or clean up, it seemed that as soon as I found out I was pregnant, I just got tired all of a sudden.

"Thanks baby for the food. I appreciate it."

"You're welcomed."

Keith and I had small talk while eating, then he hit me with the question that I thought he forgot about.

"So how do you know that nigga Red?" Keith asked.

"I met him when we were in Las Vegas for the *All Star* weekend. Why you ask me that?"

"Because I can. I saw you talking to him in front of my place. Don't ever disrespect me again and talk to a nigga I do business with unless I say so," Keith said.

I knew that he was in one of his moods, so I didn't want to edge him on and get into it. So I just left the subject alone and continue to eat my food.

After dinner we took a shower together and got in the bed to watch television. While watching television Keith said, "If I find out that you fucked that nigga, I'm gonna kill you both. The nigga told me that he was just asking you *was I in the office*? So I wonder which one of you are lying. I told you before, you got to play by my rules."

"Nigga are you crazy, I don't even know that nigga. I met him at the party in Vegas, and then I saw him again at the party at The Spot, you were there. We just spoke, and he asked me were you in the office that's it. Why are you always tripping? If you think I'm fucking somebody, why won't you just leave me alone. I'm tired of all these threats and accusations," I said.

"I'm not gonna leave you alone until I'm ready to leave you alone. You not gonna play with my heart," Keith said. I wasn't in the mood to argue.

"Alright baby, I love you. Goodnight," I said, and turned over in bed and fell fast asleep.

Chapter Nineteen

That's What's Up

December 31st, 2007, New Years Eve. I was two and a half months pregnant and Keith was getting on my nerves. He didn't want me doing anything or going anywhere. It got to the point that the only place that he didn't trip on me going, was to my mother's house and church. He even wanted me to quit my job.

"Baby, since you're in school and pregnant, I think that working is too much for you right now. I promise you that if you quit your job, you don't have to worry about money anymore. I want my little man to be stress free. With work and school, it's too much," Keith said.

The only people that I told that I was pregnant was Keisha, Simone, and Sheretta. Sheretta and I had gotten close over the last several months. She recently settled down with a man and stop partying so much, that's what brought us closer together. She was in a relationship like me. Everyone was happy about my pregnancy but Simone. When I told her, she was just so negative about the whole thing.

"Girl, you should not have that baby. You know that nigga is crazy. All he gonna do is beat your ass and keep you locked up in the house. You'll be a fool to have a baby now, plus you're back in school and working. Stop the madness and have an abortion," Simone said.

I couldn't believe her comments. I told Sheretta what she said. Sheretta told me that Simone just feels left out due to the fact that everyone she hangs with has a man, and she felt that the only chance she had with a man died when Blunt got killed. I could understand that, but to be so mean to her best friend is a whole other issue. Ever since I told Simone I was pregnant and she tripped on me, we hadn't talked much.

It was New Years Eve, I had plans to go to church with my mother to bring the New Year in at church. My mother had been doing this for years. I figured this would be the perfect time to tell her that I was pregnant as well. Keith said that he might come to church, but he had made prior plans a few months ago to hang out with his boys.

As I was getting ready to go pick my mother up, Keith said, "So are you going anywhere else after church? I know how you get down, you might have made plans with your girls."

"You can say some stupid shit some times. No, I don't have any plans after church. I'll probably go back to my mother's house and chill there until all of the shooting and craziness settles down," I said.

"Yeah, I feel you on that. Well, I'm about to go take care of some business. So I'll try to make it to church. If not, I'll see you when I get home, love you," Keith said.

"Yeah whatever."

"What? You better tell me that you love me back," Keith said.

"I love you back. I'm playing, I love you too."

I got to my mother's house around 9:15pm. The service was starting at 10:00pm, so we had some time. I called her from my cell phone to let her know that I was outside. When she got in the truck, she looked at me funny then said, "I've been having dreams about fish and you look like you've put on some weight, so are you pregnant or what?"

"Damn, Hi would have been nice."

"Girl you better watch your mouth when you talk to me. I'm not one of your little friends," she said.

"I apologize," I said.

When we arrived at the church, it was full to capacity. It seemed like everybody and their mother was there, but we managed to find two seats in the first floor pews. It was so cold outside, that it looked as if all the homeless people where just there to get away from the hulk. It wasn't a lot of preaching going on just singing and testifying. Thirty minutes before midnight hit, Pastor Dewayne Morrison, the senior pastor of the church got up and asked people to come and speak about what they wanted to achieve for the year 2008. A couple older women got up and said the usual things. My mind was on how I was going to tell my mother about my pregnancy. When I heard the pastor say "Brother Keith Jackson has something to say," I looked up and saw Keith walking up to the podium from one of the pews in the front of the church.

Keith got up to the microphone and started to speak, "Giving honor to God who is the head of my life and to my pastor, I stand before you all as a God fearing man wanting to make some changes in my life. The first is that I would like to start by contributing more money to my church." When Keith said that, the congregation started to stand up and clap and worship out loud. Keith, went on to continue, "So I stand before you all with a check for ten thousand dollars."

Everyone started shouting and dancing, the musicians starting playing the get crump music. The pastor had to settle the crowd down so that Keith could go on with what he had to say. My mother and I just looked at each other. I didn't know what to expect with Keith. The pastor had to know that this was drug money, but I was fooled at first. Maybe the congregation believes that Keith is a hard working honest businessman.

My mother whispered in my ear, "That nigga is going straight to hell, he's all in here like he's so sanctified and holier than thou."

"Momma, just chill out. I already know how you feel, I feel the same way. Let's just see how this plays out," I said.

Keith went on to say, "I've been a member of the church for four years now. Here is where I met the love of my life, whom is here tonight. Tomika Smith would you please stand up?"

I was shocked. I did as I was told and stood up in front of the whole church.

Keith continues to say while walking towards me, "Ever since you came in my life, you've made me a better man and an all around better person. I believe that God brought you to me. You are my queen and the woman that I want to spend the rest of my life with. We are about to become parents, and I don't want my child to come in the world into a broken home. I'm asking you in the house of God in front of your mother and my fellow believers, will you do me the honor and become my wife?"

I didn't know what to say, all I was thinking was that he asked me in front of all these people, so I wouldn't say no.

Yes, I did love Keith, but could I deal with his controlling and jealous ways, I'm not quite sure. But when Keith got to my pew, I looked down at my mother and she gave me a look that would kill. I walked out to him not knowing what I would say, but when he got down on one knee and pulled out a little pink ring box from his pocket, my eyes started to water up.

When Keith opened the box up, I was staring at the most beautiful ring I have ever seen. It was a four carat diamond ring with a two carat marquis diamond cut as the center stone, surrounded by a two carat princess cut and round baguettes on the side.

"So Tomika, will you marry me?" Keith said.

I looked at my mother, I looked around the church, and then I looked down at the ring and said, "Yes Keith, I will marry you."

Everyone in the congregation got up and starting clapping…that is everyone except my mother.

Then Keith returned the microphone back to the pastor. The pastor made a couple of jokes about the proposal, and then he preached for fifteen minutes about a new season.

I brought the New Year in with a fiancé and a baby on the way. My mother never said congratulations to us. The streets wasn't bad out, so I decide to just drop my mother off and go back to the house to celebrate with my man. Keith told me that he had some bottles of sparkle grape juice.

On the ride home my mother started in on me, "You know, you ruined your life by getting pregnant by that good for nothing nigga. What's gonna happen to you and the baby if he gets killed or end up in prison? I thought you were smarter than this, but I guess you're not."

"It's not that serious, I'm well taken care of. I have money saved if anything happens, plus I have a degree to fall back on. I'm going to receive my Master's in a year, I'm good. I'm grown, I can make my own decision," I said.

"You know what, you're right. Bought sense is better than told sense, thanks for going to church tonight. I'll call you tomorrow," My mother said as she exited the truck.

"O.k., love you," I said.

"Love you too, Tomika please be safe."

2008 started off good for me, I was engaged. I was going to have a baby and I started going to school full time. Keith was being real cool and calm, and our relationship was good. He wasn't even tripping when I would go shopping with Simone or out to eat or anything evolving her, but that would soon change.

In late February, I had put my truck in the shop because someone had put a big dent in it with their door while it was parked. Since Keith had a couple of cars, I figured I'd drive his BMW 750. Keith was at work, so I called him and asked could I drive his car. He said yeah, but to drive the Audi, so I did. I picked up Simone and Sheretta and we headed to Somerset to go shopping. While we were shopping, Simone notices some girls following us and just staring hard. I didn't want any problems because I was with child now. We all just figured that Simone probably fucked one of their men because the girls all looked like they were being well taken care of.

When we all were in the Gucci store, Simone finally had enough and said something to them, "Excuse me, but I couldn't help but notice that it seems as if you all are following us and staring us down. Do you know one of us or something like that?" Simone asked the two women.

The bigger one of the two stood up and said, "Yeah, we want to know which one of y'all is Keith's woman."

I couldn't believe this shit, I felt so embarrassed. I just knew these bitches were on some shit due to Simone. But as it goes, I stepped up. I'm glad we all were looking good, so we could give these bitches something to talk about.

"I'm Keith fiancé. Why is that any concern to you?" I asked.

The bigger girl said, "I don't care, my sister just wants to see who her competition was."

"What the fuck are you talking about?" Simone said as she jumped in front of me, not wanting me to fight because I was pregnant.

The smaller of the two stood about 5'2in. She was light skinned with medium length hair. Her hair was almost the same color as mine. I could see why Keith fucked with her if he did because she was a pretty girl. I'm not even gonna hate. But I was about to get to the bottom of this shit.

The smaller girl began to speak, "My name is Tiffany, and I've been fucking Keith for the last six months. I knew he had a woman. I just wanted to come see for myself what the big deal was, and I see it ain't anything."

Before I could react and smack the bitch, Sheretta had already punched her dead in the eye. The security guy for the store grabs Sheretta and Tiffany, and told us to leave before they call the police.

We all grabbed our bags and headed to the valet area outside to retrieve the car. As the car was pulling up, Tiffany and her sidekick came running behind us, I thought it was about to be on, so I grab my pocketknife from my purse. I was mad that I left my gun in my truck. I'm so use to having it in my glove compartment that I forgot. Sheretta being on point, had her can of mace out. It was about to be on. From the looks on their face, they knew we weren't for any games, so they didn't come any closer to us.

When we got in the car, the bitch Tiffany gonna say, "I've gave Keith head many of nights in that car."

I wanted to jump out and kick her ass, but I didn't want to take the chance of losing my baby over that bitch.

I dropped Simone and Sheretta off at Simone's house. Before I pulled off Simone said, "Girl don't do nothing stupid, don't worry about that hoe. She just sick because you got him, and not her. You the one living the life, not having to work. You that bitch, not her. Keep them bitches hating. Love you, stay up."

"I love you too, but I'm about to go check this nigga for even having his bitches come up to me like that. Girl, I would have never thought that he would play me like that," I said.

"Don't even feed into that bullshit. Take your ass home and get some rest, that shit is petty," Sheretta said.

"Alright y'all I'm out."

I called Keith's phone three times and I didn't get an answer. I thought about what Sheretta and Simone said; I wasn't about to play myself and go up to his place of business. I was better than that. After the third time that I called and I got no answer, I left a message:

"Tell your hoe Tiffany not to follow me anymore, because next time I will have my gun on me. And by the

way, I'm leaving your sorry black ass. I see you like fucking with little girls. I hate you and hope you die."

I had some errands to run, so I didn't get home until 6:00pm. Keith hadn't returned my phone call and I wasn't gonna call him back. I took a hot bath and ate some Taco Bell. I had dozed off to sleep and woke back up around midnight, when I turned over, Keith wasn't there. I got up and called him, still no answer, so I left another message:

"Nigga, wherever your ass is at, I hope you stay there. I'm gone. Don't call me anymore, it's over! Your ring will be on the dresser. It's been one nigga."

I got up out the bed and began packing my bags. I had no idea where I was going, but I wasn't staying here another night. Thirty minutes went by and I heard Keith coming in the house. He ran up the stair to the bedroom where I had my suitcase on the bed packing. He looked as if he had just came from the gym or something. He was sweating and looking tired, like he had been working hard.

"What the fuck you think you're doing? You not going no fucking where. Put all this shit back! You are taking this petty shit a little too far."

"Fuck you, you got my messages and I'm just now hearing from you. What, you were out with that bitch, Tiffany?! I can't believe you let that bitch get close to me like that. Do you know how embarrassed I was for her to tell me that she's fucking you, right in front of my girls?" I said.

"She's nothing but a hood rat hoe. I made a mistake and let her give me head a couple of times. Baby, I promise that's it," Keith said.

"If you think that I believe that, you must be out your rabbit ass mind. You was fucking that bitch and I don't know what you told her about me, but she followed me to the mall...but she got her ass kicked, how about that?" I said.

"I don't give a fuck about that bitch, she's nothing to me," Keith said.

"Just get out my way, I'm outta this. Bitch you can keep all this shit!" I took off my ring and threw it on the bed, grabbed the suitcase and started to walk out the room.

Keith grabbed me by my arm forcefully.

"Bitch, don't play with me. The only thing that's saving your ass right now is that you're carrying my seed. I suggest you put them clothes back up and take your ass back to sleep," Keith said.

I yanked my arm out of his hand and started walking down the stairs.

"Tomika bring your ass back up here! If I got to come get you, it's gonna be a problem."

I made it to the kitchen to get my keys and purse. When I walked out of the kitchen, Keith was right there. He smacked me in my face and told me to take my ass back upstairs. I didn't want anything to happen to my baby, so I did as he asked. I walked back to the room, put on a pair of his boxers and a wife beater and got in the bed.

"I brought your suitcase up. You can unpack in the morning. Don't play with me like that anymore. I love you and want to be with you only. That's why I asked you to marry me. Tiffany was just something to do before I proposed to you. You don't have to worry about her anymore, I promise," Keith said.

I woke around 5am with bad stomach cramps. Keith was lying beside me with his back turned to me. I got up, went to the bathroom, open the medicine cabinet, and took two Tylenols, dry mouthed. I figured that would settle the pain, and plus I knew they were safe to take being pregnant. I laid back in the bed.

Thirty minutes past and I was in more pain than before. I nudged Keith to wake him up. "What? What's wrong? I hope you not on some more bullshit, it's too early in the morning for that shit," Keith said.

"It's not that, my stomach is hurting real bad. I don't know what's wrong. I ate some Taco Bell earlier, maybe that's got my stomach hurting. I don't know, but I took two Tylenols a minute ago, and it hurts worst now," I said.

"Well, let's go to the hospital just in case. Can you put your clothes on?" Keith asked.

"Yeah, I'm gonna throw some jogging pants on and a t-shirt."

We arrived at Beaumont Hospital fifteen minutes later. There wasn't a wait so the nurse checked me in right away. After she did the mandatory check, she rushes me in to see the doctor. She told Keith and I that it seemed as if I was having a miscarriage. The doctor confirmed what the nurse had told us. I was indeed having a miscarriage, they took me in a private room in emergency and cleaned me out and sent me on my way.

After the second miscarriage, I couldn't take looking at Keith. Because of him, I've had two miscarriages. All I could think about was him and that bitch Tiffany had stressed me out so much, that day that my body couldn't take it. Keith tried to make it up to me by buying me all types of purses and clothes, but that material shit couldn't bring my babies back.

I began feeling like a zombie. I had a routine, which started off each day with going to school in the morning, and coming home cooking for Keith, because I barely ate much after the miscarriage.

Keith and I became roommates. We weren't having sex like we use to, that's because I couldn't stand him anymore. I actually started hating him. My mother was furious when I told her about the miscarriage.

"I don't know what happen to cause you to have the miscarriage, and I'm sorry that you had to go through it a second time. But baby, I think it's God way of telling you that you shouldn't be having a baby with that man. It just seems like he's bringing you down mentally and physically. You're losing weight, and you're always looking stressed out; he's not beating on you is he?"

"No, he's not hitting on me. Maybe you're right. I'm just tired and school has got me stressing, but besides that, I'm good," I said.

My mother didn't believe a word I said, but she let me live my life the way I saw fit to. From the outside, I was living the good life. I didn't have to work, I had everything I wanted, plus a man that loved me. Simone and Sheretta had the same thought that my mother had about the miscarriages. Maybe it was best that I didn't have a baby with Keith.

Chapter Twenty

This Nigga Is Crazy

New York, May 21st, 2008, Keith's friend and business partner Chris had a big birthday party at Jay Z's 40/40 Club in New York. Every baller from Detroit was there, and of course I ran into Red at the party. Keith and I were getting back on track. He was giving me my space and I was just going with the flow. Everyone around me could tell that I had started to drink more than usual. Keith practically bit my head off because I told him that I wanted Simone to come out and hang with me.

"What are y'all dikes or something? Why does she have to go every place that you go to?" Keith said.

"It's not even like that. I don't want to be around all your friends in a city I've never been to before. Plus, Simone knows some people in New York, so we can hang out and do our thing, and I don't have to be up under you the whole weekend."

"You not gonna be hanging with that bitch like that. She can come to the party with you, but that's it. You let that bitch be a hoe all by herself, and if I hear that you been going to clubs with her, it's your ass." Keith had such a negative attitude towards Simone. Yeah she was about that money, but that was my friend.

The club was so off the hook, there were a lot of celebrities there, from rap stars to radio personalities. Simone was getting much play. A few guys tried to talk to me, but every time I walked off to mingle with Simone, Keith was right on my heels. Since it was his boy's birthday party, I thought that he would be chilling with his people not watching every move I make. Red was peeping me out all night, the first chance he got to talk, approach me he did.

"What's up beautiful? I see your man got you on a short leash tonight," Red said.

"I guess so," I said.

"Why are you in such a bad mood tonight?"

"If you were going through the shit that I've been going through the last few months, you wouldn't be so cheery either," I said.

"Well I bet. I can put you in a better mood if you let me."

"I bet you could, but I don't want any extra stress in my life. I got a crazy ass man, and he's not buying any bullshit," I said.

"If you hang out with me, you don't have to worry about your man," Red said.

"That's what your mouth says, but anyway, you need to leave before Keith comes back around."

"O.k. pretty lady, I'll see you around again."

"I know, enjoy the rest of your night," I said.

"I will."

Right after Red walked away, Keith came behind and said, "Why is it that every time I look up that nigga is in your face? Are you fucking him or something?"

"First off, talk that shit to that nigga, not me. I've been at the same spot since you saw me last. I'm not fucking that nigga, but you need to be in his face not mine," I said.

"First off bitch..." Keith said.

"Nigga don't be trying to disrespect me because you scared to say something to that nigga," I said. After that comment, Keith smacked the shit out of me.

Not too many people saw him smack me because it was so crowded, and everyone was either high as hell or drunk as fuck. The two people that I didn't want to see him hit me, did.

Simone just shook her head and called me over to where she was at, and Red did the same but he gave a disappointed look.

"Bitch if you go over there to that tramp bitch, I will smack your ass again. I kept telling you watch your mouth when you're talking to me. I'm not one of your little friends. I will beat your ass! And as far as that nigga Red go, I'm about to holla at him now. You go back over to the VIP area and sit your hot ass down." When Keith left to talk to Red, Simone came up to me and walked to the VIP area with me.

"Girl, you need to leave that nigga alone. He's crazy, all he does is beat your ass and buy you things. I'm gonna start calling y'all Ike and Tina," she said laughing.

"Bitch, that's not funny," I said.

"Well, shit! Everybody else is laughing at your stupid ass; that nigga gonna kill you. That's not gonna be funny, but you staying with that nigga is funny," Simone said.

"Whatever, I don't comment on your sexual rendezvous. Don't comment about me and my man," I said.

"Fuck you and your man. I'm just telling your dumb ass something you need to hear, but I guess you not gonna learn until that nigga puts you in the hospital," Simone said.

"Whatever, you do you and I'll do me," I said.

"That's what's up. I'll see you tomorrow. Tend to your face before it swells up," Simone said as she walked away.

I know she was being sarcastic, so I responded back by saying, "Tend to your pussy and make sure it doesn't swell up either."

I saw Keith and Red talking from the corner of my eye. You could tell that they were having a heated discussion, but it didn't get serious. Keith came back over to where I was at and apologized to me.

"Baby I'm sorry about that. I just get so jealous, and it seems as if you just add fuel to the flames by making those hoe ass comments," Keith said.

"Keith, can we just go? I don't feel like this anymore, and my face is starting to swell up anyway?" I said.

As Keith and I were walking out of the club, I saw Simone all up in Red's face. She know that I'm kinda digging him. I don't know what type of shit she's on, but if she fucks him, I'm gonna cuss her ass out, I thought to myself.

The next morning, Simone called me around 9am, asking if I wanted to go out to breakfast with her. I responding by saying, "I thought you would probably still be in bed with Red."

"Whatever, I didn't leave with him. I left with this dude name Jay-Bone, he's supposed to be some local rapper from Philly. Girl he had a big ass dick, my ass hole is hurting like a motha fucka," she said.

"Girl, you nasty. How you gonna let a nigga you just met, fuck you in the ass?" I said.

"Because that's what he paid for. Don't go acting like you all that, since you got a man. Don't let me pull your hoe card," she said.

"Pull it, I ain't never let a nigga fuck me in the ass or trick with no nigga."

"Anyway, you have tricked for some money, but that's neither here nor there. Do you want to go eat and do some shopping, since I'm leaving tonight?" she said.

"Yeah, that's what's up. I'll be in your room in an hour."

"O.k., see you then," Simone said.

Simone and I didn't get ready in time to eat breakfast, so we decided to go eat at Junior's. Ever since P. Diddy made the band walk and get him a cheesecake, we wanted to see if the cheesecake there was so good that people would walk miles for, and it was. As Simone and I were finishing up our lunch, I asked her about Red.

"So what were you and Red talking about last night, when y'all were all booed up in the corner of the club?"

"Nothing much, he was asking a lot of questions about you and your relationship with Keith," Simone said.

"Like what?" I asked.

"Girl, I really can't remember much, but I do think he asked me if you and Keith lived together, and where did y'all live at."

"And what did you say?" I asked her.

"I told him that y'all did live together, and that y'all stay way out somewhere," Simone said.

"You sure, you didn't tell him where we lived at?"

"Girl you know me better than that. He kept pressing to know, but I told him that I hadn't been to your house yet. I told him that it was somewhere around Troy."

"I wonder why he's so interested in where Keith and I live at," I said.

"Maybe he wants to send you some flowers or something like that," Simone said then she started laughing.

"Girl, Keith's ass would kill me for sure then."

"I don't want to be all in your business, but you my dog, and if you like it, I love it. But you need to leave that nigga. All he does is hurt you; after last night when that nigga slapped you in the club. That shit was foul," Simone said.

"I know, it's just that I'm in love with him. He doesn't always act like that, just when we're out and he see niggas trying to talk to me or all up in my face," I said.

"Girl, you sound stupid. That nigga has done that a couple times that I know of. Why don't you just leave him? I know you got some money stashed away, so you'll be straight, plus you got a job and a new car," Simone said.

"To be honest, I sometimes think about leaving, but I'm scared of what he might do to me. Shit, I've gotten use to this lifestyle. I don't want to have to move back with my mother. If I get my own place, it's gonna be hard for me to make it with just one job, and I don't feel like struggling right now," I said.

"Do what you want, just don't wait too late because that nigga scares me," Simone said.

Before we got up to leave to continue shopping, Simone caught me off guard by asking me, "Do you think Keith had something to do with Blunt and Eric getting killed?"

I responded by saying, "Yeah."

And that was it, no more holding it in. Simone never brought the subject up again. I think that it kind of brought a peace of mind to her, to know that I thought Keith had something to do with them getting killed. I know, I felt much better finally getting it off my chest. I just hope Simone doesn't tell anyone what I had said to her, but if she knew any better, she would just kept her mouth closed.

We shopped all day; we returned to the hotel at 6:30pm. Simone's plane was leaving at ten, so she had to rush and pack all her clothes. Keith and I communicated by text all day. He was hanging with his boys, doing their thing. We had plans on hitting some clubs up later that night. I finished helping Simone pack and stood outside waiting for a cab with her. We said our goodbyes and hugged as a cab pulled up. The cab driver got out and put her luggage in the trunk.

Before she got in the cab she said, "You're the only real friend that I have, please be careful and don't let that nigga kill you, I love you."

"I love you too. I'll see you in a couple of days," I said.

Keith and I partied hard the last night in New York. We hit two clubs and a strip bar. The cost for a lap dance was ridiculous. Thirty dollars was a little too steep, but we were having fun and I wanted to continue to have a good time, so I paid for Keith and Chris to get a couple dances each. I knew that Keith wasn't going to pay for a dance his self. All the dancers were flocking to our table because they saw all the bottles of Remy, Ace of Spades and Patron. They knew money was in the house by the way we all made it rain in the club. We didn't leave until the club was closed down.

One of the girls that was with Chris's other boy Ronnie, suggested that we head to an afterhours place that one of the dancers told her about. We were all for it, shit this was my first time in New York, I wanted to live it up. When we got to the afterhours place, it was a big ass country house about an hour out of New York City. I was glad that we got a car service. We didn't have to worry about driving drunk. I really didn't want to go in because I've never been to an afterhours spot before, but when we got out of the cars and heard all the loud music and seen all the parked cars in the back, I felt a little safe.

The spot was off the hook, there were a couple of New York rappers in the place, niggas were shooting dice, playing pool, girls were walking around half naked, some completely naked, giving dances or more, depending on the money. I stay close to Keith while we walked around the place. Down in the basement they were betting on dog fights; there was something for everyone to do. I notice some card games being played upstairs, and that's what I wanted to do. They were playing for money, so I asked Keith if he would be my partner. He said that he wanted to shoot dice and I should ask one of the girls that were with us to play with me. He asked if I need any money. I said no, and head upstairs to find someone to play cards with, while Keith headed upstairs to play dice. I couldn't find any of the chicks that we came with, so I stood by the tables waiting for someone to get up so that I could play spades. Across from me was a guy standing, waiting to get in the game as well.

"Hey, baby girl can you play?" he asked.

"If I couldn't, I wouldn't be standing here?" I said.

"Well it's a hundred dollars a game, that means each person puts in fifty. You game to be my partner?" he asked.

"That's what's up," I said.

"By the way, my name is Ricky. You must not be from New York," Ricky said.

"Naw, I'm from Detroit, and my name is Tomika."

"Well Tomika, we up- let's do it," Ricky said.

Ricky and I were kicking ass all night. Well it was morning, rather time was flying by. We got up about two times and by the course of three hours, we were up six hundred dollars all together. I didn't see Keith around, so I guess he was winning on the dice as well. I was having a good time talking shit with my partner Ricky from New Jersey. As we started another hand, I felt a presence behind me. I thought that it was Keith, but when I turned around to see, it was just the same group of people that were there all night. Ricky and I were on a roll, then out of nowhere Keith comes up and says, "Get up. It's time to go."

"O.k. baby, but can I at least finish this hand?" I said.

"Did you hear me, you know that I don't like repeating myself. Get your ass up, it's time to go," Keith said.

"My man, baby girl and I are on a roll. We are already up six hundred. Won't you let her finish this hand?" Ricky said.

"Nigga, I don't give a fuck about some hoe ass six hundred dollars, this is my woman and I'm telling her it's time to go. You need to stay out of grown man's business, matter of fact keep the six hundred. You look like you need it," Keith said as he was pulling me up out of the chair.

The ride back to the hotel room was hostile; Keith was talking shit to me the whole ride back. I was so embarrassed by him. Everybody in the car was just looking at him like he was crazy. When we got inside the hotel room, Keith pushed me on the bed and starting pulling my pants down.

"What are you doing? I'm on my period," I said.

"Bitch, this is the type of shit that you like. You want a nigga to man handle you, you don't appreciate when a nigga trying to be good to you. I can't believe how you disrespected me tonight," Keith said.

"How did I disrespect you? I was chilling playing cards."

"No, you were all in that nigga's face," Keith said.

"You are fucking crazy. I don't want no other nigga but you, why can't you see that? I don't look past you."

"Whatever bitch, I'm tired of you out here playing me like a fool. I'm out here trying to get money for us and you can't stay out a nigga's face," Keith said.

I knew that he was drunk and I didn't want to go at it with him all night, so I just laid there with him on top of me trying to take off my panties and spitting all in my face while he talked.

"I'm gonna teach your ass how to respect a gangster."

He ripped my panties off with the maxi pad still in it. He then pulled down his pants, turn me around so that my ass would be in the air and rammed his dick up in me. I started screaming and telling him to stop, but he didn't. All I could do was cry. I couldn't believe that he was raping me.

The next morning when I got up, I notice that blood stains were all over the sheets. Keith wasn't anywhere to be found. I packed my clothes and called Keith to see where he was at because we had to be at the airport by 1pm, and it was already 10:30am.

He didn't pick up so I left a message;

"That was some real foul shit that you did last night but it's cool, though the same thing that makes you laugh makes you cry. Anyway, where are you? We have to be at the airport by one o'clock. I'll be in the lobby waiting for you. I packed all your stuff up. Just meet me in the lobby."

Keith didn't call me back. At first, I thought he left without me but I had our plane tickets, plus his stuff was still in the room. He had packed most of his stuff yesterday, so I figured he went to holla at his people before he left because Chris and his girl were staying another day.

Around 11:15am, I got a text saying he would be there in ten minute. I was so frazzled that I went to the bar and had an early cocktail. While I was enjoying my second Long Island, Red came up to me.

"What's up baby girl?"

"Nothing, waiting on Keith to get here so we can go to the airport," I said.

"I know we can't talk too long, so I'm just going to get right to the point. You're too good for that nigga. All he does is dog you out. I want you to take my number and call me when you're ready for a real man."

"Boy, you know I can't get your number, but you can have mine and call me when you think I'm ready for you," I said.

I swallowed the rest of my drink and went back to the lobby and waited for Keith. Keith had me so stressed and discombobulated that I began to drink heavily. I left the bar with Red just in the nick of time, because as soon as I got ready to sit back down, Keith came walking in my direction with a big ass Hermes bag. He was smiling like he hadn't just beaten my ass and raped me the night before.

"What took you so long? Don't you know we have a plane to catch?" I said, not looking at the bag in his hand, as I started grabbing my luggage and heading for the door.

"That's how you greet your man now? I had to stop and pick my baby something up. I know, I tripped last night and I'm sorry. Do you forgive me?" Keith asked.

"Whatever, I'm getting tired of you tripping on me, you need to get help. I'm not going to be dealing with your bi-polar ass," I said.

"Baby, please forgive me, I was wrong. I'm trying to be the bigger person and apologize. You are making a big deal out of nothing."

I didn't say a word, I didn't want to get him started all over again. I just couldn't believe that he was trying to turn the shit around on me.

"Anyway, open your gift up. I know you're going to like it."

I already knew what it was, plus I didn't care for Hermes purses anyway. I thought they were too big, overpriced, and ugly. Just as I thought when I opened up the box with the purse in it, he got the biggest, ugliest purse he could find. It was a dodo brown, black leather and suede purse. The price tag read five thousand five hundred and fifty six dollars. I thought to myself, he could have kept the purse right where it was at, and just gave me the money. I smiled, gave him a hug and a kiss and said thanks.

The plane ride home was a smooth one. When we got to the house, Keith told me not to try anything slick and leave because if I did, he would fuck me up. I took his word and just chilled. I was starting to feel like Farrah Fawcett in the movie *The Burning Bed.*

Two weeks later, Keith left to go handle some business and pick his girls up so that they could spend the rest of the summer with us. I was happy that the girls were coming because I would have company in this big ass house of mine. Keith didn't like me having people come over. Simone would tease me and say that he's trying to isolate me from the outside world. I laughed, but in all honesty, I believe he was. He got so upset when I went back to work that I thought he was going to actually kill me.

Chapter Twenty-One

That's the Way Love Goes

The summer was ending and Keith was going to take his daughters back home so that they could go school shopping with their mother, and get ready for school. This particular time Keith asked me did I want to ride with them; Brooklyn and Paris was so excited about me riding with them that I couldn't say no. I secretly wanted to go because I wanted to see what their mother looked like. I figured she had to be light complexed since their kids were a golden brown complexion, and Keith was dark as hell. We got up early Saturday morning and packed the kids suitcases and the school clothes that Keith bought them while they were staying with us. No matter how Keith treats me, he is a great father.

While the girls were staying with us, Keith took them to the zoo, the state fair, the movies, shopping, and we all went out at least twice a week. I knew that if we had children together, he would love them and treat them like his other kids. When I had the first miscarriage, I could look in his eyes and feel his pain and guilt.

As soon as we entered Ohio, we stopped to eat at Waffle House and ate breakfast. "Ms. Tomika, when we get to my house, I want you to come see my Cabbage Patch dolls," Paris said.

Keith told the girls to call me Ms. Tomika. He told them by calling me Ms. Tomika, they were being respectful.

ASA Publishing Company

"I don't think your mother would like that, but if you get permission from her, then I would love to see your dolls," I said.

"My mommy won't mind. We talk about you all the time to her. She said you sound like a really nice lady," Paris said.

We had a nice ride to the girls' house. We played car games and listen to the radio. Keith whispered in my ear while he was driving, "You know my babies love you, right?"

"I know, and I love them too. I just wish we could work out our differences so we can be one big happy family," I said.

"There's no differences to work out, you have to realize that I'm the man in this relationship, and what I say goes. If you can abide by my rules and do as you're told, everything will be fine. I love you baby," Keith said.

"I love you too, but you have to respect me as well," I said.

We pulled into a beautiful subdivision in the Cincinnati area. Keith pulled into their driveway which was connected to a two car garage. The kids' home was beautiful on the outside; it was a ranch style house that was all brick, red brick to be exact. Keith called the mother whom name was Rolonda, and told her to open the door that they were outside. A pretty light-skinned woman came to the door. I assumed it was their mother. She was petite with a nice shape, she had long hair with blonde highlights. When she started walking to the truck, I noticed she had a deep gash across her left eye that went through it.

The girls ran to her and started to tell her all the places they've been and the clothes that Keith and I bought them. Keith didn't say a word to her. He just popped the trunk and got the girls luggage and bags. Rolonda walked over to me an introduce herself.

"Hello, I'm Rolonda the girl's mother, and you must be Tomika."

"Yes, I am. It's nice I finally get a chance to meet you. The girls talk about you all the time. You have two beautiful respectful young ladies," I said. Before she could respond, Keith jumped in our conversation.

"Why in the hell would you just assume that this was Tomika? What if I had brought another woman with me to drop the kids off? You need to keep your mouth shut and wait until I introduce you all," Keith said.

Rolonda didn't say anything to him, she waved bye to me and grabbed the girls and headed to the house.

"Damn, you not even gonna let me say bye to my girls?" Keith said.

"My bad, girls go give your daddy a hug goodbye," Rolonda said.

"Mommy, can Ms. Tomika see my dolls? I want to show her my room," Paris said.

"Yeah, she can. Take her in the house," Rolonda said. The house was neat, clean, and homely inside. Rolonda has nice taste in furniture. I could tell by the way she was dressed that she had style.

When Keith told me about his kids, he mentioned Rolonda. He told me that she was his age, so that would make her thirty now, and that she didn't want to be in a relationship anymore. So they parted ways on good terms. He said that one of the reasons why they couldn't get along was that she liked to go out and party too much, but from the looks of it I didn't get that vibe from her. I went inside both girls' rooms and they were fit for princesses. Both of them had full size canopy beds with a cartoon character theme to them. Their bedrooms look like something out of a catalog. Paris showed me all of her Cabbage Patch kids, and I could have sworn that she had everyone that was ever made. I gave the girl's hugs and I showed myself out.

When I got to the door, Rolonda was coming in the house and she looked like she was mad. Before I walked out she said, "Be careful."

I turned around and asked her, "Why would you say that?"

"I'm just giving you a heads up. Have a safe trip back," Rolonda said.

Keith started blowing the horn and yelling, "Hurry up, we got to find a hotel and check in. I got stuff I got to do today."

"See you next time, I hope," Rolonda said.

I wanted to check her about her smart ass comments, but I let it ride, said thank you and left.

Keith dropped me off at the hotel, and he left to go handle his business. I already knew it was drug related, I just hope that he wasn't gonna try and bring anything back because I've heard stories that niggas didn't want to break any laws in Ohio, because they were giving niggas life for any and everything.

What Rolonda said stayed on my mind so I decided to call her and get to the bottom of her slick talk. Brooklyn had called me from their home number a couple of times and I saved it on my cell phone. I knew it would come in handy one day.

The phone rang twice before she answered.

"Hello," Rolonda said.

"Hey, this is Tomika calling. I have some questions to ask you. I hope you don't mind me calling?" I said.

"Does Keith know that you're calling me?" Rolonda asked.

"No."

"Well, I don't think it's a good idea for us to be talking. I don't want it to get back to Keith," she said.

"I promise I won't say anything. I just need to know why you told me to be careful. Is there something that I should know about Keith?" I asked.

"Look, I don't know anything about you and Keith's relationship, my girls told me that you were a nice lady. I just let it slip out. I didn't mean anything by it. I'm happy that he found someone else. Let me ask you this, are you happy with him?

Because if you're not, that means he's putting his hands on you and it's only gonna get worst," she said.

"Why would you say that he's putting his hands on me?" I asked.

"Please don't call me anymore. Keith is a crazy ass nigga, the scar on my face is from him. The nigga almost killed me. He threw me out of a car on the freeway with my baby in the car. He doesn't care about anyone but himself and his girls, his whole family is crazy. His mother is a money hungry bitch who lets her sons do whatever they want to do. As long as they're giving her money- it's all good. Just watch what you do and say around him and his family. And if you want to be with him, just do what he says and it will be all good," Rolonda said.

"Let me ask you this, how did you get away from him?" I asked.

"I didn't get away, he left. I wanted to call the police, well actually I did call the police one time, but when they came, he told me if I told them what happened he would kill me. So when they got to the house, I said that I was just mad at him and everything was fine. And you know what, they sent me to jail for making a false call. After he knocked my eye socket in and beat me up so bad, I guess he didn't want me anymore. So one day, I packed up my shit and moved back here with the girls. Once I got settled in, I called him to let him know where I was at. He sent money and helped me get this house, but we don't talk unless it's about the girls. Also, he made it perfectly clear to me that I can't have any man around my girls, but he can have you around them. He is such an ass," she said.

"Thanks for talking to me. I got a lot of thinking to do. I promise I won't tell Keith that we talked, and I won't mention anything that we discussed today, thanks again," I said.

"No problem, it was nice talking to you. But for real girl, you need to leave him now before it gets worst. I saw that scared look on your face earlier. Girl he has beat my ass enough to last me three life times," Rolonda said.

"One more thing before I let you go, did he hit you in front of the kids?" I asked.

"Sometimes, why you ask that?" she said.

"Just something that was on my mind, bye."

"Bye," she said.

After talking to Rolonda, I got a better understanding about Keith, he was crazy for real. While waiting for him to get back to the room, I started putting a plan together on how I was going to leave him. I didn't want to leave with battle scars like Rolonda or even worst, ending up dead. I didn't say a word to Keith about what Rolonda told me or what we discussed. It would be a secret that I would take to the grave with me.

When we got home the next day, Simone called me and asked if I wanted to go to this new club called Escape. I told her that I was tired and just wanted to relax.

"Bitch you are so lame, now that you're playing house. You and Sheretta kills me, y'all got men now, y'all don't know how to act. I guess I'm gonna have to roll solo tonight," she said.

"I guess so, or you can call Keisha's money hungry ass. I know she wouldn't mind rolling with you," I said.

"That's your people not mine. I just deal with her on the strength of you. She was cool to hang out with in Las Vegas, but that's where it ended," Simone said.

"I hear that, but I'll holla at you tomorrow," I said.

Later that night, Keith was getting dressed to go out.

"What's up? You want to roll with me and my man? We going to some new club that just opened up," Keith said to me.

"Are you talking about Escape?" I asked him.

"Yeah, how do you know about it? Did you have to do some research on it at work?" he asked.

"Nope, Simone called me a couple hours ago asking if I wanted to go with her. I told her no, I don't feel like going anywhere tonight, I'm tired."

"Alright, I'll holla at you when I get back. I shouldn't be gone that long," Keith said as he walked up to me and gave me a kiss.

When he does little things like kiss me, it makes me forget all the foul shit that he does as well.

Around 2am, I hear Keith coming in the house. He must have been a little intoxicated because he was making a lot of noise. When he got to our bedroom, he had a beer in one hand and a wingding dinner from Coney Island in the other hand.

"Damn, you loud as hell. Fuck me being sleep," I said.

"My bad, you want some of these wingdings and fries?" Keith asked.

"Yeah," I said.

Keith sat on the bed. We ate the food and he went and got me a beer to drink as well.

"So how was the club? Did you see Simone there?" I asked.

"Did I? Your girl was all in me and my man's face. I thought she was on some pills or something. She knows I can't stand her ass," Keith said.

"How was she in y'all faces? What was she saying to y'all?" I asked.

"I mean she was all on us, following us and shit like that. She even tried to cut into me about paying for some ass," Keith said.

I didn't believe that shit. Simone was my girl, she wouldn't do me like that. Or would she? I know how she gets down for money, but she wouldn't play me; we grew up together. We know each other's deepest darkest secrets. She was talking about Keith scares her and all the other shit. Maybe she was just saying that to throw me off. She is money hungry. I'm gonna have to get to the bottom of this shit.

"How the fuck did she try to cut into you about some money?" I asked.

"Your girl Simone asked my boy what's up? Did he want to get together later and do something for some cash? And she told him I could come along too if I was paying," Keith said.

My mouth just dropped, that sounds like some shit she would say. Plus, I've seen in person how she gets downs with two niggas, my thoughts went back to Las Vegas. "Well, I'm gonna call her and get to the bottom of this shit," I said.

"Call her ass, I told you she wasn't anything but a gold digging hoe. She ain't shit but an undercover prostitute, but you didn't want to believe me. My man Chris dissed her ass a couple of times. You saw how she was trying to be all on him in New York in front of his girl. She ain't shit and that's why I be tripping on you because you hang out with her. And you know what they say, birds of a feather flock together," he said.

"Whatever," I said as I picked my cell phone up to call her.

The phone rang four times, then the voicemail came on which was Junior Mafia song, **Get Money**, "*You have reached the baddest chick. I'm unable to get to the phone right now, so leave your name and number and I'll get back to you as soon as possible, thank you.*"

"What's up? This is Tomika, call me back when you get a chance, one," I said.

I was so much in my own little world, that I didn't pay attention to Keith laying next to me watching Sports Center and smiling a devilish smile.

The next day while I was at work, all I could think about was the shit that Keith said about Simone last night. It was 10am and Simone still hadn't called me back yet. I didn't want to call her again, I already left a message. I figured I'll wait until I get off work, then I'll call her again. I couldn't focus on anything at work. I had to get to the bottom of this, so at 10:45am, I called Simone; the phone rang three times before she answered.

"Bitch you know it's too early. I don't have to be at work until 1pm," she said.

"I was just calling to see what the fuck went on last night? Keith was telling me that you were all in his boy's face talking about you wanted to fuck both of them for some money," I said.

At this point, I was too pissed off to be tactful. I wanted to know what went down last night.

"What? Girl, don't be calling me early in the morning talking some bullshit about what you're crazy ass man said."

Simone was testing my patients, all that smart shit wasn't called for. All I wanted to know is what went on last night.

"Girl miss me with that slick shit. I just want to know, did you come on to them like that?"

"You should know me better than that. I did not approach ole boy, he came on me, and Keith's name was never brought up. I only seen them once together, so I don't know why he would say some hoe ass shit like that," Simone said.

"I don't know either, that's why I'm calling you. I know your past and that sounded like something you would do." I said.

"That nigga got you over there brainwashed. But let's not forget I know your past too. That nigga ain't got enough money for me to fuck with his ass," Simone said.

"Whatever. I didn't call you to beef. I just wanted to get your side of the story from last night. But let's not forget that nigga had enough money for you a couple years ago, when you were on his head at The Spot," I said.

"You know what, I ain't got time for this petty shit. You over there getting your ass beat and dogged out every day; trying to bring me into that bullshit with y'all. Your man probably wants me to fuck him or join y'all. Sorry, ain't enough money in it," she said.

"Fuck you and the five muthafucka's who look just like you. He don't want nothing to do with your disease filled ass. You ain't shit but a walking STD," I said.

"You so stupid, you don't know when a nigga's playing you. That crazy ass nigga don't want you to have any friends, and you're stupid enough to let the shit happen. So fuck you and fuck your hoe ass man," Simone said, then the phone went dead.

After I hung up with Simone, I called Keith to tell him what happened. He swore up and down that Simone was lying, and was so convincing, that I didn't have any other choice then to believe him. From that day on, I didn't talk to Simone for a long ass time.

Chapter Twenty-Two

Who Can I Run To

October 9th, 2008, another birthday, and I didn't have my girl Simone to celebrate with me because we were still beefed out. I don't know what to think. In a way, I kinda believed Simone, but I can't block out the past. Simone has fucked some of her closest friend's man before, so what makes me any different?

Keith was in Atlanta. He wanted me to go down there with him, but since I've been back to work after the second miscarriage, I didn't want to keep asking for time off, plus I needed a break from Keith. Keith and I relationship was on its last leg, especially after the incident in New York. I need to start getting my plan together to leave him ASAP. My first instinct was to call the police on him and give information on his drug dealings, but I couldn't live with myself knowing that I had snitched on him. If he was gonna get caught up, I would hope it would be on his own.

I began hanging with my cousin Keisha. She was cool to go out with, but she likes to go to all the hood bars and Keith didn't like that. He has his reservation about me getting so close to Keisha, but she was family and she was young. I was trying to expose her to other shit besides titty bars and hood niggas.

On this particular birthday, I decided to just spend it with my mother. We went out to dinner, a movie, and she came back to my house to spend the night with me. Our relationship was starting to get back on track, she just hated the fact that I was with Keith. She even told me that she could tell that he was putting his hands on me. Of course I lied and told her he never touched me.

I only had a few more months of school, then I would be receiving my second degree; my job was going quite well. I was helping out more with the producing, a lot of my segments that I suggest were getting put on the news. I was really proud of myself. A couple of weeks after my birthday, Keith and I were sleeping in the bed and the house phone rang at 1am. It was my job saying that they needed me to come in and cover breaking news for the 4am broadcast, I knew that I couldn't say no. I wanted to make a name for myself in the news business, so I got up and went in at 3am.

Everything was just so hectic at work, there was a body founded on the Westside of Detroit; around midnight, and it was a rush as to which station would have the breaking story first. When I started working on the intro for Jennifer, I noticed that the description of the dead woman was somewhat familiar. Then when I got to the name I automatically thought about; the girl Tiffany from the mall, the name of the deceased woman was Tiffany Steward. She was described as a twenty-two year old light-skinned woman with long hair.

I skimmed through the information that I received from the police department and the homicide detectives, but when I got to how she was killed, I knew it had to be the same girl that Keith was messing with and that he must have killed her. The report read that the body was found in an abandoned car on the city's Westside. She was found with her tongue cutout and a gunshot hole through her head execution style. This was so familiar with how Blunt and Eric got killed. I was waiting for the police department to fax me over a picture of Tiffany so that I could be one hundred percent that this indeed was the same girl. I didn't have anyone to share this information that I trusted but Simone and we weren't speaking, so I was a nervous wreck all morning at work.

Twenty minutes before the news was scheduled to air, we received a picture of Tiffany Steward and it was in fact the same girl. I was overcome with sadness, and asked if I could have the rest of the day off. I lied and told Jennifer that Tiffany was my best friend's cousin and I had to go inform the family and catch my composure.

When I got home around 6am, Keith was turning over in the bed sleep. I couldn't believe that he could kill people and sleep so comfortable. I thought about packing my things and leaving, but then I thought about what Rolonda said and about the dead chick Tiffany, Keith wasn't going to let me go so easily. When I got in the bed, Keith must have felt my body because he put his arms around me. I couldn't go to sleep for anything, so I tuned on the T.V. The story about Tiffany Steward was on all the news channels. I wanted to wake Keith up so he could watch it and get his reaction, but I knew the truth, and he probably would have just blown it off anyway. When I finally got to sleep around 9am, my phone started vibrating. I looked over at it and noticed I had a text from Simone, it read: ***You are a dumb bitch if you don't leave.*** I wondered if Simone had seen the news and remembered ole girl from the mall, or was she just fucking with me. Anyway, I didn't even bother to respond to her text. Shit, I couldn't even get mad at her, she was right. I'm a dumb bitch if I do stay with him, but I knew one thing for certain, I had to find a way to leave him without getting hurt.

A couple of weeks later, Keisha called me wanting to know if I would go to the bar with her. She said that she broke up with her baby daddy and she wanted to clear her head and go out. I wasn't up to going to a hood bars, so I suggested that we go to one of the casinos downtown. She was cool with that. I told her that I would be there in an hour. I wanted to put some clothes on. Keith wasn't at home, so I called him to let him know that I was going out with Keisha. He was talking shit at first, but said that I could go out. I didn't want to drive my truck so I asked

Keith if I could drive one of his cars. He said yeah, so I opted to drive the Audi.

I thought I was the shit in that car. Keisha was geeked up when she saw me pull up. We rode around for a minute before we went into the casino; niggas was on our head, and I guess it was the car. Keisha wasn't use to all the attention that we were getting. Niggas never came on her unless she was naked and dancing at the club.

We were in the bar area having drinks, chilling and talking to some guys, just passing time. Keisha wanted to gamble a little bit, but I was in no mood to lose any money, so I told her to do her thing and I would be here waiting, having drinks. I wasn't doing anything wrong. I was just having conversations with a couple of guys in the bar and letting them buy our drinks.

While I was at the bar Keith called me, "Hello," I said.

"What the fuck you at the casino doing?" Keith asked.

"Nothing, at the bar chilling. Why you calling like this?"

"Bitch don't make me come up there, I heard you all up in niggas faces."

"You got a fucking problem. I can't even go out and chill without you tripping on me. What's up with that?" I asked.

"You better get your ass out of the casino in the next ten minutes, or I'm coming up there and drag your ass out!" Keith said, then he hung up.

I didn't know what was going on. Who could have called him and told him that I was up in niggas faces. Knowing Keith, he probably got somebody watching me in here, but why would they lie on me? After I got off the phone with Keith, I found Keisha and told her about the phone call that I got from Keith and that we had to leave.

I decided not to go home just yet, so we grabbed something to eat at J Alexander, and then we went back to

Keisha's house. Keith called me when I got to Keisha's house and asked me why I didn't go straight home.

"I'm tired of being in the house all day by myself, so after we left the casino I decided to get something to eat," I explained to Keith.

"Bitch you need to be heading home right now. You think that you can disrespect me and not have any consequences. You a damn fool, now get your stupid ass home NOW!" Then he hung up on me. I didn't pay him no mind. I didn't feel like dealing with all the bullshit, so I bought a pint of liquor and kicked it with Keisha.

We talked about the beef between Simone and I and what was going on with Keith and I. Keisha turned out to be a cool person to hang around with. She never judged me or gave her opinion about my current situation. Keith was blowing my phone up, leaving message after message.

"*Bitch when I see you. I'm going to knock your fucking head off.*" That was the first one.

"*You got five minutes to get home or I'm coming to get your stupid ass.*

Bitch you like hanging with hoes, like I said before birds of a feather flock together.

You a hoe, your cousin a hoe, all y'all some hoes, but you a part time dike and a full time hoe. What a nigga got to do to get your mind right?"

After hearing these messages, I decided to cut my phone off. It wasn't any reason for me to run home, shit he was gonna trip no matter what. I just wish I knew who told him I was at the casino in guys faces. They just got me a long night with his crazy ass. Keisha told me not to pay any attention to him and that I should look for someone else, because he was causing too much trouble between my friends, family and me. She told me that my mother had called her mother and said that I've been acting different ever since I got with Keith and moved out. She even told her that she suspect that he's beating on me, but she doesn't know for sure.

I could tell that Keisha wanted me to let her in on what was really going on with Keith and I, but I don't tell all my business to just anyone, and I know how messy she is. My business would be all over the city by morning if I told her anything.

It was around 11pm, I was getting ready to go when we heard a knock on the door, and it was two neighborhood niggas coming over to smoke a blunt with Keisha. I turned my phone on as I was heading out and I had twenty missed calls, five voice messages, and three text messages- all from Keith. When I was heading for the door, Keisha asked me to chill until she finished hitting the weed. I was hesitant at first, but I said what the fuck. Keisha's mother wasn't at home, so they went to smoke in the kitchen, I stayed in the living room.

Five minutes later, there was a knock at the door. I got up and looked in the peephole to see Keith standing outside. I wasn't about to open the door. Keisha came in the living room asking me who was at the door and why I didn't answer. I replied by saying, "That's Keith crazy ass, and I'm not in the mood for his bullshit tonight."

"Girl let that nigga in, he's not gonna trip with us in the house," Keisha said.

"You don't know him. The nigga is crazy for real. Seriously, don't answer the door," I said.

While we were talking, Keith continued to knock on the door. He started cussing at me saying, "Tomika, I know your hoe ass is in the house. I see the lights on. You better open this god damn door right now before I knock it down. You know what, you ain't nothing but a hoe and a slut just like all the bitches you hang around with. You ain't shit but a part time hoe and a full time dike, open this fucking door!... Then you have the nerve to be riding around town in my shit getting numbers and making me look like a fool. I'm gonna teach you a lesson about playing with a real nigga. After tonight, you gonna learn to respect a real nigga when you meet one!"

I wasn't about to open the door with all the commotion going on in the front. One of the guys that was smoking with Keisha came into the living room, "What's going on outside? Who is that nigga? Keisha that's your man out there?" he asked.

"Naw, that's Tomika's man, and he on some bullshit right now. She's scared to go out there," Keisha said.

"Do y'all want us to say something to the nigga?" The guy asked.

"No we cool. I don't want to cause any more trouble with him. He'll cool off in a minute," I said.

The other guy came in the living room, talking shit, "That nigga out there is lame, acting like this over a female? He's blowing my high!"

I wanted to tell the nigga to say that to Keith's face, but I had other shit on my mind like how I was gonna leave without getting my ass kicked.

A couple minutes past, then out of nowhere a rock bust out my auntie's picture window. We couldn't see what Keith was doing outside because the blinds were closed. Keith came in the house through the window. Before I had a chance to run, he grabbed me by my hair, turned me around and punched me in the mouth. Then he proceeded to punch me in my head and eye. I could have sworn that Keisha had a smile on her face when I looked up for a second, but all I could remember is the guys trying to pull Keith up off me, and Keisha going off about the window.

I woke up a couple hours later at Sinai Hospital, my whole body was aching. I looked around and notice Keith sleep in a chair next to my bed. I called his name out and he woke up.

He walked over to the bed, kissed me on my lips and said, "I'm sorry for putting my hands on you. You make me so mad sometimes that I just blank out. You know I love you and don't want anything to happen to you. That's why I get so upset when I don't know where you're at or what you're doing. You know that there's a lot of people out here that want to see me dead and I don't want you to get hurt because of me. That's why I'm so protective of you."

I didn't even say anything. Keith was crazy and I didn't want to set him off again. All I wanted was for him to just leave me alone.

"Do you hear me, I love you Tomika. You just have to learn how to talk to a nigga. Your mouth is too damn smart and it's gonna get you killed if you don't watch it," Keith said.

"Are you fucking kidding me? You beat my ass, got me laying up in the hospital, and it's my fault? Why don't you just leave me alone? I don't want to be with you anymore. Please, just go," I said.

"Bitch, I'm not going anywhere and neither are you. This the shit I'm talking about; your smart ass mouth, ain't no other nigga gonna want you. And if I ever hear about you being up in a nigga's face again, you are dead. I told you before, this shit we got is blood in - blood out," Keith said.

"So you saying the only way I can leave is if I'm dead, that's some sick shit. If you feel that way, why don't you just leave? Why are you still with me if I get you so angry? Please Keith, let me go. I can't take this anymore. You almost beat me to death last night," I said.

"Baby, I've invested my heart and soul into us. I'm not letting you go. Either you gonna get down, or lay down. It's your choice. The police should be here in a minute, just tell them that some niggas tried to rob you and they broke into your auntie's house. That's the story Keisha and I told them when they came to the house."

Before I could say anything, the doctor and nurse walked in, "Good to see you up, Ms. Smith. I'm doctor Black Morgan, all your test came back. You have three broken ribs and a sprain ankle. The swelling in your face and arms will go down in a couple of days, but other than that, everything is fine. I hope the police find the man who did this to you. I can't believe people are still breaking into people's houses and assaulting them."

Keith didn't say anything while the doctor was talking. When the doctor finished, he did ask, when could I go home? The doctor said as soon as I wanted to.

"So can I go to work on Monday?" I asked.

"Yes, just get plenty of rest for the next two days. You will be in a lot of pain, but there's no reason why you can't go to work, as long as you don't do any lifting and or excessive twisting and turning." He prescribed some pain medicine for me, and two hours later, I was at home in my own bed.

It was Saturday and I had a day and a half to get better before going to work on Monday. I didn't want Michael and Jennifer asking questions about my face, so I stayed in the house the whole weekend with an ice pack on my face and stomach. Keith was waiting on me hand and foot, but it still couldn't make up for what he did to me and how he had embarrassed me.

I talked to Keisha Sunday afternoon, she informed me that Keith paid her and the two guys that where at her house money to lie to the police.

How the story was told to the police, *Keisha and I were coming home from the club when we got to the porch, we notice the window busted out. Keisha stayed on the porch to call the police, while I went in the house. When I got inside, that's when I got attacked. Keisha ran in the house to help, and the so-called man pushed her down and punched her in the stomach and ran out the backdoor. A couple minutes later, her two friends arrived then Keith.* Keisha told me that Keith gave her a thousand dollars for the window and gave each one of them five hundred dollars each.

My mother didn't come to the hospital, but she called and came by to make me something to eat. She stayed the night with me. I was happy about that, I really missed her. She got up the next morning to go to church, but promised to stop by with some food for me before she went home.

The police officer called me Sunday evening and I concurred with the story that Keisha and Keith gave them.

# # # # #

Monday morning at work, Jennifer called me into her office, "Tomika, you're doing a good job here, you're the best assistant that I ever had, but I can't help but notice that you are coming in to work looking disheveled and tired. I don't want to pry, but is there something going on with you at home?" Jennifer asked.

"No, I've just been stressed out with school, having two miscarriages, there was a break-in at my cousin's house this weekend, and I was attacked," I said.

"I'm sorry to hear that, do you need some time off?"

"No, I'm fine. I just want to get back to work."

"Before you go, I have some good news, there's an opening at CNN headquarters in Georgia for an assistant to the VP of Public Relations. I figured since you will be receiving your Master's in Public Relations, this would be a good opportunity for you. I think that you need a change in scenery, so I have all the information that you need. I really think you should look into it," Jennifer said.

"O.k., thanks a lot, I will. Are you trying to get rid of me?" I said jokingly.

"No, I just want the best for you, and this is a great career move for you."

I went on with my day. Michael kept asking me, what was wrong? He said that I wasn't my usually annoying self today. I didn't want to, but I just broke down crying and told him about the whole weekend. He just sat there listening to me not saying a word or showing any emotion until I was finished.

He got up, walked over to me, and said, "You're a dead woman if you stay with that sick ass nigga. Why are you so stupid? You are a smart, beautiful woman any man would be happy to have you in his life. You need to get some counseling and get yourself together, I love you and don't want to see you hurt or much worst, dead."

I decided to go out by myself for lunch. I needed some time to myself. I had Keith on my back at home and Michael and Jennifer on my back at work. When I returned from lunch, there was a fruit basket on my desk. I already knew who it was from. The card read;

Baby, I'm sorry for what happened on the weekend. I promise it won't happen again. You are my world, and I don't know what I would do without you. I'll love you even after I'm dead, to death do us part.

I was so caught up in the card, I didn't notice that there were two brochures on domestic violence on my desk. I picked them up and put them in my purse. I was a little upset that Michael would just leave them on my desk. He could have just handed them to me. When he came back around, I asked him about the brochures. He said that he didn't leave them on my desk. The only other person that could have done it was Jennifer.

I figured I would ask Jennifer about the domestic violence handbooks before I got off work. So at the end of the day, I went into her office and asked why did she leave them on my desk. She responded by saying that she needed me to read them because we were going to be doing a week long segment on domestic violence. She wanted me to do the research and the booklets were just the beginning of my research, which we never ran a series on domestic violence.

The following weekend Keith took me to Miami to party for the weekend. I guess this was his way of apologizing for putting me in the hospital. While we were there, we partied hard with the biggest rap stars in the game. I shopped the entire time I was there. I actually had a good time with Keith. He was behaving like the Keith I fell in love with. While we were in Miami, he kept saying that we need to go to Las Vegas and get married soon. I made up excuses why we should wait; such as my job, not having time, and the best one was that I wanted to have a big wedding in a church. Keith agreed that we should wait and that I should start planning the wedding as soon as we get back home.

When we got back home, everything was falling into place. I really felt like Keith was changing for the best. We were spending more time together and getting to know one another better as well. All that changed in less than a couple of weeks. The police had a warrant to search Keith and Chris's Real-Estate Company due to an informant that they said they had. When they searched the place, they found two unregistered guns and less than a quarter ounce of weed. Keith said that they were looking for drugs. Both Keith and Chris got arrested, but was let out on a ten thousand dollar bond. After his arrest, Keith laid low and basically stayed around the house. He didn't like it when I would hang out after classes, and go out with some of my classmates to a bar or restaurant. He wanted me to be with him every moment of the day, and that was driving me crazy. Keith and I were having sex so much since he had so much free time on his hands, that I had to buy tubs of K-Y jelly. Keith had my insides raw, and my pussy was sore. My asshole and my jawbones hurt too. Some nights I would beg him not to fuck me.

We were having sex at least three times a day, and he love to have oral sex just as much. I thought in the back of my mind that Keith was trying to get me pregnant. Or maybe he was punishing me in a different way because he knew he was hurting me. I guess this was a different sign of domestic violence.

I wasn't worried about getting pregnant because of all the miscarriages that I've had, and I hadn't gotten pregnant yet.

Chapter Twenty-Three

Life's A Bitch

November 25th, 2008, two days before Thanksgiving, Keith and I were lying in the bed sleep when all of a sudden we both jumped up due to heavy banging on the door. It was around 11:30 at night; we had gone to bed early because we were up all day grocery shopping and getting the house together for Thanksgiving. We decided to have thanksgiving dinner at our house since we had so much room, and I wanted to prove to everyone that I could cook a whole meal without any help. Plus Keith's mother was coming and I was finally going to meet one of his brothers.

He finally told me the real deal with them. He said one was in prison for murder. The one that I was going to meet, be in and out of the city so much, Keith said that he only gets to see him on holidays, maybe twice.

After about the third knock, Keith went downstairs to see who was at the door, "Who is it?" Keith asked.

"The police, open up."

"Baby, put some clothes on, the police are at the door," Keith said to me.

I threw some jogging pants on and a t-shirt, and ran downstairs to see what was going on. When I got to the doorway, Keith opened the door.

"Keith Jackson you have the right to remain silent, anything you say, can and will be held against you."

Everything was a blur from there on.

A S A   P u b l i s h i n g   C o m p a n y

"Tomika, Tomika," Keith called out my name and I snapped out of my daze, "Call my mother and let her know what's going on. Tell her, I'll call her tomorrow. Then I need you to call John Glenn, my attorney, and let him know what's going on. He'll know what to do, his number is in my cell phone. Don't mention any money because he's already been taking care of. I'll call you after I get processed," Keith said.

Keith called me early the next morning letting me know the charges that they had against him and what was going on. Apparently they have two informants that's willing to testify against Keith with the murder of Eric and Blunt, and some drug conspiracy charges. Keith said that he'll let me know more when his attorney fills him in with all the evidences that they have on him.

Before we got off the phone, I told Keith that I don't think that we should be together anymore, and it wasn't because he was in jail. I was just tired of going through the bullshit with him and that I would be his friend through his court situation, but we need to part ways.

When I told him that he got enraged, "Bitch, I'll kill you before I let you leave me. Just holla at my mother and Chris and see what's up. I'll be in touch. Tomika, don't make me do no foul shit to you. Just get at my people and I'll call you and let you know what my visiting hours are when I get to the county. I love you," Keith said.

"Yeah, whatever," I said back.

"Bitch don't get tough since I'm in here. I still can get at you, and one more thing, you bet not move out of that house."

Over the next couple of weeks, I didn't answer any of Keith calls. He left a lot of messages on my voicemail. I talked to his mother a couple of times, but then she started questioning my loyalty to Keith and her. I exchange a couple of not so nice words and that was the end of our relationship. She left a couple of nasty messages as well, and it made me think back to what Rolonda told me about Keith's family.

Chapter Twenty-Four

Everything That Glitters Ain't Gold
(Back to the Present Day)

After all the bullshit I've been through with Keith, over the past two and a half years. This nigga has the audacity to be fucking my nasty ass cousin. Oh it's on for real now. I can't believe I thought that Simone would do me dirty, but all the while it was Keisha. Keith must have put that bug in my ear about Simone so that I wouldn't suspect Keisha was doing that foul shit to me. I decided to call Simone and apologize to her for my rude behavior the last couple of months. She accepted my apology and we got caught up on what's been going on with me and my situations with Keith. I told her about the phone conversation between Keith and Keisha.

"We should go over her house now and beat her ass," Simone said.

"I know right," I said. "I wanted to wait and see if she'll holla at me first, I don't want her to know that I know what's going on."

"I feel you girl, but you can't let that shit ride. Sometimes family play you worst then people off the street. I just can't believe it. She watched that nigga beat your ass and put you in a hospital, and she still wants to fuck with him. These young hoes today are stupid," Simone said.

"I got to wait and see what the deal is, but I hope that hoe ass nigga gets life in prison. His court date is in a week, so I want to be there," I said. "But on another note, what's been going on with you?"

"Nothing much, ever since we left New York, I've been chilling with and messing around with all these nigga's out here. Blunt was the only nigga that I really liked. I was just out trying to get money. Out of everybody that I dealt with, he was the realist one and I knew he cared for me. He used to ask me all the time to be his girl but I just couldn't stop getting all this money that was out here. But I think I'm ready to settle down now," Simone said.

"What? I can't believe this; a hoe wants to be a house wife," I said while laughing.

"Bitch, that's not funny. But anyway, I think that I might be pregnant," Simone said.

"Bitch you lying. This is some shit," I said.

"Girl, can you believe how our life has changed in the last couple of months?" Simone said.

"I know right, so when will you know if you're pregnant or not?" I asked.

"Well, I'll go to the doctor tomorrow so I'll know then," Simone said.

"Let's have lunch or something tomorrow. I'll call you when I get out of class," I said.

"That's what up," Simone said.

Soon as I hung up the phone with Simone, Red called. I've been dodging his calls for about a month, so I figured I might as well see what he wants. It couldn't hurt, and after the day I had, I needed to talk to someone.

"What's going on beautiful?"

"Nothing much just got off the phone with my girl, I haven't talked to her for a while because of Keith, but we're back cool now," I said.

"I'm glad to hear that. But what's up with me and you? I want to take you out to dinner tonight. You can't keep running from me, and you sure can't use your man as an excuse because he's not going to know," Red said.

"You're right about that, but I don't know who he got watching me. You could be working for him," I said.

"First off, I'm not no hoe ass nigga, so please don't let that shit come out of your mouth anymore. I don't work for no nigga, I just want to take you out to get something to eat. All you have to say is yes or no. That other garbage you talking is not necessary," Red said.

"You right, I apologize. Yeah, I would like to have dinner with you," I said.

Red was looking good as usual. He had on some Gucci gym shoes with some Rock Republic jeans on with a white tee. He was dressed hood, but classy. He reminded me of Keith, they had the same kind of authority presence when they enter a room.

I still didn't feel comfortable with Red knowing where I lived so I met him at a lounge in downtown Detroit. I arrived before he did, so I decided to order an Apple Martini to get my nerves together. I know this was against street code to be going out with a man that my ex was doing business with, but I need to have some fun and relaxation. Keith put me through enough stress to last a life time. Anyway, Keith was fucking my cheese head ass cousin.

Red and I laughed and conversed about the classes that I'm taking. Me wanting to move to Houston, Texas. Just life in general.

"I've been wanting to ask you something for the longest time, but I don't want you to get offended by it," Red said.

"I'm open, you can ask me anything. I've been through too much to get offended by anything anymore," I said.

"Are you sure?"

"Yes."

"Why did you stay with Monster for so long? Didn't you know that he was a little off? I mean, look at the way he treats you when you all go out or how he has to know your every move," Red said.

"This might sound like something out of a Lifetime movie, but he wasn't crazy in the beginning. In fact, he really wasn't checking for me. That's what made me like him," I said.

"Well, just to let you know, I think that you're a real beautiful, smart, sexy woman, and I've been wanting to get with you from the moment I saw you in Vegas," Red said.

"You're just blunt with your shit, I see," I said.

"There's no need for me to lie. I know I can treat you a lot better than your nigga- man, fiancé, whatever he is to you can," Red said.

"I'm not even looking for that right now. I just want to kick it and have a good time," I said.

"That sounds like a plan. Why don't we leave here and go get a room somewhere, where we can chill and talk some more?" Red said.

"O.k.," I said.

"Well follow me, I'm gonna get us a room at the Hotel Baronette.

"Well, let's stop and get something to drink," I said.

"You don't think that you already had a little too much to drink tonight?" Red said, referring to the four Apple Martini's I had.

"No I don't."

"O.k. then, we'll stop. I'll grab you something, but I'm good. I don't want you to be drunk. I want us to have a good time and I don't want you to do anything you don't want to do. And I don't want you to blame it on the liquor," Red said.

"I'm a grown ass woman. I'm good. Let's ride out."

Red didn't have to worry about me blaming anything on the liquor. I've wanted to fuck him for a while too, so it was all good. I needed some dick, and it was just going to be a one night stand. I was cool with that.

When we got to the hotel room, Red was so horny that his dick was standing straight up, through his pants.

"Damn nigga, you must have been waiting a long time for this," I said, while laughing.

"I told you that already. I've wanted to fuck the shit out of you for a long time. I can't believe that you let that nigga Monster all up in that and he be beating your ass," Red said.

"His name is Keith, and he doesn't have shit to do with what's going on right now. Do you want to hit this ass, or do you want to talk about Keith? Because right now you're blowing my high," I said.

"You know I want to fuck you," Red said.

"Then act like it," I said. Red grabbed my drink from my hand and starting kissing on my neck, then he starting kissing me in my mouth.

"Let's go to the bedroom," Red said.

When we got to the bedroom, he asked me to take off my clothes so he could look at my body naked. I did as I was asked.

"Damn baby, you got a nice ass body. I can't wait to get up in that."

"You have some condoms?" I asked.

"Yeah."

"What's up, you scared?" I asked.

"I ain't never scared," Red said.

I pulled the cover and sheets back and laid in the bed with my panties and bra on. Red got on top of me and kissed me from my forehead to my toes. I was getting so hot, I couldn't take it. He then came back up from my toes and started licking on my thighs. While he was licking on my thighs, he put his index finger in my pussy.

"Damn this pussy wet," he said.

"I know, it's waiting on you to get up in it," I said.

"I got to taste it first," Red said. He pulled my panties off and got to licking and sucking in my pussy like there was no tomorrow.

"Damn baby, slow down. This pussy ain't going nowhere, you can eat this all night," I said.

"I know, it tastes so good, just like candy," he said. He flipped me over on my stomach, spread my butt cheeks open and started licking my ass hole. He was running his tongue in and out my ass fast but gentle. I wanted to return the favor. So when he was finished, I told him to lay on his back while I tried to put his whole dick in my mouth. Since he was already rock hard, it was a tough challenge, but I got the majority of his dick in my mouth and I was licking and sucking on it like my life was depending on it. I didn't have his dick in mouth for a good five minutes before he was about to cum. I wasn't gonna let him nut in my mouth, so I stop sucking his dick and started jacking him off with my hands. I came three times before he even ran up in me, but when he did, it was the worst pain I've felt in a long time.

Red had a dick like a horse, it was big and long. I've only seen a dick like that in porn movies. I took it like a champ though. I could tell he was use to fucking hoes, because the only way he wanted to fuck was missionary style. He was fucking me so hard that I wanted to cry, but the pain didn't last long. He came three minutes later. I really couldn't get into fucking him because he was wearing that same cologne that Eric wore when he and Blunt tried to rob and kill Keith and me.

"I see you still wear that cologne," I said.

"Yeah, I know you like it, and this shit just smell good as hell," he said.

"Well, I don't like it anymore, so please don't wear it again around me, thanks," I said. I didn't want to go into details with him about why I didn't want him to wear the cologne again. I'm glad he didn't ask either.

"Damn baby, you got some good ass pussy, so I'll do whatever you want me to do."

"I know you came quick as hell," I said in a joking way.

"I had to get the first nut out the way, are you ready for round two?" he said.

"Yeah, let me get another drink. You working with a lot." I said.

I got so fucked up that I didn't realize that we ran out of condoms, and the last time we fucked we didn't use a condom. We had sex all night and morning. I didn't get home until 10am. Before we left, he handed be five hundred dollars.

"What's this for?" I asked.

"I just wanted to show you that I can pay to play."

"I hear that. I know it's too late to ask, but do you have any sexual transmitted diseases? Because we didn't use a condom the last time we did it."

"No, I don't have any diseases, and no I didn't cum in you either. Do you want to go grab some breakfast at one of the casinos?" Red asked.

"No, I need to go home and get some rest and recuperate from last night. How about we get some dinner later on tonight?" I said.

"That would be nice, hit me up when you finish recuperating," Red said with a smirk on his face.

"I'll do that."

"Let me walk you to your car."

As we were walking through the garage to get to our cars, Red was on the phone talking to someone about some business. I could tell he was getting irritated, but what caught my attention was what he said at the end of the conversation "*All is well.*" What the fuck, that's the same shit the robbers said when they broke in my house. What the fuck?! I got it all wrong. Red broke in my house that night, not Blunt and Eric. My keys dropped right out of my hand when I heard him say that.

"Baby girl, you alright? You look like you just saw some scary shit or something," Red said.

"My bad, I was thinking about what all I had to do today. Well let me get going. I'll call you tonight," I said.

"Damn, a nigga can't get a hug or a kiss? You cold blooded."

"No, I think you the one that's cold blooded," I said and then I gave him a hug and a kiss.

I couldn't wait to get home to call Simone and tell her what was up. I had to get in contact with Keith. I guess, I was going to have to make that trip to the County to holla at him and let him know what's up. I can't believe that I had just fucked the nigga that killed my baby, tried to rob my man, and kill us. This shit seemed like a movie or some shit you read in a book.

When I got home, I called Simone to let her know what happened and broke down the whole situation with Red and me.

"Girl, you sure can pick them? Every nigga you fuck with is crazy. So what are you going to do?"

"I don't know. I'm going to go up to the County and see Keith, but I can't tell him that I fucked Red. That's how I found out about him being the nigga that tried to rob him."

"Well, how are you going to tell him?" Simone asked.

"I don't know yet."

"So Keith killed Blunt and Eric for nothing, and probably killed that girl Tiffany all over some shit he thought they did," Simone said.

I never told her about Tiffany. I wonder how she found out about that; maybe the news. But she would have mentioned it to me when we first talked last night. I played it off and asked her, "Who is Tiffany?"

"You don't remember, the girl that followed us in the mall that day when we all went shopping, it was all on the news in shit. Matter of fact it, was on the station that you work for," Simone said.

"Yeah, girl you're right. I must have forgotten all about it. But anyway call me after you come from your doctor's appointment and we can go get something to eat," I said.

"Alright, I'll talk to you later," Simone said.

Since it was Saturday and I didn't have to go to work or school, I figured I would go get my hair done before I left the house. I transferred my house phone calls to my cell, just in case Keith called I would be able to talk to him. Simone called me while I was at the hair salon and told me that she was in fact pregnant. I was happy for her. I hoped that the baby would calm her down now.

"So, are you going to tell the father?" I asked.

"Yeah, I'm about to call him now. He's probably gonna be tripping talking about a paternity test, but whatever. I know it's his baby because I'm eight weeks pregnant, and he's the only one I was having sex with at that time," Simone said.

"Alright, I'll talk to you later," I said.

"I'm going to come up to the shop and get my toes done. Do you want me to bring you something to eat?" Simone asked.

"That's what's up."

Later that night, Red called me to see if I wanted to go out to dinner. I lied to him and told him that I was tired and had a lot of homework to do. He told me to just get at him when I had time. He tried to come over but I told him that I didn't want to disrespect Keith anymore by bringing a man into his house. Red understood.

The next day, I got up, went to church, and rode out to see Keith in the County jail. I waited for an hour before I got on the elevator and took that ride up to the fourth floor to see Keith. I didn't want to touch anything in this little nasty ass booth. The walls were dirty with spit stains and dried up cum, it looked like. Keith came strolling out like he owned the world. He looked better than ever. He had lost a little weight and gain more muscles. He smiled at me then picked up the phone. I did the same. The glass even smelled like shit. I couldn't hear him that good, so I had to press my face up to the glass.

"Hey baby girl, I see you finally came up here to see your man," Keith said.

"Sorry that it took me so long, but I figured since Keisha was fucking and sucking your dick so good that you would want to spend all your time with her." His mouth dropped when I said that. He was about to try and explain himself but I cut him off.

"I don't want to hear it. I came up here to tell you something," I said.

"It bet not be that you're fucking with a nigga or a bitch, Keisha told me how you get down. I don't want to have to kill your ass when I get out," Keith said.

"You mean, if you ever get out. Keisha doesn't know shit about me. I never fucked with a girl and she knows that. You stupid if you gonna believe a cheese head bitch over me. But you ain't shit anyway to be fucking my cousin, you a dirty ass nigga," I said.

"Don't talk that slick shit to me, when a nigga is behind this glass. If I was out, you wouldn't be talking this jazzy. Slow your roll, get your words in order, and talk like you got some sense. And another thing, I ain't never fucked your cousin. I let her suck my dick a couple of times and that's it," Keith said.

I didn't feel like going there with him, so I just left that shit alone. I told him about Red and why I thought that he was the one that tried to kill us. I left a few details out like us fucking and going out to eat. I told Keith that I was at the restaurant with some group member from school, and Red walked up to me to speak and he asked about him. I noticed his cologne, then he got on his phone and was talking to someone, and that's when I heard him say the famous words, "All is well."

Keith wasn't even concern about what I was saying about Red. He got mad because I smelled his cologne.

"Why the fuck was you all in that nigga's grill to smell his cologne?" Keith asked.

"It wasn't like that, he came to our table and his cologne was loud, and that's a smell I'll never forget.

"I don't think you're telling me the truth, but I'm gonna give you a pass. Don't worry about that nigga, I'm gonna handle that. Just stay away from him and watch your surroundings. Don't be having anybody in the house. I'm gonna have Chris check up on you every now and then," Keith said.

Keith and I talked for thirty more minutes before I left, since inmates could only have an hour visit. He told me that his case didn't look good because they had an informant that was going to testify against him about the killing. He said that they're trying to get him on Tiffany's murder as well. That was a topic that we never talked about because I already knew that he killed that girl. I asked him who he thought was snitching on him. He said that he didn't know, but as soon as he found out they would be dead. He even had the nerve to say that he thought that I had told on him. He also informed me that his mother would be coming back to Michigan to get his things in order and to keep an eye on me. He said to expect her phone call. I told him about the last conversation that his mother and I had, and informed him that she wouldn't be calling my phone again. He then started going off on me about disrespecting his mother. Keith and I said our goodbyes and I left. He told me that he loved me, and I told him I loved him too. I couldn't lie, I did still love him after all the shit he did to me and put me through.

Chapter Twenty-Five

The Same Thing that Makes You Laugh, Makes You Cry

Ain't this some shit, my cousin Keisha had the nerve to call me Sunday night asking me did I go visit Keith.

"Bitch you have some guts calling me after you've been fucking my man. I knew you were a hoe, but I didn't know that you got down like that with family. But one thing that gets me, you were fucking him, but you still didn't have shit. Did he give you any money? Did he buy you a new car? He didn't do shit but fuck your stupid ugly ass. To answer your question, yes I did go see him, and he said you were nothing but a head doctor to him, that you're a nasty dirty hood rat bitch."

"Bitch, you the one a hood rat, that's why he's fucking with me. He don't want your ass. He said you can't even fuck right," Keisha said.

"You know what, I'm not about to waste my time on you. You're nothing to me, you're garbage. If Keith wants to be with you, then do the damn thing and tell him to stop calling me, because I don't want him anymore. And when I see you bitch, it's gonna be on," I said. Then I hung up the phone.

Keisha was the last thing on my mind. I was wondering how Keith was going to handle Red, and if I had anything to worry about.

A month went by and Red was still calling me. I was avoiding his phone calls. I didn't know what he knew, and I wanted to stay away from him just in case Keith had someone watching him and they saw us together. I was going to see Keith once a week to see where his mind was at and what he knew about Red and my relationship. If he knew anything, he never let it show.

His mother hadn't showed up yet and his trial was scheduled to start on January 6, 2009. I was planning on moving to Atlanta, and work for CNN as an assistant to the President of Public Relations after my graduation in May. Jennifer already sent a letter of recommendation to the CNN President of Public Relations in Atlanta. It didn't hurt either that her cousin was a producer for CNN, so I was basically guaranteed the position as long as I graduated on time, and was able to pay for my on relocation fees.

Simone called me late in the afternoon crying hysterically.

"Tomika, I need you to come over my house as soon as possible," Simone said.

I knew that she had bad news to tell me. I didn't know if someone was with her and was trying to get to me or what. So I asked, "Is there anyone with you? It's not a set up or anything is it?"

"She tried to laugh, but she was blowing her nose.

"Girl, you know me better than that. After what you went through, I would just as well die than to get both of us killed. But I have something to tell you."

"I'm kinda of tired, and I've had a long day. Why can't you tell me over the phone or come over?" I asked.

"Tomika, I really need you. Please come over, I have some important things to talk to you about," Simone said.

"O.k., just give me a minute to get myself together."

I arrived at Simone's house fifteen minutes later. When I got to the door, it was slightly open. I thought to myself, this is some bullshit already. I stepped back pull out my cell phone and dialed Simone's number. Simone picked up on the second ring.

"Hello," Simone said.

"What's up girl? Are you at home? Because your door is open," I said.

"Yeah, I'm here. I must have left it open when I got home. Anyway come on in, it's all good," Simone said.

She didn't sound like herself. The voice in my head told me to turn around and leave, but my heart wouldn't let me. Simone said she needed me. I took my gun out of my purse and walked in her house with caution. I found Simone in her bedroom, sitting on the bed smoking a blunt. It looked as if she had been crying all day, her eyes were red and puffed up.

"What's wrong with you?" I asked as I sat next to her.

Simone was looking in a photo album, and she had pictures all over her bed. I was in some of them along with Sheretta, Keisha, Tory, Keith, and a lot of guys that she dated in the past.

"What you doing? Taking a trip down memory lane?" I said in a joking way.

♫"I stumbled on a photograph, it kinda made me laugh. It took me way back, back down memory lane. I see us standing there, such a happy, happy pair, with love beyond compare." ♫

I started singing, Simone looked up at me laughing and said, "I'm HIV positive, I found out today when I went to the doctor's office to get my results and get some prenatal care pills. Don't look at me like that. I need you to be by my side right now Tomika," Simone said.

"I'm not looking at you like shit, I can't judge you. You my girl, I'm gonna ride with you. Are you gonna have them test you again to make sure?" I asked.

"I had them give me a swab test after they told me that I was HIV positive, and it took two hours for the results to come back; in it was positive too. What am I going to do? I can't have this baby knowing that I might infect it."

"You know, now they have all types of medication that can prevent a baby from being infected, so if you want to have the baby, have it. This might be the only time that you're able to have a baby. So, do you know who the father is for sure and have you told him yet about the baby?" I asked.

"Yeah, I told him about the baby, it's John Blake's. He plays for the Lion's. He told me that he wants to take a paternity test before he does a thing to help me out. Now he wants to call me all type of hoes and sluts. I told him I wasn't a hoe or a slut when he was eating my asshole," Simone said. We both started laughing.

"So are you going to tell him about you being HIV positive?" I asked.

"I don't know yet, right now I just don't want to think about it. I want us to chill and hang out. You feel up to it?" Simone asked.

"Not really. But for you, I'll hang. Put some clothes on and you can ride with me to my house so I can change my clothes if you want. You should spend the night with me. I'm lonely staying at that big ass house by myself," I said.

"O.k., I'll do that. I don't want to be alone anyway. I might try to kill myself," Simone said, then laughed. But I knew she wasn't kidding.

Simone and I went to Outback to eat that night. She ended up staying with me for a week. I didn't want her to leave, but she said that she had to face her life. She said that she was going to tell John about her having HIV. I told her to be careful, because this day and age, you don't know what a man is capable of doing after getting that type of information. She said that she was going to tell him over the phone. I dropped her off before I went to work. We said our goodbyes, and I told her to call me later that night. -Simone called me later that night crying, talking about John said that he was going to kill her.

"Do you think that he's for real?" I asked.

"Tomika, I really don't know. I told him that I had HIV. He hung up the phone on me, then an hour later he called back talking about if he test positive, he's going to kill me. My life is all fucked up!" Simone said.

"Do you want me to come over and chill with you?" I asked.

"No, I'm good. I just can't believe that I have HIV. I guess all these years fucking with no condom, finally caught up with me. I wonder how long I had it, and who I caught it from?"

I wanted to say *maybe you caught it from them niggas you was fucking with in Las Vegas who were fucking each other than you without a condom*, but I decided not to.

"So, are you going to call any of your ex's and tell them to go get tested?" I asked.

"Hell naw, I don't want my business in the streets. They gonna find out just like I did."

"Girl, you cold blooded, but let me get ready to go to class and I'll call you when I get back home," I said.

"Tomika, I have something to tell you, but you have to promise that you won't get mad."

"Girl please, don't tell me you fucked Keith or Red, because I don't want to beat your ass and be over here worrying about if I got HIV?" I said.

"Bitch, you know I wouldn't play you like that."

"Whatever."

"But for real, it's nothing like that. It is serious though," Simone said. Simone was beating around the bush. I don't know what she had to tell me, but I was in a rush to get off the phone.

"Girl what's up? I have to change clothes before I go to class. Just tell me."

"Tomika, I was the one that told the police about Blunt and Eric murders. And that I thought Keith killed them, but I only did it after they found that girl that he use to mess with dead, Tiffany. Tomika, I know he killed all of them, and I didn't want him to end up killing you. I know he was beating your ass. Keith is crazy. I wanted to get him back for killing Blunt," Simone said.

"O.k., I'll talk to you later." I needed time to process all the information that Simone just told me.

"That's all you got to say. You're not mad at me?" Simone said.

"Girl at this point, nothing surprises me. Why would I be mad at you? You got that nigga out of my life. I'm hurt that you didn't tell me this earlier, but you're right, he might have killed me if he was still out."

"Girl, I thought you were gonna come over here and try to beat my ass. I guess you're over that nigga. What are you going to do about Red?" Simone asked.

"First off, what you mean I was gonna try to beat your ass? You know I would have did it," I said, then we both laughed. "I don't know what to do about Red. I'm starting to think that it was a bad idea to tell Keith about Red. What if he finds out that I had sex with him?" I said.

"Yeah, you right. But that nigga Red did you dirty. You should have told Keith. What do you think Keith is going to do?" Simone asked.

I didn't know whether to trust her or not. She could be taping our conversations to give to the people that are handling Keith's case, so I played it cool. "Knowing Keith, he's probably not going to do anything until he gets out and knows what really went down. He's not going to do anything while he has those cases pending," I said.

"Well, I'm about to go to class. I'll talk to you later. Oh before I get off the phone, I'm going to Atlanta next week to look for an apartment and to check out the scene to make sure it's where I really want to live, so do you want to roll?" I asked Simone.

"Naw, I'm good. If I don't talk back to you, just holla at me when you get back," Simone said.

My trip to Atlanta was uneventful. I went for my face-to-face interview with a man named Steven Scott, who would soon be my boss if I decided to take the job. I was offered the position and had a week to think about it, because I would have to start in a month with no relocation fee from CNN Production Company. I had two more classes to take from December to May of 2009, my graduation date, but I could take those classes online.

While I was in Atlanta, I hung out with Jamal. A lot has changed since the last time we talked. He had two kids by two different women, plus he was getting a name for himself down there. I didn't want to get mixed up in any of his drama, so we kept it on a friendship level. Fucking was not an option for us. I didn't tell Keith's mother Brenda that I was coming to the ATL. I didn't want to be bothered, and I know she had some shit she wanted to get off her chest with me.

Chapter Twenty-Six

I Can't Believe It

When I got off the airplane from my trip to Atlanta, I turned my cell phone on and noticed that I had eight voice messages and a couple of text messages. Immediately, I thought that the messages had something to do with Keith.

The first message was from my mother.

"Tomika call me as soon as you get this message, it's important."

The next was from Michael.

"Tomika did you see the news? Call me."

The third was from Red.

"Baby girl, sorry to hear what happened to your friend, call me if you need anything."

That message struck me as strange; everyone knew that I was out of town. So whatever went down, everyone knew about it but me, so it must be important if they called me while I was on the plane.

I didn't want to listen to anymore messages until I called my mother back. I dialed my mother's phone and she picked up on the second ring.

"Hello," My mother said.

"Yeah, what's going on? I just got your message," I said.

"I got some bad news for you."

"What is it? Did anything happen to my sister?" I asked.

"No, but the police found Simone and some NFL player dead in her apartment. They say it was a homicide, suicide.

Apparently, she was dating him and they must have had an argument. He came over there and killed her, then himself," my mother said. Before she could continue, tears starting rolling down my eyes.

"Who is they?" I asked my mother.

"The news and the detective that's working the case. He was on the news," my mother said.

"What was the football player's name?" I asked.

"John Blake. Baby, do you want to spend the night at my house tonight?" my mother asked.

"Yeah, I'll be over there in about an hour or so. Let me go home and pack a bag, put my clothes away, and check my mail," I said.

"O.k., do you want me to pick you up?"

"Nawl, I'm good. I'll see you in a minute, bye," I said.

On my way home, I checked the rest of my voice messages and my texts. I returned Michael's phone call, and he told me how sorry he was to hear about Simone. We talked for a couple of minutes. I told him that I was going over my mother's house, so he said he would meet me over there. While talking to him my phone clicked. It was a private call. I told Michael bye and answered the call, "Hello."

"What's up baby girl? Where the fuck you at? I've been calling the house for the last couple of days," Keith said.

"I had to take care of some business out of town. Why, what's up?" I said.

"Bitch, you must be outta your fucking mind. How the fuck you gonna leave and not tell me?" Keith said.

"Look, I don't want to hear that shit right now. I just found out that Simone got killed and you want to call with this bullshit," I said.

"Well, you wouldn't have to hear it if you would play your position, and know what the fuck you should do."

"You know what Keith, Fuck You! You on some stupid shit right now. I just told you that my best friend got killed and you didn't say that you're sorry to hear it, or asked how I was doing? You are a cold hearted muthafucka, and I hope you rot in prison," I said.

"Bitch I'm gonna kill you when I get out. You better watch your back."

"Whatever, if you're gonna kill me, do it now!" I said.

"Don't worry, you're gonna get what's coming to you. You un-loyal bitch. Your girl did. Oh, tell your man Red I said *what's up* when you see him," Keith said, then he hung up the phone.

The phone conversation with Keith had me nervous. I didn't know what to think with that last comment he made about Red. Did he know that Red and I had sex? I wondered, but right now all I could think about was Simone. I can't believe she's dead, all the shit we've been through together. I knew she had my back. I never should have believed Keith when he said that she tried to get with him. I missed months from her life.

When I pulled up to the entrance of the subdivision, a funny feeling came over me. There was a guard at the gate that I had never seen before. So I asked him, "How long have you been working here? Where is John, the regular guy at?"

"Well Ms. Smith, my name is Nathan, and this is my first night. I don't know where John is. I hope you have a goodnight," he said.

"Same to you."

I pulled up, opened the garage, and pulled all the way in. I didn't bother letting the garage door down because I was only going to be in the house for a minute. I was just grabbing some clothes. When I got to the door that connects the garage to the house, it was unlocked. I thought it was strange, but maybe in my rush to leave I forgot to lock it. But I figured it was all good because my garage door was down. I walked in the house, turn the lights on in the kitchen, and sitting at the kitchen island was the most handsome man I've ever seen in my life. I wasn't so much scared as I was shocked. All I was thinking was who was this man? Before I could ask the question he spoke, "How are you doing tonight, sister-in-law?" the man said.

"Not so good, especially since there's a stranger in my house," I said.

"Well let me introduce myself, I'm Marcus," He said while extending his hand to me to shake. "Your brother-in-law, your man Keith's brother. He called me and told me to come over and check up on you, and make sure you were alright," Marcus said.

"Thanks, but I'm good as you can see. I just came here to pack a bag. I'm going to stay at my mother's house for a couple of days." While I was talking, I was digging in my purse; acting like I was looking for something which I was,…my gun.

Then I realized I left it in the glove compartment of my car, I put it there before I got to the airport to leave for Atlanta.

"What you looking for?" Marcus asked.

"My keys to my wallet," I said.

"Won't you sit down and get a little comfortable. I want to get to know the woman that got my brother ready to settle down with."

As he was talking, I noticed a duffle bag on the floor next to his leg. So I asked, "Are you planning on staying here for the night? I see you have an overnight bag with you."

"Oh this, it's not an overnight bag. I have something in it for you."

I looked suspiciously at the bag, as he was grabbing it to put it on top of the island. What he pulled out of the bag made me vomit instantly; it was Red's head. This sick muthafucka had cut Red's head off and was carrying it around in a duffle bag. Blood and veins were dripping and hanging from his head, where his neck and rest of his body was attached to it.

"I guess you don't want to fuck him now," Marcus said.

I didn't respond, I just turned my head and began to cry.

"I know that my brother taught you the code of the streets, its death before dishonor. I just don't understand how you could be fucking the same guy that tried to kill you and Keith, plus he's one of the informants in Keith case. You got to be the stupidest chick in the world," Marcus said.

Marcus sat Red's head down on the island and started going through the duffle bag and pulling out all types of knives, and other looking dangerous tools as I looked closer at Red's head. I noticed that his tongue had been cut out, that made me throw up again.

"So what do you plan on doing with me?" I asked.

"What do you think I'm going to do? You're a big liability for Keith. You were unfaithful, and the price of that is death?" Marcus said, as he was trying to decide what tools to use to kill me, I assumed.

I had to think quickly and figure out a plan to stay alive, because this nigga did not play any games.

"How are you going to kill your niece or nephew?" I asked.

"So you're saying that you're pregnant with Keith's baby?" Marcus asked.

"Yeah," I said.

"That's the same line your girl Simone said. But you, I'm gonna give you the benefit of the doubt."

"What does Simone have to do with anything?" Then at that moment, I realized that Marcus must have killed Simone and John.

"What do you think she has to do with it? She was an informant as well. So, she had to get dealt with. But if I didn't do it, I had a funny feeling that football player would have. I don't understand how you could socialize with such rats, but I guess it's true what they say, birds of a feather flock together," Marcus said.

ASA Publishing Company

Marcus walked up to me, nose-to-nose and said, "We have to take a little ride. And if what you said is true, then you don't have anything to worry about."

"What do you mean by that?" I asked.

"You said that you're pregnant. So we're going to CVS and get a pregnancy test. If you're pregnant, then you'll live to see another day or maybe you won't. It might be that nigga Red's baby, and don't deny that you fucked him, because he already told everything. It's amazing what a nigga will tell when they're facing death. But anyway, we digress. Leave your purse, and let's go."

"Yeah, you're right, I did have sex with Red. But it was only once, and we used a condom. I've been fucking your brother for the past two years without a condom, and I've been pregnant twice by him. I know this is his baby," I said.

All I thought on the ride back to the house is that I hope the test comes out positive. I didn't think I was pregnant, I had to say something to kill some time.

When I was in the bathroom peeing, I said to Marcus, "You know Simone was really pregnant, and it was John's baby? So you killed a whole family, you don't feel bad about it"?

"I've done worst," he said.

The pregnancy test turned out to be positive, I couldn't believe it. But the worst part about it was that I was pregnant with Red's child. I knew it had to be Red's because I haven't had my period for the last couple of months.

Marcus looked at me and said, "You dodged a bullet, literally."

"So what are you going to do with me?" I asked.

"Nothing right now, I have to see what Keith has to say about the whole situation. I know he's gonna want you to go to the doctor and find out how far along you are. But for now, just do you and go over your mother's house, but don't try anything stupid. You know how we get down," Marcus said.

Chapter Twenty-Seven

Keith

I can't believe Marcus dumb ass let that bitch go. I don't care if she did say she was pregnant with my child. He wasn't suppose to let her go; now we don't know where that hoe is. Marcus always was a sucka for dark skin bitches. But anyway, with all my informants dead, I don't have anything to worry about. Doing two years for the gun possession ain't shit. They're sending me to a level two correctional facility in Coldwater, Michigan, that ain't shit. I can do that time in my sleep. There ain't nothing but young ass punks, white boys and niggas with petty ass dope and marijuana cases there. I'm still gonna be the man when I get out.

The first thing I'm going to do when I get out is find that bitch and kill her ass, unless that baby she's pregnant with is really mine, then she'll get a pass. But if not, it's a wrap for her. What really got me heated, is that fucked up letter that I received from her yesterday.

February 14ᵗʰ, 2008

Dear Keith,

I can't believe that you would go to that extent to be free, that you would do all those terrible things. I used to ask Simone all the time, why did they call you Monster, and she couldn't tell me because she didn't know. But after everything that I've been through with you, I see why people call you Monster. It's because you are a Monster! You had me fooled. I thought that you were a man of God, everything you did in the streets contradicted what you did for the church and the community. You had everyone fooled. I can't believe that you had the pastor to speak on your behalf at your hearing. I wonder how much you contributed to the church for that. But anyway, I just wanted you to know that I forgive you. I know that you're a sick person, and that you need help. I just want you to let me live my life with the child that I'm carrying.

So far so good, I haven't had any complications with the pregnancy, and I want to keep it that way. Keith, I'm begging you to leave me and my family alone. I hope you find happiness and I hope you repent for all your sins, and you make peace before you pass away. Just so you know, I never went to the police about anything that you've done. I did learn something from you, death before dishonor.

Happy Valentine's Day!

Tomika Smith

P.S.,
Everything is how you left it. I didn't take anything from the house, and I left all the keys to the cars and trucks on the counter and the engagement ring.

She really got me fucked up if she thinks I'm gonna let her go. We'll see each other in the near future. I'll bet my life on that.

Epilogue

Nine months later and I have a beautiful two month old baby boy. It turns out that I was indeed pregnant with Keith's baby. That night after Marcus let me go. I packed all my important papers that I needed, and grabbed what money I could from the house without Keith knowing something was missing, and headed straight to the airport. I've been living in Atlanta and everything's been chilled so far.

From what Michael and my mother has told me, and what I've read, all charges were dropped against Keith due to insufficient evidences, but he got sentenced to two years for possession of an unregistered firearm. I hope he turns his life around and leave me and my son alone.

I named my little man King Montgomery Jackson. I wanted him to have his father's last name. I pray to God every night that King doesn't grow up to be like his father. I named him King because he's my man and the king of our little castle. I'm finally free from all the madness. I wish I could share this moment with Simone, but I know she's looking down on me and smiling.

ASA Publishing Company

CPSIA information can be obtained at www.ICGtesting.com
Printed in the USA
LVOW07s1324170315

430898LV00019B/362/P

9 780982 813577